Maureen Peters was born in Caernarfon. She obtained an English and Philosophy degree, as well as a teaching diploma, from the University College of North Wales.

TRUMPET MORNING

The Petrie family live on a farm in Anglesey, North Wales. Grandfather Taid is a Revivalist preacher; his wife, Nain, an Irish gypsy who casts spells to annoy her husband. Then there is the aunt who's sworn off men forever, and another always ready for a lark. Also an uncle married to a wife who doesn't fit in, another whose marriage will benefit the farm, and the youngest facing a darker destiny in 1940 with Great Britain at war. As eleven-year-old Nell prepares for grammar school, and the shadows of war creep closer, comedy and heartbreak mingle in this story of a most eccentric family.

Books by Maureen Peters
Published by The House of Ulverscroft:

KATHERYN THE WANTON QUEEN
PATCHWORK
ENGLAND'S MISTAKES
WITCH QUEEN
THE LUCK BRIDE
BEGGAR MAID, QUEEN

THE *VINEGAR TRILOGY:*
THE VINEGAR SEED
THE VINEGAR BLOSSOM
THE VINEGAR TREE

THE MALONE TRILOGY:
TANSY
KATE ALANNA
A CHILD CALLED FREEDOM

MAUREEN PETERS

TRUMPET MORNING

Complete and Unabridged

ULVERSCROFT
Leicester

First published in Great Britain in 2006 by
Robert Hale Limited
London

First Large Print Edition
published 2007
by arrangement with
Robert Hale Limited
London

British Library CIP Data

Peters, Maureen
   Trumpet morning.—Large print ed.—
Ulverscroft large print series: general fiction
1. Farm life—Wales—Anglesey—Fiction
2. Anglesey (Wales)—Social conditions—Fiction
3. Domestic fiction 4. Large type books
I. Title
823.9′14 [F]

   ISBN 978–1–84617–672–2

01 169 590 7

Published by
F. A. Thorpe (Publishing)
Anstey, Leicestershire

Set by Words & Graphics Ltd.
Anstey, Leicestershire
Printed and bound in Great Britain by
T. J. International Ltd., Padstow, Cornwall

This book is printed on acid-free paper

1

Christmas mornings always felt different. I was certain that even if I found myself in a heathen country without a calendar my bones would tell me when Christmas Day arrived. It wasn't the faint frosting of snow on the window pane, nor the scent of candied peel that was chopped into the mincemeat, nor the sound of the bells pealing across the low meadows. On that particular morning, there was a spattering of rain instead of snow and the bells wouldn't be rung until the war was over. That would be any day now, Taid said, since the war had been going on three months already and everybody knew German tanks were made of cardboard.

Taid was the name we called Grandfather and being Welsh we pronounced it Tide, as we pronounced my grandmother's name Nine. Their real names were John and Hannah, but nobody ever called them that. Their children called them Mam and J.P. and everybody else called them Nain and Taid, as if they were grandparents to the whole village as well as to me. They didn't address each other by name at all if they could help it,

1

mainly because they didn't get on.

'Chalk and cheese,' said Aunt Ellen who lived with us and was considered touched in the head by everybody except me. I thought she spoke good sense most of the time.

'Never got on from the day they met,' Aunt Ellen said.

'They must have got on sometimes,' I argued, 'else they wouldn't have begat children.'

I knew the right word was begat because Moses kept using it when he was writing down where all his people came from.

'They're married,' she said in faint surprise. 'It stands to reason.'

Whenever Aunt Ellen stood something to reason it meant she couldn't explain it. That was partly why I was fond of her. The other adults in the family claimed to know everything, but Aunt Ellen, who was actually Taid's youngest sister and therefore my great aunt, was not omnipotent. I had been named for her but, to avoid confusion, was addressed as Nell. Actually, that is not quite accurate. Both of us had been called after another aunt, long since dead, who had been a genius.

'A genius!' Taid said, dragging the word out to the full length of its splendour. 'She wrote a book that was published in London and there is a copy of it in the British Museum.'

There was a copy of it in our parlour too. It was on a shelf, propped up by bookends that were shaped like a lion and a lamb.

'The day cometh when the lion shall lie down with the lamb,' Taid said.

That day had not yet cometh, at least not in our parlour. The book separated them still, bound in calf leather and so thick that neither lion nor the lamb could have taken a good look to discover if they wanted to lie down together.

A parlour is a room where one talks, but nobody ever talked in our parlour. It wouldn't have been respectful. The room was on the left of the narrow entrance hall and it was always chilly, even in the summer. The walls were of panelled wood, paler than the rest of the furniture, and there was a dark-red carpet on the floor with dull, cold leaves all around the border. There were gold cords and over the window panes themselves two thicknesses of frilled and spotted net.

There was a small fireplace in which no fire was ever lit. In winter the hearth contained an arrangement of holly branches and, in the summer, a huge spray of everlasting colours and honesty. In our house, summer began on the first of May and ended on the last day of October. Taid had decreed it so and since he had no patience with spring and autumn, those unreliable seasons never stuck their noses over the threshold. On the narrow slate mantelshelf there was a little ebony clock on which two gold-coloured cherubs sat, glaring at each other, and on the wall above hung Taid's trumpet.

There was an upright chair at each side of the fireplace and on the wall opposite the door, tall narrow bookshelves, with a separate shelf containing the book my genius relative had written, a little to one side to emphasize her superiority to Dickens, Shakespeare, Thackeray and the rest. There was a small table beneath the shelf, crowded with framed photographs of various members of the family. The other articles of furniture were the square, high-backed armchair in which only Taid ever sat and the long table, its surface of gleaming black slate, on which he wrote his sermons and where our dead were laid out, though since my birth everyone had been very healthy.

The front of our house was directly adjacent to the road, the garden at the side with its low stone wall being a continuation of the main building. At the back the land fell sharply away creating an extra storey, so that what was the ground floor when one entered from the street became the middle storey when one approached it through the meadows. The staircase went up out of the narrow hall and also twisted down into the back quarters which was where Nain held sway.

On the other side of the hall was the dining-room and, when I woke on that Christmas morning, I could hear the clatter of knives and forks. The long table was being set for Christmas dinner which would be as plentiful as in previous years. The government had introduced rationing, but Taid had squashed that idea.

'It'll never catch on and I'm not encouraging it in my family,' he said firmly.

So there would be pheasant, well hung and basted with butter, a pudding thick with nuts, raisins, sultanas, sugar and mincemeat into which Nain surreptitiously mixed a tot of rum. As a family, we were strictly teetotal so she had to do it on the sly. We did have cowslip and elder wine to drink though because, being made from Nature's bounty, they were not considered to be alcoholic. That they packed a hefty punch only proved that Taid was right when he said you didn't need alcohol in order to enjoy yourself.

My room was actually a tiny loft buried between the ceiling of the top landing and the rafters. One reached it by shinning up a ladder and pushing open a trapdoor. The room had a dormer window that couldn't be opened but let in the light, and a braided rug on the floorboards. It hadn't been possible to get a bed up there, so I slept on a thick feather mattress under blankets of good Welsh wool and a top quilt that was made out of dozens of triangles of patterned cotton, all stitched together. There was not sufficient room for a wardrobe or tallboy, but I had a low chest of drawers with a mirror on it and a couple of shelves where I kept my books. Now that I was going to Holyhead Grammar School I needed books and a place to study. I had a small table too with a hinged lid which lifted up to disclose a chamberpot. That chamberpot was the most beautiful object in the room and I often regretted that I couldn't display it. There were red cabbage-roses all over the outside and the two handles were shaped like green stems. The chamberpot was only ever used in dire emergencies for we had a proper chemical toilet next to the wash-house outside the back door.

It was still early, but the strengthening light was stripping away the darkness and I could see the spattering rain as it drove in gusts against the window pane. Half of me wanted to get up and half of me wanted to cuddle back into the warm hollow between mattress and quilt. On this morning of all mornings, however, it would have been a sin and a shame to remain in bed. I wriggled out and reached for my clothes, all laid out in twos with each upper garment laid crosswise over its fellow. It was my way of warding off evil, crosses being a powerful protection against anything that might creep up in the night.

Usually I spared a moment to regret that I didn't have any breasts yet, but today I didn't bother since the effort of hoping for a miracle that never came might dull the pleasure of the holiday. Not that the pleasure was upon me yet. First there was the ritual with Taid to be endured.

It was a ritual that was carried out on special occasions — those being first Sundays in the month, Christmas, New Year, Ash Wednesday, Easter, Whitsun and whenever some important event occurred in the family. Before my birth and for about five years after it, my Uncle Guto had been the acolyte on these occasions, but since I could remember, I had been the one and if there had been any way of avoiding it, I would have avoided it.

I took my wellington boots in my hand and climbed down the ladder to the landing at the top of the stairs. Here a round window with bits of red, blue and yellow stained glass in it looked across the street to the whitewashed chapel. Taid didn't really approve of the

7

stained glass. It made us look as if we had Catholic ideas, he said. Sometimes I used to kneel down and look through one of the coloured segments and imagine I was a Catholic, seeing the chapel opposite dyed scarlet or emerald.

The large back bedroom and two smaller bedrooms opened off the landing. The bedroom on the left was where my Aunts Marget and Catti slept. They would be downstairs, laying the table and getting everything into the oven before chapel started. The right-hand room was where my Uncles Ben and Guto slept. The big room was for Nain and Taid. There was flowered paper on the walls there and a carpet on the floor to match the one in the parlour. All the furniture in that room was massive but it was dominated by the huge, brass-railed bed with its high mattress and fringed covers. This was where all the begetting had gone on, though I found it hard to visualize. The door stood partly open and I could see that, as usual, Nain's side of the bed was neatly made with the cover smoothed flat and Taid's side was still littered with the coats he'd taken from the hallstand the previous night.

I never learned the reason for it but Taid refused to cover himself with sheets and blankets when he lay down to sleep. Instead, he used to pile his share of the bedcovers on top of Nain and then spread over himself all the coats he took from the hallstand every night on his way upstairs. It meant that everybody in the family had to have a rummage to find their own garments the next day.

I went in now and pulled out my navy-blue mackintosh. It was slightly too wide in the shoulders and too long in the sleeves and covered the tops of my wellington boots, but as Nain said, 'Better to have it on the loose side to allow for growing. One can't rely on Mathew being in a position to send anything this year.'

Mathew was my father and the eldest son and Nain was quite right not to rely on his sending anything since during the twelve years he'd been in Australia seeking his fortune, he'd never sent back as much as a picture postcard. Nobody except Nain ever troubled to mention him and she did so only occasionally as if, by speaking his name aloud, she could keep some part of him alive and with us. My mother had died when I was born, so I was by way of being an orphan which made me feel rather proud and not in the least wistful.

I sat down to pull on my wellingtons and my Uncle Guto looked in at the door on his way downstairs.

'Happy Christmas, Nell. The old man's waiting,' he said.

I almost fell over in my haste to jump up and hug him. Guto was the youngest of my five aunts and uncles, eleven years younger than the next one up. He was seventeen years old and his birth had been a tremendous surprise.

'Shock is the right word,' Nain had reminisced. 'I went to Dr Gareth because I thought I was going into the change. Putting on weight like a Michaelmas goose I was, and all in the same place! 'Looks to me as if you might have a tumour there', Gareth said. 'I'll arrange for you to go in for a few days' observation'. Well, that put the wind up me proper, but halfway home the tumour starts kicking me! Well, I didn't need any observation then to know what was wrong. Tumour indeed! Guto it was.'

Guto it was now too, his eyes laughing at me and his sunstreaked hair flopping over his brow. All the Petries were dark or red-haired, but Guto's hair was light brown and his eyes were hazel and he was near enough to my own age to be not like an uncle at all. He was slim and wiry in contrast to his thicker-set older brothers and there was a lightness of heart about him even on grey mornings when the fields were sodden and the mud sucked hungrily at one's boots.

'Happy Christmas, Guto!' I put my arms about him and kissed him hard on both sides of his face. He smelled of the brilliantine he was always putting on his hair to try to make it lie flat and I sniffed at him with a pleasure I could almost taste.

'Better go on down,' he advised. 'The old man's waiting.'

I considered asking Guto to take my place but I knew that would annoy Taid as much as my being late, so I unwound myself and clumped down the stairs.

Taid was standing in the hall, his tall figure black against the rectangle of morning revealed by the open front door. He was tapping his foot, which was a habit of his whenever the impatience that continually bubbled below his surface threatened to erupt. I was never able to see my grandfather piece by piece. I saw him always finished and complete, fashioned out of rock and slate, his spade beard streaked with silver, his eyes glowing dark coals in his tanned and weather-beaten countenance. I could not recall his ever having praised me or given me one gesture of affection, but I had never resented the lack. One did not expect the 'mountains to bend down and acknowledge one's existence'.

'Happy Christmas, Taid.' I smiled at him brightly, but I didn't hug him.

'Happy Christmas, Nell.' He took out his watch, frowned at it as if daring it to be fast or slow, then said, 'I will give you three minutes to wash your face.'

'Thank you, Taid.' I hurried down the stairs that led into the back quarters.

Three minutes was not really sufficient time. The big kitchen on the left of the stone-flagged passage at the foot of the stairs deserved leisure in which to savour its myriad colours and scents, but there was no sense in lingering when Taid had his watch out. On the right were the pantry and the dairy and, outside the back door, the covered yard with the wash-house and toilet.

I did the necessary, rubbed a damp sponge over my face, and put up the hood of my mackintosh to conceal the fact that my hair was still in its night-time plait. Then I clumped back up the stairs to the front door again.

I always had a wild hope that Taid might change his mind at the last minute, but Taid changed his mind less frequently than God did. Already he had his Bible in his hand and the trumpet beneath his arm.

'You may carry it,' he said, and held out the instrument to me.

'Thank you very much, Taid,' I said, and wanted to die. Bad enough to have to walk at his side while he carried the wretched thing. It was ten times worse having to carry it myself and be seen by the neighbours. I could only pray silently that the neighbours would be too busy to have time to watch, but as we skipped out into the street I could feel curtains being twitched and smiles beginning.

'Shall we go through the meadow, Taid?' I asked hopefully.

'Too wet,' he answered.

It was a sensible answer, but that wasn't his real reason for going round by the road. Taid actually liked being seen by the neighbours as he strode past the row of cottages and the corner shop and headed down the lane that led to the beach.

There were beaches all around the island, some golden summer places where the tourists came and others narrow inlets of shingle and seaweed where the gulls wheeled and dipped in search of scraps. This morning the rain on the wind blew salt spray into my face and the waves were choppy. The suspension bridge was still veiled in mist and across the water a slow rising sun outlined the battlements of the ancient castle.

By the time we were crunching over the pebbles, past the white sea-holly that clung to the tufts of grass at the edge of the shingle, I knew my prayers had been ignored again. Nothing short of an earthquake would stop Taid now. Nothing did.

He held his Bible open but he didn't lower his eyes to the printed page. Why should he when he knew the words as well as if he had written them himself?

'And I saw a new heaven and a new earth,' he said in a voice so loud that it defeated the wind. 'For the first heaven and the first earth were passed away and there was no more sea. And I, John, saw the holy city, New Jerusalem, coming down from God out of Heaven, prepared as a bride adorned for her bridegroom.'

It did no good to remind myself that it was St John the Evangelist who had written all that. When Taid raised his powerful voice, shaping the words against the wind, the words and the thoughts behind them became his alone. Out of his mouth came the angel with the jar of seven plagues and the holy city with its jewelled gates glittered near enough to touch.

'And behold I come quickly,' Taid announced, 'and my reward is with me, to give every man according as his work shall be. I am alpha and omega, the beginning and the end, the first and the last.' The Bible snapped shut and was handed to me and Taid took the trumpet from my numbed fingers, raising it to his lips and blowing on it one long sustained note that hurt the eardrums and hung in the air. As its last echo quivered into silence his voice thundered forth, each word rolled out with a passion that had in it all the primitive grandeur of rock and sea and sky.

'If today is the day of your coming, oh Lord, then John Petrie is ready!'

I cringed inwardly as I always cringed, knowing that his words could be heard by others besides me, pricked by imagined ridicule and at the same time absolutely terrified lest the clouds part and the chariots of the Lord whirl into the world. Taid might be ready to be judged. I was not.

The mist had lifted a little but only the gleaming grey-silver chains of the suspension bridge were revealed. There were no angels. Taid was looking at me and I hastily said my one word.

'Amen.'

'Amen, amen!' Taid had not removed his hat, the Quakers having some habits of which he approved. Now he tugged it more firmly over his thick grey and black hair and turned inland again, crunching back up to the lane, with me scrambling behind.

'Going to be a good day.' There was

satisfaction in his voice. 'Rain's veering towards Ireland.'

The pleasure in his voice had increased. In his eyes the Irish were all pagans and Papists and a good wetting might bring them to their senses.

'Sun's coming out,' I said.

'Go and get your breakfast.' He waved me on ahead with the hand holding the trumpet.

It was not done out of compassion for any embarrassment I might be feeling. Taid would not have understood an emotion like embarrassment. He merely wanted to walk back down the street accepting the greetings of anyone who might be around, without a small granddaughter tagging behind. Nevertheless, I took it as a release and ran, the hem of my mackintosh flapping against my wellingtons, along the road, through the garden gate and along the path, down the outside steps at the back and thence to the kitchen door.

I never entered that kitchen without a sense of joy. It was a large room, its far wall tucked into the hollow of the cliff, its near wall bright with diamond-paned windows. This was the oldest part of the house. The foundations went back to the eighth century and the walls were early medieval, four feet thick and stone. The floor was grey-blue slate, washed and scoured every Saturday, and an open range ran down one side of the whole. Nain still did all her cooking over glowing charcoal, or in the huge bake oven at the side of the fire. Everybody else in the world had gas or electricity. We had oil lamps, and bits of ash in the crusts of our loaves.

There were yellowing sheepskin rugs on the floor and pots of scented geraniums along the wide window ledges and strings of apples and onions and walnuts hanging from hooks in the ceiling. The table would have seated twenty, with elbow room, and there were benches ranged down both sides. A half-dozen spool chairs and a rocking chair stood about and on the wall, protected by glass, was a picture of the Duke of Windsor. Nain had been in love with the Duke of Windsor for years and knew that he'd only married Mrs Simpson because he'd never visited our village and met his true love. She had lost all patience with the government when he'd been forced to abdicate and, though she had accepted King George, she made it very clear that she only did so because he had a good Celtic wife.

She was at the stone sink washing her hands, alone save for a couple of tramps who were finishing off some bacon and eggs at one end of the table. There were always tramps in

17

our kitchen eating their heads off and flirting with my aunts. If there were no tramps around there were dark-eyed Lawsons and Bohannas and Lovells. Nain's mother had been pure Romany, her father Irish tinker, and Taid hated the gypsies nearly as much as he hated the Irish. For that reason he scarcely ever descended into the kitchen. Nain was undisputed monarch of the nether regions, though she wore her royalty with all the modesty of a true aristocrat.

She was more than ten years younger than her husband, a fact she took care was made known to people as soon as possible after introduction. She looked young for her age, people said, but to me she had always looked ageless and unchanging. Had I been told she was forty or ninety I would have accepted it. Her hair was jet black with a white streak that looked as if it had been put there on purpose and her skin was the colour of lightly toasted almonds with scarcely a line to crease its smoothness. Her eyes were hazel like her youngest son's, flecked with green and yellow like the eyes of a cat save that no feline creature ever carried with it such an air of tender innocence. If she had been a cat she would have been a round tabby, licking her kittens by the fire, with claws sheathed beneath velvet. Yet the claws were there. She extended them now and again to scratch my grandfather a little.

'Happy Christmas, Nell!' She swooped upon me, her hands still soapy. 'Give your old Nain a kiss then!'

I kissed her with enthusiasm. She smelled of mincemeat and warm dough and her lips were soft. I thought her beautiful though she was almost as broad as she was tall, her wedding ring nearly buried in the flesh of her finger, her ankles swollen above dainty Cinderella feet.

'Taid said I was to have breakfast,' I said.

'I've bacon and eggs ready.' She glanced over to where the tramps sat. 'I've my granddaughter to feed now and you'll want to be on your way, I'm sure.'

The dismissal was courteous but firm. Those who believed Nain was a soft touch all through didn't know Nain very well.

They rose, tipping their battered hats, sweetened on their way with thick slices of ginger bread. Nain wiped the table and put my breakfast before me.

'Did the old sod get his nonsense out of the way then?' she enquired.

The 'old sod' and sometimes the 'old bugger' were her customary ways of referring to her husband. Nain, as deeply religious in her own way as any woman who ever drew breath, had inherited from her tinker father a gift for cursing that would have made a navvy envious. She did not consider it to be cursing, since to her it came as naturally as breathing and there was no sin in breathing.

'The Lord didn't come,' I answered, with my mouth full of fried bread.

'I should bloody well think not,' she said. 'The Lord's got more sense than to land here on His birthday and with the old war going on! Drink your tea, Cariad, while it's hot. You've not got much time before chapel.'

She would be going to the evening service since without her supervision the dinner might burn to a crisp or the pan in which the pudding was steaming boil dry. There were always two services on Christmas Day but on ordinary Sundays, there was Sunday school as well. Wednesday night was Band of Hope night which was better fun, and on Mondays and Thursdays there was choir practice. Social life revolved about the chapel, though Nain took it all more lightly than Taid approved and had been known to skip Band of Hope in favour of a visit to her cousins over in Menai Bridge.

'I don't suppose — ?' I stopped, glancing at her from the corners of my eyes.

'In the dining-room. You can open it now.'

I forsook the rest of my breakfast and

dashed up the stairs, almost colliding with Aunt Ellen who was just coming downstairs. Had there been a collision I'd have got the worst of it since my great aunt was nearly six feet tall and could have deputised for the local blacksmith without anyone noticing much difference.

'Happy Christmas, Aunt Ellen!' I hugged as much of her as I could get my arms round and went on into the dining-room.

This was a handsome chamber extending from the front to the back of the house. The front windows were screened by lace curtains from the street but the ones at the back gave a clear view over the yard and the barn and milking shed to the meadows that ran down to the shore. Today I had no interest in views. My attention was riveted on the square parcel tied with scarlet ribbon that was placed, with a pile of smaller gifts, at the foot of the tree.

There had been an argument over the tree. There was always an argument over the tree, my grandfather declaring it was pagan and my grandmother saying they always had one at Windsor Castle.

'Hung with coloured paper chains and glass balls and with candles. The King lights them and all the footmen stand round and sing carols,' she said.

For one who had never been presented at

court it was incredible how much she knew about the habits of the royal family.

In the end, as happened every year, we had a tree, cut with great reluctance from the firs on the estate where my grandfather was bailiff. It stood in a red pot, its green branches unadorned save for a dusting of tinsel and a small, bright star fastened to the highest branch. There was a half-jaunty, half-apologetic look about it as if it knew it was defying Taid but had decided to put the blame on those who had carried it here.

The smaller gifts would all be exchanged and exclaimed over after dinner but I was intent on wresting the ribbon from the big parcel. I knew what was inside. I had been praying for it for months and, to be on the safe side, I'd made sure that the rest of the family knew exactly what I was praying for. It was folded in tissue paper and it was exactly what I had seen in my mind. A red cloak with a narrow collar of real fur and a matching tam-o'-shanter. More! There was a muff made of the same fur as the collar, with a ribbon threaded through for me to loop round my neck. It was beautiful, so infinitely superior to my school mackintosh that I felt tears brimming in my eyes as I touched it with reverent hands.

And it fitted! The hem, which could be

turned down later, reached my knees and the back swung in a mass of unpressed pleats from the yoke.

'For heaven's sake, Nell, we're due in chapel in five minutes!' Aunt Marget exclaimed, sweeping in. Aunt Catti was at her heels as usual. It was rare to see one without the other. There was two years difference in their ages but they were almost like twins with their dark hair and brown eyes and perfect white teeth. Marget was the plumper of the two and Catti had the rosier cheeks, but otherwise there was no difference to the casual glance. They both wore their chapel coats, Marget's of bottle green, Catti's of navy blue, with white gloves and small felt hats. Aunt Catti wore hers tipped slightly over one eye to show she was ready for a bit of a lark. Their voices were soft and when they laughed, people said it sounded as if they had bells on their teeth.

'I'm ready! Happy Christmas!' I spun before them, my plait swinging.

'Better put your shoes on instead of your wellies,' Aunt Marget advised, 'or the old man'll have a blue fit.'

'Or a pink one!' I said, repeating an old joke. Their ready laughter pealed out. Where they went it was always summer.

My chapel shoes were in the rack under the

hallstand. I put them on and stood up again as Taid came down the stairs, black coated and hatted, with the Bible under his arm. I wondered what comment he'd make on my outfit but he merely shook his head, intoning under his breath, 'Vanity of vanities, all is vanity!' and marched past to the front door.

'Silly old sod,' Aunt Catti mouthed at his retreating back and winked at me from beneath the tilted brim of her hat.

I fell into step behind them as we went out into the street and Aunt Ellen came plodding after with the hairpins already beginning to escape from the coils of reddish hair bundled at the nape of her long neck.

The chapel door was open and we could see the lesser members of the congregation filing in. The minister would not begin the service until the Petries had arrived. He would not have dared, even though he was ordained and Taid only a lay preacher.

My uncles were coming. Ben, the eldest of the three remaining, took his place between his two sisters. His face was red from scrubbing since, even on Christmas morning, the sheds had to be mucked out. Mark was coming down the street with his wife on his arm and their only son, Johnny, whom I hated with a deadly hatred, trotting ahead with an insufferably priggish expression on his face.

He was eight to my eleven and I never could reconcile myself to the indignity of having to walk into chapel at his side.

'Happy Christmas, J.P.' My Uncle Mark nodded to Taid and, having received a grunt in return, edged his wife, my Aunt Flora, into place.

'Guto isn't here,' Aunt Ellen said, looking round her with a helpless air as if she feared to cross the road without her nephew.

But even my Uncle Guto, who had the courage of all King Arthur's knights, didn't dare to be too late. He came now, vaulting the garden gate to show he took religion lightly, and grasped Aunt Ellen's arm.

Taid turned his head and swept his eyes over us, over his dark-browed sons, his pearl-toothed daughters, his sister and daughter-in-law, Johnny and me. Then, not looking to left or right, he led the procession across the road with as much majesty as if he left a sea of drowning Egyptians behind.

2

I had been up in my bedroom under the eaves struggling half-heartedly with a problem ostensibly in arithmetic which I hated with a deadly hatred, but actually with the decision as to whether I wanted to be Meg in *Little Women* or one of her three younger sisters.

Meg was the eldest and had married happily and had nice babies but her life had been rather boring in my view; Jo had more life about her but had been fobbed off on the old professor; Beth had been saintly and being saintly appealed to me, though not if it required any mental effort, and she'd died young. Dying young had a limited appeal. Amy had been much prettier and an artist into the bargain but as I couldn't sketch anything that resembled what it was supposed to be that character was out too. I was lying full-length on my mattress, the books jumbled around me, having begun to consider seriously the possibility of being Lady Macbeth who went round muttering about ravens and made my blood curdle when we read it in English, fourth period,

Friday afternoons, when Nain tapped on the door.

She had climbed the ladder, the rungs of which creaked under her weight, and stuck her head through the aperture when I crawled to open the door.

'You're needed downstairs, Cariad.'

She spoke in English which denoted a serious matter.

'I was just going to do my arithmetic,' I began.

'Duw! Never mind the mathematicals. You can guess what we're worried about. The cows in Rhiannon's field that's blocking our way to the river.'

She spoke English slowly and sweetly though one had to notice her tongue stumble now and then. She had never had more than a few days schooling anywhere, but she knew everything that was worth knowing and created the rest out of her boundless imagination.

'Is it true that Widow Evans is going to charge rent for taking our cattle to the river?'

'So she says. The old man's talking of going to see Price Cheat-his-mother-in-law, but that'd be good money thrown away, since she's the deed to the meadow.'

I had never asked how our local lawyer had cheated his mother-in-law, if indeed he ever had. Most people had descriptions tacked onto their surnames to distinguish them from their neighbours and the origins of some of those descriptions were obscure indeed. Who would have guessed that Ceri Napoleon was so called because to have named her Ceri Nelson might have drawn attention to the fact that she had only one eye?

'What will happen?' I asked.

'There's to be a discussion about it.' She spoke with gravity, family discussions being convened only on rare occasions. There'd been one the previous September but war had been declared anyway.

'A big discussion?' I sat up straighter. Since I'd passed the scholarship I'd been promoted to what might have been termed a very junior position on the family board.

'Pretty big. You'd better put your chapel dress on.'

My chapel dress was grey with a pleated skirt and a white Peter Pan collar decorated with a pale blue bow. It was rather a nice dress and certainly fitted the solemnity of the occasion.

When I was ready I smoothed down my hair which had a tendency to straggle free from the thick plait in which it was confined, and climbed down the ladder to the landing. From the hall below I could hear my Uncle

Ben greeting my Uncle Mark. Their voices blended into a grave harmony and then Guto's lighter voice intervened, weaving a gayer melody.

My two oldest uncles reminded me always of two massive sheepdogs with infinite experience. Ben was the second son in the family, coming after my father, and he seemed determined on proving to the world how responsible and serious minded he was in contrast to his eldest brother who had deserted after his wife's death leaving their daughter to be brought up by the rest of his family. Ben was thirty-seven but weighty responsibilities had aged him into his forties before the years had actually caught up with him and he trod everywhere with a heavy step that matched the slight frown on his face. The frown was no more than a mask to conceal the kindness of his nature, for Uncle Ben had a horror of being thought 'soft' and went to great pains to conceal the broad streak of sentiment that ran through his character. Uncle Mark, who was three years his junior, also looked older than his actual age. He was of the same height and breadth as Uncle Ben, but his features were slightly longer and his voice a mite sharper. Ben ran our farm and was officially bailiff, though since Taid never admitted that he was now retired, Uncle Ben found himself in the rather awkward situation of being Henry IV, with Richard III smilingly abdicating, but still hanging onto the crown. Uncle Mark had decided to turn his back on farming and enter the modern industrial world. He managed the garage on the outskirts of the village and lived in a house with bay windows that was joined onto the garage. His wife was not with him though, having married a Petrie, she had every right to be present. However, she often stayed away because she didn't like leaving Johnny by himself.

'Just an excuse,' Aunt Catti had remarked to me. 'Flora never could stand up to the old man, so she stays out of the firing line.'

As I went down the stairs I saw Guto, a slim tow-headed puppy in comparison with his elder brothers, and thought it was rather sad that he was my uncle and there was no chance of my marrying him when I grew up. I'd said as much to Aunt Ellen once and she'd considered the remark for a long time before pronouncing, 'Well, in my opinion, I think incest ought to be kept in the family.'

Incest had been not uncommon in remote parts of the island in the old days. There was a belief that if father or brother took a girl's maidenhead the act provided her with a natural immunity against having babies

30

before she was married, or so Aunt Ellen had told me.

'But they must have had babies anyway,' I argued.

'All the time,' she answered serenely, 'but that doesn't alter belief.'

'And nowadays?'

We were in her room over the stables and I put my arms about my knees and looked across at her enquiringly.

'Largely died out on account of the wireless,' she said. 'There's more to do in the evenings what with that and the picture houses. Mind you, even before that the Petries never went in for it much. Father took the Biblical view of such matters. If he'd kept to the old ideas I might not have had my unfortunate experience.'

By which remark I gathered that incest was also a preventive against rape — or in Aunt Ellen's case almost rape.

There were no Victorian euphemisms in our family. Taid would never have dreamed of pasting bits of paper over the impolite words in Genesis. He used the terms himself often enough, thundering them from the pulpit, his dark eyes flashing as he castigated the whore-mongers, the fornicators, the despoilers of virgins. Everybody enjoyed John Petrie's sermons and assumed he was referring to the English.

Being farm bred I knew all about reproduction, having seen the bull being brought to the cow and the tomcat busy with the queencats. Nobody had actually sat down and explained anything to me, but I'd worked it out to my own satisfaction and it still seemed to me to be a pity that my Uncle Guto and I couldn't make a match of it.

'Better go in,' he said now, giving me a gentle push.

I went into the dining-room. Tea, which was a cooked meal we ate around six-o'-clock, would be delayed because of the conference. The midday meal we called dinner though Nain said it was different at Windsor Castle.

The tree was still in the corner, shedding its needles like crazy. The long table shone and there were ashtrays along its length. Taid had no objection to tobacco provided the use of it was confined to men. He himself smoked a pipe as did Ben and Mark. Guto smoked cigarettes which caused Taid some anxiety. He had an idea that cigarettes were intended for fast women and men who were not really men, but as he had not yet pronounced a verdict Guto went right on smoking cigarettes.

The chair at the head of the table was, of course, for my grandfather. He sat there now, beard jutting, the Bible before him. If all else failed the Good Book would be opened at random and its advice taken. First there would be the conference however, the Lord having given everybody a brain to exercise before we went bleating to him with every little problem.

The rest of us sat as if we were at a board meeting, my uncles alternating with their sisters and Nain, Aunt Ellen and me at the foot of the table. An extra chair had been put ready for Aunt Flora but it was no more than a gesture since she hardly ever came. Smiles and decorous greetings were exchanged though not one of us had been absent from any of the others for more than a few hours.

'Let us begin by saying a prayer for guidance,' Taid said and launched into one immediately. 'Almighty God, who created and put in motion both heaven and earth allotting land according to measure, guide us to a rightful decision in the matter of the disputed territory between Mrs Rhiannon Evans and us. Amen.'

It was a much shorter prayer than usual, which meant Taid was eager to get on with the business in hand. There were echoes of amen all round the table. Then Taid reached for pipe and matches and his two elder sons followed suit. In a few minutes blue-grey spirals of smoke and the heavy scent of shag tobacco filled the air.

'The problem,' said Taid, 'concerns the disputed meadow that runs along our fences and blocks us from the river.'

'The meadow is not disputed,' said Uncle Mark, 'since we all know it belongs to Rhiannon Evans. The right to cross it is disputed.'

'It's the same thing,' Taid said.

'Not in law,' Uncle Mark began, but was interrupted.

'Since when did you know anything about the law? Manager of a garage is what you are. I don't remember you taking any degree in law. If I'd wanted a lawyer I'd have got Price Cheat-his-mother-in-law. I'm not interested in the law. I'm only interested in getting my cattle down to the river, and that means the meadow is disputed.'

'The right of way is disputed!'

'That's just what I've been saying!' Taid snapped.

'We've always had right of way,' Uncle Ben said. 'There was never any question when Geraint was alive.'

'Geraint was a reasonable man,' Taid said. 'You can't expect a woman to be so reasonable.'

'If you ask me women are more reasonable

than men in lots of ways,' Aunt Catti said.

'If they were they'd be running the world, not filling it with babies,' Taid said.

'I'm not filling it with babies,' Aunt Marget said indignantly.

'And never will be if you don't put a bomb behind Emyr Jones,' her father retorted. 'Eight years you've been wearing that ring and he hasn't named the day yet.'

'We're getting off the point,' Uncle Mark reminded us. 'The point is our right of way through that meadow. We've no paper to prove right of way. Now if we went to court it could be argued that the right isn't automatic since we can take our cattle round by the road nearly as quickly.'

'With cars and lorries thundering through, those cows that weren't killed would miscarry with fright,' Uncle Ben said.

'We could send a petition to the government and ask them to re-route the traffic,' Aunt Ellen said.

'Those lorries are taking aeroplane parts to Valley,' Guto objected. 'The government isn't going to hold up the war effort just because we can't get our cows across the road.'

'If only Lloyd George was in power we could drop him a line,' Nain said wistfully. 'I remember when he came to speak at the drill hall in Caernarvon and we all went to hear him. A peach of a man! The way he looked — '

'Didn't stop at looking either,' Uncle Mark said. 'No, not you, Mam! But there were tales coming from the valleys even before he was elected. It's a wonder he wasn't called to the penance seat.'

'He's a politician,' Taid said. 'They need a bit of relaxation.'

'Well, he did a lot of relaxing up in the valleys,' Uncle Mark said.

'It's not for us to criticize,' Taid said. 'He wasn't a member of our chapel anyway.'

'Not only miscarry,' Uncle Ben said, pursuing his own train of thought. 'Breathing in those old petrol fumes can't do them any good either!'

'Has anyone actually talked about it to Mrs Evans?' Aunt Catti wanted to know.

Aunt Marget was turning the ring round on her finger and looking very thoughtful.

'She told Dai Post that unless we offer payment she's going to take out an injunction,' Taid said.

'Perhaps it was just a threat,' Nain said hopefully.

'That was what they said about Hitler when he was talking about Austria,' Uncle Mark said, 'and the next thing anybody knew he was sitting in Vienna.'

'Mrs Evans isn't bringing her herd over into our meadow, is she?' Uncle Ben enquired.

'Did she happen to mention to Dai Post how much money she wanted?' Aunt Ellen asked.

'What difference does that make since we've no intention of paying one penny?' Taid demanded. 'If you can't think of something more sensible to say you'd do better to keep quiet, Ellen.'

'She's a right to an opinion, the same as the rest of us,' Nain said.

'Not when it's a bloody stupid question!' Taid never used strong language but 'bloody' in his opinion, was a lively adjective.

'Well, if you're not willing to pay and Ben won't take them by way of the main road, what are we going to do?' Guto demanded.

'You could hex her cows until she gave in,' Taid said to Nain.

'I thought you were against hexing,' Aunt Ellen said.

'As a general rule, yes,' Taid said cautiously, 'but when it's in a good cause then I don't object. I'm against making war but when you're attacked it's only common sense to fight back, otherwise we'd have Huns running all over the place.'

'Rhiannon Evans is as Welsh as you are!' Uncle Ben said.

'Her father was a Monmouth man, bit of the Saxon in him somewhere.'

'I don't like wishing ill.' Nain was looking unhappy.

'I don't suppose many people like going off to fight either,' Taid said scornfully, 'but they do their duty.'

'You could hex a little bit, Mam,' Aunt Marget coaxed. 'Give them a touch of milk fever or something?'

'Not milk fever,' Uncle Ben said. 'That can spread to our herd.'

'What about bubonic plague?' Guto said brightly.

'I wouldn't do anything so wicked!' Nain exclaimed. 'And I don't have a spell for that anyway.'

'Why punish the animals? It's not their fault. Give Rhiannon Evans the flu or something,' Uncle Mark suggested.

Nain still looked unhappy. She was tender hearted even towards her enemies, and I knew it would weigh on her conscience.

I heard myself saying, 'Why doesn't Uncle Ben marry Mrs Evans and then we'd have right of way all over her farm.'

It was the first time I'd ever spoken up at a family conference and my voice trailed away into a complete and utter silence. Every eye was upon me.

'I only thought,' I began lamely but Taid interrupted, banging the palm of his hand down so hard on the table top that the Bible jumped.

'Out of the mouths of babes and sucklings!' he cried.

'She'd make a lovely wife for you, Ben!' Nain's face was glowing, her conscience relieved.

'A blue dress and hat since it'd be her second time around,' Aunt Ellen said. 'One bridesmaid. More wouldn't be fitting.'

'Her father died about seven or eight years ago, so we'd have to find someone to give her away,' Aunt Marget chimed in.

'Mark could do that and then Guto could be best man,' Aunt Catti suggested.

'It's a bit of a responsibility for a young boy.' Aunt Ellen primmed her mouth.

'I've been best man twice before so I'll give you a few tips,' Uncle Mark said.

'I don't want to marry Rhiannon Evans,' Uncle Ben said. There was another brief silence. Then Taid said, his voice rumbling slightly, 'Of course you want to marry her. Don't be so bloody silly.'

'And she doesn't want to marry me.'

'How do you know that for heaven's sake?' Nain demanded. 'Have you asked her?'

'I've not asked her and I'm not going to ask

39

her,' Uncle Ben said.

'Of course you're going to ask her.' Taid bent upon him the full ferocity of his glare. 'It's not natural for a man of thirty-seven to be unmarried. You'll have people talking.'

'You've heard them, have you?' Uncle Ben's voice was deadly polite.

'She's a very attractive woman,' Nain said encouragingly, 'and I've heard she sets a good table.'

'Let her set it for somebody else then!'

'You see what you've done!' Taid turned wrathfully upon Nain. 'Brought them up soft as butter, encouraged them to rebel against me. You see!'

'Don't you go heaping blame on Mam!' Uncle Ben shouted. He shouted so seldom that we all jumped. 'I'll get married when I'm good and ready, not before. Right now I'm comfortable as I am.'

'Too comfortable, if you ask me.' Taid scorned. 'You don't know the meaning of hard living. Time you stood on your own feet and raised your own sons!'

'I've run this place practically single-handed the past five years and had the Squire's estate to manage.'

'Meaning I'm too old to be useful any longer? Time for me to be six feet under, I suppose? Sharper than a serpent's tooth — '

'Wasn't it clever of Nell to think of it?' Aunt Ellen said.

'She passed to the grammar, didn't she?' Taid said. 'She's going to be a genius. I'd say she's made a promising start.'

There were approving nods and murmurs, even from Uncle Ben, though in his case they were somewhat perfunctory.

'Right then!' Taid folded his arms, speaking through teeth clenched on his pipe.

'It's all settled. Ben starts courting Rhiannon Evans and that's the end of any right of way nonsense. You're a good girl, Nell.'

I sat, looking suitably modest with all the promise of my genius on me. Only Uncle Ben was glowering, but in the general atmosphere of satisfaction I was the only one who noticed.

3

We were entering a cool damp February,
which nobody minded since Februarys were
supposed to be cool and damp, except in
Australia where everything was upside-down
anyway. I was back at school where, after
having been there a term, I was settling well,
or so my teachers said. I was learning Latin
and spent hours muttering 'amo, amas, amat'
and 'hic, haec, hoc', as if the words were a
mysterious conjuration.

'Such a lot of ways of saying 'love',' Nain
marvelled.

'I'd be happy if Ben found one way of
saying it,' Taid grumbled.

There was some justice in what he said.
Since the family discussion my uncle had not
exactly implemented the decision taken. He
had not argued or shouted again. He had
simply gone on as usual, tipping a cool nod to
Rhiannon Evans if he chanced to see her
while he was driving our cattle across her
meadows, otherwise ignoring her.

'Ben's a good boy. He knows his duty,'
Nain said.

'Knowing and doing are two different

things. It says in the Bible that we're better off married. You hear that, Ben?' He raised his voice slightly as my uncle came through from the back. 'St Paul tells us it is better to marry than to burn!'

'I'm not burning,' Uncle Ben said placidly as he stomped through.

Nain and I exchanged glances. Matters must be serious if Taid had started quoting the New Testament. The Gospels had too much forgiving in them for his taste, Taid's maker being the stern Jehovah of the Israelites.

'Perhaps he's a bit shy?' Nain excused.

'He wasn't so shy when he was taking out Maggie Chip Shop,' Taid said.

'I wasn't sorry when that broke up,' Nain observed. 'The smell got into his clothes something dreadful.'

'Well, something will have to happen soon,' Taid said. 'Mrs Evans was measuring the gate in our fence day before yesterday with a look in her eye.'

'What sort of look?' I asked with interest.

'A look that told me she's thinking of buying poles or barbed wire so that she can block off the gate from her side,' Taid said darkly.

'Did you ask her what she was doing?' Nain demanded.

'I wouldn't give her the satisfaction.' He opened the parlour door and went in, shutting it firmly behind him.

'That I can believe,' Nain muttered. Then her expression lightened as she saw my enquiring face. 'A grown-up joke Cariad,' she said. 'Haven't you got any homework to do?'

'I did it last night,' I said virtuously. 'I'm waiting for Auntie Catti.'

'It's your day for going into Bangor! I'd forgotten all about it with all the worrying over the right of way,' she said contritely.

The aunts, Marget and Catti, took me out for the day once a year each. Aunt Marget took me on the first Saturday in September and Aunt Catti took me on the first Saturday in February. With Aunt Marget I always went to Holyhead and with Aunt Catti I went to Bangor. I enjoyed both outings immensely though we always did exactly the same things, but that made the outings as warm and secure as a familiar blanket snuggled round one on a cold night.

I was wearing my new cape with my grey chapel dress underneath and I had a shilling to spend. I never received regular pocket money. Nain never had anything over from the housekeeping that Taid grudgingly doled out and Aunt Ellen always said she was penniless, though it was generally believed in the family that she had a secret bank account somewhere. Uncle Ben turned over his coppers to me after I'd helped him muck out and Uncle Mark gave me five pounds on my birthday, but that wasn't until April and I'd spent the last lot. Guto never had any money, but he let me take a drag at his cigarette sometimes and now and then, if there was a Walt Disney film on, he'd take me to the cinema. He didn't actually take me to see Walt Disney as the rest of the family believed. We used to whip round the corner and see something with Barbara Stanwyck in it instead.

Aunt Catti was wearing her light blue waisted-coat and a little white felt hat that dipped over one eye. She had unruly black hair that curled at its own will and the hat looked like a gallant white boat anchored to the waves of a dark and stormy sea. She was nearly twenty-eight years old and had walked out with a whole string of young men but until Aunt Marget was married there wasn't much point in getting too serious about anyone, Aunt Catti being too devoted to her sister to be the first one to be wed.

We went out to the corner to wait for the bus. It was only a short ride over the gleaming suspension bridge and through the town. We always got off at the Plaza Cinema and spent ten minutes looking at the stills in the frames at each side of the entrance. Next to the cinema was an even more fascinating place. Set back from the road behind a jumble of granite, marble and slate was the stonemason's house. He carved all the local tombstones and always put the latest examples of his work in his front garden. Aunt Catti and I would linger, trying to decide which ones we'd choose for ourselves.

'The angel one looks very nice. Everybody would notice that.'

'That's the problem.' Aunt Catti's smooth round face wrinkled with indecision. 'I'd not want a load of strangers gaping at me and leaving litter.'

'The marble is nice.'

'Now there I agree with you. It's got a lovely sheen and the gold lettering would set it off a treat.'

When we had made choice of tombstone we walked up the long curving hill past the Willow Pattern Tea Shoppe and the hospital to the tiny bookshop on the corner. There were bigger bookshops in the town but this one was the most fascinating for it sold second-hand volumes and there was a tale that someone had once picked up a first edition there.

The shop was on two floors with books piled to the ceiling and the proprietor almost buried behind a desk piled with more books. There were always college students, lordly in their black gowns, coming in and out to sell and buy. Outside the door on a three-legged stool sat a tramp. The same tramp had sat there for as long as I could remember and he was always reading a book. I didn't know his name or anything about him but once, as we'd gone into the shop, he'd raised his shaggy head and said, 'We are such stuff as dreams are made on . . . '

He'd bent his head again immediately, not finishing the quotation, but his voice had been rich and strong, full of echoes.

We went past him today and I dived into the books. They were not arranged in any order, save that the heavy volumes were at the bottom. Some of these volumes were beautifully bound in vellum and calfskin. Other books with covers ripped and pages missing were flung into a wire basket at the side. I ignored those and crouched down by the bookshelves, running my finger along dusty spines. I had my shilling but, if the book cost more, Aunt Catti always willingly paid the difference. Most books were well within my range, however.

'This looks interesting.' I pulled out a fat volume and opened it. 'There are lots of pictures.'

Aunt Catti bent to look at it with me and we both uttered a small squeal, Aunt Catti ahead of me since she had taken in what the picture was all about and I wasn't sure.

'Good Lord!' She snatched the book from me and burrowed her way to the desk where her voice was lowered into a furious tirade of which I caught the odd phrase like 'check your stock more carefully' and 'ruination of innocence.'

I went back to searching the shelves and found a thin red book marked at a shilling. '*Shirley* by Currer Bell', the front cover informed me. The print inside was very small but there would be plenty of reading. I took it outside to have a closer look. It had been printed in 1854 and a couple of the pages were loose. I didn't think it was a first edition but it was old enough to be interesting. I looked at the name of the author again, shaping it with my lips. Currer was an odd name. I didn't know if it was male or female.

'Charlotte.' The tramp had raised his head. 'Currer Bell was the pseudonym used by Charlotte Brontë.'

It was as if he'd read my thoughts, which was not too difficult since, born in April, I had an April face which reflected every shade of my passing moods.

'The one who wrote *Jane Eyre*?' I looked at

the title with renewed interest.

'*Shirley* is the weakest of her novels,' the tramp said. 'The story is diffuse and it tails off badly towards the end, but there are some splendid character studies.'

'It won't be too old for me?' I said doubtfully.

'All great literature is too old for everybody but in striving to understand it we grow in stature ourselves,' he said and bent his head again, the cadences of his beautiful voice dying until the air was as still as if he had never spoken.

I went in and paid for the book with my shilling. It was all I'd managed to hold back from the weekly Band of Hope collections, and I felt no sense of sin as I handed it over. The Band of Hope did very well out of me as a rule. Aunt Catti was still rather pink in the face after her tirade and Mr Gregson, the proprietor, put the book into a red and white striped bag as if he were doing us a very special favour to mollify my aunt's wrath.

'Is it a nice story you've bought?' she asked me as we turned into College Road.

'It's by Charlotte Brontë, the author of *Jane Eyre*. Currer Bell was her pseudonym,' I said.

'Heavens! The things you know!' She gave me an admiring look.

Clearly she hadn't seen me talking to the tramp and I didn't enlighten her. My aunts were not as tolerant about tramps as my grandmother was, though they were proud of their gypsy blood.

We strolled down College Road, heading for the neo-Gothic building of grey stone that looked exactly as a university ought to look. There were lawns and trees about it and students were passing in and out of the high gates. Those gates stood open and there was nothing in the world to prevent us from walking through them and up the path, but that would have seemed to us both as immoral as marching past St Peter at the gates of heaven before our credentials had been checked out. The university was for those who had passed their Higher School Certificate with flying colours and were launched upon a degree.

'There are no lectures on Saturday afternoons, of course,' Aunt Catti said as she had said before, 'but the library is kept open so that the students can study.'

We stood by the gates for quite a long time, our minds accompanying the black-gowned young men and women — far fewer men since the war had begun — and then, with a mutual accord, we went on down the road to a small gate that led into the terraced parks and tennis courts. In summer the azaleas splashed pink and blue and mauve over the steep, twisting paths and the slap-slap of tennis balls sounded on the courts, but now only the pussy willows were beginning to feather forth and beyond a thin line of peering snowdrops the courts were deserted, the nets sagging and grass springing without permission between the stones.

Aunt Catti wore high-heeled shoes that made descending the steep paths a perilous exercise, so that she frequently had to pause or go a little out of her way to avoid a fall of pine needles. I went ahead, clutching my book, passing now and then a bench on which a couple sat holding hands. One young man was in a uniform, with a peaked cap over his head. He sat holding both the hands of the girl he was with and neither of them was talking. As I went by I felt a kind of quiet desperation emanating from them, though I hadn't then the words to express it.

The courts were not entirely deserted. As I reached one of the lower paths I saw another couple, not sitting, but walking on the court itself, touching finger tips across the sagging net. Their heads were turned towards each other and, if the court had been surrounded by spectators, they wouldn't have noticed it. Even at eleven I recognized the chain that bound them and I stopped dead, staring after them, as they reached the far side of the court where there was a large hole in the wire. They ducked through the hole into the dense shrubbery at the other side and the slight bumping of their bodies as they moved close to each other ran through me like a physical shock. I felt as I had felt years before when Taid, taking me to the fireplace, had knelt with me inside the circle of his arm saying,

'Fire is hot and burns. You must never go near the fire.'

And, so saying, had taken my small hand and placed it for the fraction of an endless second on one of the glowing red coals. I remembered the shock of pain dying into a white throbbing, the sense of betrayal and after that the curiosity with which I had regarded flames that licked and leapt out of the coals, writhing in orange and scarlet with a line of blue curving at the heart.

Guto had never talked about girls save in general terms. As far as I had been aware, when he'd finished his chores about the farm he went over to lend a hand at Uncle Mark's garage and then went off to play football or cricket. I had never imagined him with a girl and the sight of him, oblivious to my presence, with a female I'd never seen caught my breath with a thrill of intense pain and intense curiosity.

'I ought to have worn my sensible shoes,' Aunt Catti said, panting slightly as she joined me.

She said the same thing every year though we always walked this way even when the first Saturday in February rained cats and dogs.

'I saw Guto,' I heard myself say.

'Guto? Where?' She looked about her.

'The other side of the tennis court,' I said, adding, 'with a girl.'

My announcement fell sadly flat. Aunt Catti merely inspected her legs carefully in case her stockings had a run in them and said 'That'll be his new girl, I suppose. Olive something or other, her name is.'

'New girl' implied there had been others. And Aunt Catti pronounced the words as if they had no significance at all for me.

'I didn't know that he had a girl,' I said, making my voice very light and grown up to show that it didn't matter to me at all.

'Well, of course Guto has a girl,' Aunt Catti said. 'Only natural that he'd have a girl, probably will have plenty of them before he's through. No need to mention it to the old man. He still thinks of Guto as a baby.'

My aunt had been in the gravest danger of falling in my estimation, but that remark sent her soaring back to her high eminence. In a couple of phrases she had enlisted me in the ranks against Taid, made me part of the family conspiracy designed to keep him ignorant of what his kindred really did as opposed to what he fondly imagined they did.

'I'll not say anything,' I said solemnly and we walked together in perfect amity along the path and beneath the memorial arch.

'Seems funny,' said Aunt Catti glancing back at it, 'that it was put up in memory of all those who were killed in the last war.'

'Will they put up another arch when this war is over?' I asked.

'Oh, I don't suppose it will last long enough to make it worth while. All be over by Christmas,' she answered as we crossed the road and cut up the lane at the side of the Castle Hotel. The main street ran at right angles to the top of the lane. On one side, sunk in a wide corner, was the cathedral. I had been inside once or twice, but the interior had been suspiciously elaborate with a high carved altar and glinting candlesticks. We therefore turned the other way, past the shops, the Recruiting Office, the Italian ice-cream parlour, to the café where we always had tea before we caught the bus home.

Robert Roberts was a confectioners on the

ground floor with two tea-rooms above. There was always an enormous wedding cake displayed in the left-hand window, four tiers of white icing swirls, silver bells and horseshoes and a plastic bride and groom on top. As the same cake was always there I had begun to suspect that it too was made of plaster, but if so it was very regularly dusted.

All the cakes in the other window were real. The rationing didn't seem to have bitten very deeply yet in our part of the world. There were maids-of-honour, and Eccles cakes, and chocolate log, and bara-brith, and seed cake and flaky rolls filled with vanilla custard.

We went through the shop and up the staircase at the back to the tea-rooms above. Everything in those two rooms was brown except the tablecloths on the round tables and the net curtains at the windows and they were so sparklingly white that they hurt the eyes. The front windows looked down into the main street, the back windows looked out across a huddle of slate roofs up the hill to the grey mass that crowned the hill. Seen from this distance and at this angle, the university looked more like a cathedral than the cathedral itself.

We took our usual table in the bay of the window and the waitress rustled forward in her black silk dress and starched lace apron, her notebook and pencil poised. There was a menu on the table, propped between salt cellar and pepper pot and, having greeted the waitress, Aunt Catti and I bent our heads over the handwritten card.

The menu never varied, at least not when we went there in February, but we always read it through from top to bottom, earnestly debated each item and then ordered exactly the same things each time.

'A pot of tea for two, some buttered toast and a plate of chocolate éclairs,' Aunt Catti said.

'Would you like some jam?' the waitress asked as she always did.

'Perhaps — if you have gooseberry?' Aunt Catti gave me a look of slight anxiety. 'Is that aright with you, Nell? You look a bit peaky.'

I was still thinking about Guto. Seeing him with the girl had cast a shadow over the afternoon. But I couldn't spoil my aunt's pleasure.

'Gooseberry would be lovely,' I said and pushed my uncle to the back of my mind.

The waitress scribbled rapidly on her pad and rustled away.

'Well, this is nice!' Aunt Catti unfastened her coat and slid her arms out of it and I took off my coat and draped it over the back of my chair.

'I could do with a cup of tea.' I knew the lines of our scene backwards and forwards.

'Nothing like a cup of tea.' She had eased her feet slightly out of her shoes and drew a long breath of relief.

'Unless it's two cups of tea,' I quipped and she laughed the laugh that had bells in it.

The waitress brought the laden tray and my aunt and I sat back in our chairs, our elbows in, like two good children, while she put everything on the table. The tea came in a plump brown pot with a tall, narrow jug of boiling water, a smaller jug of milk and a bowl of lump sugar. The jam was in a flowered china pot with a curved handle from which a shallow spoon hung. The four slices of thickly buttered toast lay in a chafing dish and on the cake stand, each in a doily of lacy paper, were four éclairs, the tops dark with melted chocolate, the soft underside of the delicate choux pastry brimful with cream whipped until it was almost yellow.

'Shall I pour the tea?' Aunt Catti asked.

I nodded, pushing my cup nearer, watching the stream of amber liquid.

We ate in silence, save for the faint crunching of our teeth on the toast, the rattle of teaspoon in the saucer, the slight sucking noise made by the jam spoon as we plunged it into the cool, tart preserve. This was a ritual, to be savoured slowly and with infinite satisfaction. Even the taking of our second éclair apiece, with exchanged looks of rueful greediness, had the character of a sacrament.

'I shouldn't have had that second one. I'll be as fat as a pig,' Aunt Catti said at last.

Both she and Aunt Marget were pleasingly plump. It was impossible to imagine them thin.

'You're lovely as you are,' I said truthfully.

'They say men like a bit of an armful,' she said.

'They won't like me then.'

'They'll admire your mind,' she assured me. 'When you go to the university you'll be meeting boys from all over the country and when you get your degree — ' She drew a long breath of anticipation.

'Nain will be pleased,' I said.

'Nain will be delighted. It was always her dream that one of us should go to the university,' Aunt Catti said softly. 'Mind you, we did all go to the grammar, but none of us stayed to do our Higher School Certificate. I might have gone, but my Latin let me down. Two out of a hundred I got in my school certificate. Mind, there was a kind of distinction in that too. It was the lowest mark recorded in North Wales.'

'That was something,' I agreed.

'I don't suppose I could do it twice,' she regretted.

'I like Latin. There's a pattern to it,' I said.

'Wasn't a pattern I could follow. Would you like to go to the Ladies while I settle the bill?'

I went with alacrity, knowing that she wouldn't follow me. Aunt Catti only went to the toilet in her own house. It had made life difficult for her in school where she had held on to the contents of her bladder all day and then run home, every door opening at her approach, until she reached the haven of the yard.

When I got back she had paid up and was putting on her coat. Our afternoon together was drawing to its close. I put on my cloak and took up *Shirley* in its peppermint-striped bag and we went down the stairs and through the shop into the street again and walked briskly to the bus stop.

'Is Uncle Ben going to marry Rhiannon Evans?' I said.

'It was decided, wasn't it?'

'Yes, but — ' I hesitated, feeling a pang of guilt. My Uncle Ben had given me several glances of quiet reproach recently.

'Ben's a bit shy,' said Aunt Catti, putting out her hand to flag down the bus. 'He's had a lot to do on our place and over on the big estate and Guto's only been helping since he left school. Taking a girl out now and then is one thing, but marrying is another. A man can get too settled in his ways.'

We broke off the conversation as we climbed aboard, it being an unwritten rule that we didn't talk about family affairs in public. The bus was fairly crowded and the talk around us was mainly of the war which, I gathered, was hotting up. At home the war wasn't talked about much at all. It had arrived and I think most of the family felt it would go away again if nobody took much notice of it. But I saw there were some men in uniform and that, though the evening was closing in, no lights glittered along the way. Some of the road signs had been blacked out, so that if a German spy landed he'd not know whether he was in Beaumaris or Cardiff — it being a known fact that enemy maps were all wildly inaccurate.

By the time we reached our stop it was quite dark and the house with its white-washed wall glimmered only faintly, the blackout curtains tightly fastened.

There were no chinks of light from any of the windows along the street and the unusual gloom had about it something exciting and dangerous as if the village had become sinister, its inhabitants masked.

The kitchen, for we entered the back way, was warm and bright. Aunt Marget was carrying the dishes up to the dining room and Nain was sliding the big pot of lobscourse out of the oven. She was famous for her lobscourse with its lean, pink ham layered with turnips, onions, potato and apple and scattered with spice. There were extra potatoes, fluffed with butter and browned under the grill, and an apple tart to follow.

'You'll be ready for your tea,' she said as we came in.

She was right. The brisk walk to the bus and the journey itself had effectively disposed of buttered toast, gooseberry jam and cream éclairs.

'I bought a book, Nain.' I showed it to her. 'It is nearly a hundred years old.'

'Fancy now!' Her black hair hung about her face in little wisps and she pushed them back, bending to read the title. 'Did you have enough money?'

'It cost a shilling.'

'A whole shilling for such an old book! You think they'd have taken a bit off,' she said.

'Shall I show it to Taid?'

'He's writing his sermon.' She hesitated, then said, 'You may as well go in. The old bugger'll grumble less if it's you. It's time for his tea anyway.'

I climbed the stairs to the floor that was level with the street. I could hear Taid muttering to himself behind the parlour door. As a lay preacher he deputized for the regular minister once a month and was frequently invited to preach in other chapels too. People said his sermons were better than the minister's. They were full of 'hwyl', that untranslatable Welsh word that can be applied to any gathering and refers to the intensity of emotion with which one enters into the spirit of an occasion. When Taid preached hell-fire one knew he had had the privilege of a guided tour in the infernal regions and was describing exactly what he had seen, and when he spoke of the glories to come the wonders of heaven unrolled before the eyes of his enraptured congregation.

I tapped on the door and went in to meet his uplifted gaze as he sought inspiration somewhere between the top of my head and the ceiling. Then he lowered his head and wrote rapidly. If I spoke now I'd be damned to perdition along with the rest of the sinners, so I laid the unwrapped book on the table and sat down on the stool near the door.

'Done! Amen!' He laid down his pen and reached for the book, holding it at arms' length for he flatly refused to wear spectacles.

'It's by Charlotte Brontë, Taid,' I said.

'Plenty of reading in it.' He ran his forefinger up and down the close packed columns of print. 'Not modern?'

'No, Taid.'

'When you've read it we might read it together, after we finish the Dickens book,' he said.

I read aloud to Taid from one of the English classics every Saturday night when he'd finished his sermon and tea had been cleared away. Saturday was one evening he spent in the kitchen with Nain knitting in the big armchair nearby. My aunts and uncles went out on that evening and Aunt Ellen walked down the road to sit with Gwennie Richards who had been confined to a wheelchair for years. Gwennie was rumoured to be a little bit odd, which was probably why she enjoyed Aunt Ellen's company.

This Saturday was no exception. Having approved the book Taid crossed the hall into the dining room where the lobscourse steamed, tempting one to gluttony with its aroma. Grace was pronounced and Nain dished out the mounds of food.

'Where's Ben?' Taid glanced at the empty chair.

'He ate earlier and went out,' Nain said.

'To start courting Rhiannon Evans, I hope! She's a roll of barbed wire in her front yard.'

'I think that's to keep out the Germans,' Aunt Ellen volunteered. 'They're going to put tree trunks by the roads to stop the tanks coming.'

'Lot of silly nonsense!' Nain frowned in my direction.

'It's as well to be prepared,' Aunt Ellen said.

'You should have worn a barbed skirt, Auntie, then you would never have had your unfortunate experience,' Guto said.

I had avoided looking at him, but that remark made me giggle and, meeting his twinkling eyes, I saw he looked exactly as he had looked before I had seen him with the girl.

'Don't be cheeky,' Aunt Ellen said, but she looked coy. 'Are you going out, Guto?' I asked.

'Over to Mark's. We're working on that old Ford engine.'

I beamed, thinking he couldn't get into any mischief tinkering with a car.

'There's Emyr. Excuse me.' Aunt Marget rose as the stuttering of a motor cycle sounded. 'I don't want to keep him waiting.'

'Tell him you're practising for your wedding day,' Taid said with malice.

'I'll walk with you, Guto,' Aunt Catti said. 'I'll go and keep Flora company if you and Mark are going to be busy in that old garage.'

I helped Nain clear away and wash the dishes. We worked rapidly, in complete accord, hearing the sounds of departure above and then Taid's heavy tread upon the stair.

The kitchen range glowed crimson and the two oil-lamps wrenched away our shadows and spread them over the walls and the low ceiling where the apples and onions hung. Taid sat in the high-backed chair and I sat on the stool with the heavy volume of *David Copperfield* in my lap. A piece of paper pasted inside the cover informed the reader that this book was the property of the local lending library. Taid had borrowed it in 1931. He had no intention of stealing it, but he had a bad memory when it came to libraries. That was how we'd come to possess complete sets of Dickens, Austen and Thackeray.

I began to read slowly at first so that they could both follow all the English words and then faster as I lost myself in the twists and turns of David's flight to Canterbury and his arrival on the green where Miss Betsy Trotwood waited for unofficial donkeys. In the background Nain's needles clicked and

Taid's pipe sent grey-blue smoke up to the shadowed ceiling.

'She sounds as daft as our Ellen,' Taid said as I drew to the end of the chapter.

'A good heart though.' Nain turned the heel of a sock. 'I think she'll give David a home and protect him from the Murdstones. You read lovely, Nell!'

'We'll have another chapter next week.' Taid took the book from me. 'Time you were in bed, Nell. I'll wait until 9.30 and then I'm locking up whether everybody's in or not!'

Locking the front door was a mere gesture since anyone who was late simply came in the back door anyway, but it asserted his authority to his own satisfaction at least.

I said goodnight and went quickly up the stairs to rescue my cloak before Taid grabbed it from the hallstand to use as a blanket.

4

'I've been thinking what to do about Ben and Rhiannon Evans,' Taid said.

He was presumably speaking to me as I was the only one present, but actually he would have spoken aloud even had he not been with anybody. Taid didn't need a companion off whom to bounce his words. I said nothing therefore.

'It's plain,' Taid was continuing, 'that nothing will come of anything if I leave it to them.'

He frowned, his lower lip jutting in concentration. We were in the pony trap, so he didn't have to pay much attention to the driving since the pony knew the way blindfold. Our destination was the police station in the next village. Taid's brother's son, that is to say my second cousin, was the constable there. It rather pleased us all to be able to say, 'Our relative, Police Constable Petrie.' The village was a very small one, however, and the police station no more than a tiny office with a larger room behind it where Constable Petrie lived and slept. There was a stone cell at the side with an iron-barred window that looked out into a cobbled yard.

'My nephew will know what to do,' Taid said as we drew up before the low building. Constable Petrie was seated in a rocking chair placed at an angle that gave him an uninterrupted view of the long street. His cowboy hat, which he wore instead of the more conventional helmet, was tipped over his eyes but he pushed it back as he heard the approaching rattle of wheels and clip-clop of hooves.

'Morning, Constable Petrie.' Taid used his formal title, deeming an officer of the law too important to be addressed by his Christian name.

'Morning, J.P. Morning, Nell.' He rose, tall in the high-heeled, fringed leather boots he always wore. His navy blue trousers were tucked into their tops. His truncheon hung from his belt as did the holster of his pistol. He cut, I suppose, a somewhat unconventional figure, but my second cousin was an unconventional man. All his life he had extolled and practised the simple values of a frontiersman. His twin passions were the Wild West with its rich harvest of sheriffs, outlaws and bounty hunters and the strong conviction that he had been born to impose order on a lawless world.

Unhappily he found it impossible to conform to accepted police procedure. His habit of firing his pistol into the ceilings of interview rooms where people were being questioned about motoring offences and the like; his insistence on drumming up posses; the dreadful day when, alarmed at the sight of so many English tourists streaming into Mona, he had hung a large closed notice on the suspension bridge — all had combined to make him a difficult colleague. In the end the Chief Constable, a man of rare and sensitive imagination, had given him a police station all to himself, where the measure of his efficiency could be judged by the fact there hadn't been a lynching or an Indian massacre in living memory.

'No trouble on the way, J.P.?' He lifted me down.

'All quiet, Constable.' My grandfather looped the reins of the pony over the hitching post.

'Get yourself a chair. I'll brew some tea. You'll have some buttermilk, Nell?'

'Thank you, Constable.'

'Not for much longer.' He laid a finger along his jutting Petrie nose. 'There's a rumour of promotion. Sergeant Petrie soon, I'm told.'

'No man deserves it more,' Taid said sincerely.

'I try to serve the community. Mind, the responsibility is going to be heavy with the war and everything.' He led the way into the office.

I loved Constable Petrie's office. It held a desk so large that the walls must have been built round it, for it could never have been carried through the narrow door. There was shiny brown and cream linoleum on the floor and a large board on which wanted posters were stuck. Since the previous September new ones had been added. Messrs Hitler, Goering and Himmler stared out from among Dick Poach-Your-Last Rabbit and Smuggling Tom Rhys. I had never seen Smuggling Tom Rhys, but everybody saw Dick Poach-Your-Last-Rabbit every day. He was the best poacher in the district and, though nobody troubled to arrest him, it would have hurt his feelings to have his picture removed.

'Take a good look at those faces, Nell. Commit them to memory,' the Constable instructed. 'If you see any of them in this vicinity at any time you run and tell me or your Taid.'

I obediently fixed my eyes on them, though secretly I didn't think it very likely that I'd ever meet any of the leaders of the Third Reich, even skulking in disguise, up our street. My second cousin was brewing up tea and pouring buttermilk.

'Can I go to the cell?' I asked.

I'd played house in the cell since I was tiny and still regarded it as one of my special places.

He nodded, handed me a couple of biscuits and a cushion in addition to the buttermilk, and went back to brewing the tea.

I went into the cobbled yard and across to the stone building. A thin, dark face peered out from behind the bars, teeth flashing in a white smile as I was recognized.

'How are you then, Nell?' the prisoner enquired.

'Very well, thank you, Mr Bohanna,' I said politely.

Charlie Bohanna was some relative on Nain's side, distant enough not to render his being here a social embarrassment.

'Want to come in and sit?' He obligingly opened the door for me, so that I could put the cushion on the step and lean against the jamb.

I handed him one of the biscuits and enquired, 'You've been drinking again?'

There were no fresh scars on him so he hadn't been fighting.

'Drink is a curse, Nell. Drags a man down,' he affirmed.

'Taid says that too.'

'Your Taid is a wise man, got a good head on his shoulders.' He bit into the biscuit and crunched with enjoyment, sitting next to me with his legs stretched out. The gold hoops in his ears swung softly as he turned his head. 'How's your Nain then? She's not been to see us for a while.'

'She's been busy,' I said.

'She'll be over when spring starts, I daresay,' he said. 'She always gets restless, come spring.'

He spoke truly. In spring the Romany wagons were cleaned and painted and the slow trek south began for those who had not established themselves on any permanent site. Nain, though she lived in a house for forty years, had a wistful expression at the back of her eyes when spring came and she went over more often to see her relatives.

'I'm thinking of joining up,' Charlie told me.

'In the army?' I gaped at him.

'I wasn't thinking of the Band of Hope,' Charlie said. 'The army needs good fighting men.'

He and his brothers fought with knives when the quarrel was a serious one. They were as quick as Sicilians with the long, curved blades, and artists enough not to inflict lasting harm beyond the odd scar or two. When the quarrel was minor they used hands, feet and knees.

'What the devil d'ye think you're up to then?' Constable Petrie demanded, coming suddenly round the corner.

Charlie and I looked at him blankly.

'Get your feet inside the door! You're not due to be released till noon,' the Constable snapped.

Charlie swung his legs round and grinned. 'Does that suit?' he asked.

'Twelve o'clock, boy! Not ten to twelve! Haven't I enough to do keeping the peace round here without having to repeat myself to you? Twelve o'clock! Nell, your Taid's waiting.'

'See you later, Charlie,' I said.

'Tell your Nain to come over and see us soon,' he said.

We would go, of course, and I would talk with Charlie a few more times until the army swallowed him up and we learned long years after that he'd died as a prisoner-of-war on the Burma railroad, but that was hidden from me on that day.

'Did you settle what to do about Uncle Ben?' I ventured when we were nearly home.

There was no guarantee Taid would answer me because there were many times when he believed that children should be seen but not heard. However, as the original suggestion had come from me, he clearly felt that there was some justice in my being involved.

'Constable Petrie was of the opinion that Ben could bail her out if she was arrested for something,' he said.

'But she'd have to break the law first, wouldn't she?' I said.

'There's the difficulty,' Taid said moodily. 'Rhiannon Evans is a pillar of respectability. It's a problem.'

'If Uncle Ben is shy perhaps someone ought to stand in for him,' I said.

'Stand in? How?' He shot me an impatient, frowning look.

'Like Mr Barkis and Peggotty in *David Copperfield*. You know when Mr Barkis tells David to tell Peggotty that Barkis is willing? And Peggotty marries him.'

'Escob fawr, the child's right!' Taid's look of impatience turned to one of the warmest admiration as he slapped the reins hard across the pony's back and sent us bounding past Virgin and Child Cottage towards the next gateway that led by various twists and turns to the Evans farmhouse.

He would have turned in at the gate

without a second thought, but chance had it that Rhiannon Evans was on her way down the path as we reached the gate. She wore a flowered dress and her lips were certainly redder than could be achieved by biting. She hesitated as Taid drew up with a flourish and then walked forward steadily, a spot of colour burning on each cheek. It was obvious that she had steeled herself for an unpleasant encounter.

'Good morning, Mrs Evans!' Taid's heartiness almost blew her backwards.

'Good morning, Mr Petrie.' Her voice was chipped ice.

'I have to tell you, Mrs Evans,' Taid said in a tone that dripped conspiracy, 'that Ben is willing.'

'I beg your — ?' She had stopped, a look of blank astonishment on her face.

'Willing,' Taid repeated heavily. 'Ben is *willing*, Mrs Evans.'

With the sure instinct of an actor who knows exactly when to leave the stage he tugged at the reins, turning the trap in a circle and we trotted back to our house.

'You're a good girl, Nell!' Taid gave me an approving look as I climbed down.

I hoped Rhiannon Evans had read *David Copperfield*, but from the bewilderment on her face I doubted it.

After that, during the days that followed, we seemed to be forever bumping into Mrs Rhiannon Evans and every time Taid would utter the mysterious phrase, nod his head encouragingly, and move on.

As usual there was a variety of opinion expressed within the family. Nain torn between her reluctance to agree with Taid and her desire to think well of my brainwave, sat rather uncomfortably on the fence. Aunt Ellen leapt into the fray.

'Willing to do *what*, for heaven's sake? What will Rhiannon Evans imagine Ben is willing to do?'

'Pay the money for the right of way, perhaps?' Guto suggested.

'You don't think so, do you?' Taid said, alarmed. 'I don't want her to get the wrong impression.'

'Sounds a bit romantic,' Aunt Catti said.

'Sounds foolish to me.' For once Aunt Marget disagreed with her sister. 'Emyr wouldn't think of such a thing.'

'If we took Emyr Jones as the pattern of how to go courting, nobody in the world would ever get married,' Taid said unkindly.

Aunt Marget's brown eyes filled with tears.

'Always getting on at her!' Aunt Catti said wrathfully. 'It's a big step getting married. You can't just jump into it.'

'Jump!' Taid echoed. 'Good God, if Emyr

Jones started crawling to the chapel I'd regard it as a miracle!'

'Perhaps you want him to rape her!' Aunt Ellen shrilled. 'Will that satisfy you, J.P.? To have your own daughter stained and dishonoured, forced into wedlock — '

'Oh, do be quiet, Ellen,' Taid said, flapping his hand at her.

'I can't see Ben raping Rhiannon Evans,' Aunt Catti said, giggling.

'I'd die of shame if any of my sons did such a thing,' Nain said. 'I hope that I've brought my sons up to respect women.'

'Respect is one thing. Running away from them is something else,' Taid growled.

'Ben never ran away from anything in his life,' Nain said, narrow eyed.

'Ben ran away from a pig once! You've chosen to forget that, haven't you?'

'A sow in farrow — and he was six years old at the time! You'd have run yourself under those circumstances!'

'Rhiannon Evans isn't a sow,' Aunt Marget said.

'No, and the way Ben's going on she'll never be in farrow either!' Taid shouted and went out, slamming the door behind him with ferocity.

Uncle Ben took no part in these discussions. He behaved as if the topic had nothing to do with him at all. He ate his meals placidly, went off to his work about the farm and the estate and said not one word about Rhiannon Evans. He was like a man with a dread disease who hopes that, if he ignores it, it will go away.

'It was a good idea, Nell,' Taid said to me, 'but I'm beginning to think Rhiannon Evans is a bit lacking in the top storey.'

'Perhaps we ought to lend her *David Copperfield*?' I suggested.

He considered it, then shook his head.

'She wouldn't give it back,' he said. 'That's the trouble with lending things to people. Anyway, we've not finished reading it ourselves yet.'

'Perhaps you could preach a sermon?'

'Well, not entirely on that one subject,' he demurred, 'but it wouldn't do any harm to hint at it.'

His very next sermon centred on the blessings of married life.

'There is no condition known to man, short of being dead and beyond earthly troubles, that is more pleasing to the Lord. Look in the Bible and every great leader was married. Moses had a wife, Abraham had a wife, David had a wife! King David approved so heartily of the sacrament of matrimony that he took several wives — not that I am advocating the same! Times are different now and there are more men to go round, but that's not a state of affairs that will continue for long! It is the duty of healthy men and women to be married, to beget children, before the darkness of a new barbarism falls over our ancient land. A good wife is above rubies! Above rubies, mark you! And the immortality of a man is contained in his sons and in his daughters. A man's children are his treasures, greater than money, or land. And the mother of his children is above rubies!'

I slanted my eyes along the bench and caught a decidedly cynical twist to Nain's lips. Uncle Ben sat as stolid and immobile as wood, but Rhiannon Evans had flushed crimson and had an awakened look in her face.

'The penny's dropped.' Guto nudged me, whispering, and I saw that he had been looking in the same direction. I choked back a giggle and stared hard at my feet.

When we came out of chapel Aunt Ellen burst forth.

'Going on and on like that! Is it my fault that I had an unfortunate experience? Do you think it's pleasant to be an old maid? And your own daughters still single! Showing them up in public. Nasty, I call it! Shaming your own family and putting ideas in people's heads. Don't blame anybody but yourself if the penance seat is full next week! I never heard such nonsense — King David indeed! What kind of example is King David, I'd like to know? Messing about with the Queen of Sheba!'

'That was his son, King Solomon!'

'There you are then!' Aunt Ellen cried in triumph. 'Like father, like son. Setting a bad example to his own children!'

'Morning, Mrs Evans!' Taid, ignoring his sister, spoke loudly.

'Lovely sermon, Taid.' Rhiannon Evans used the familiar term used by everybody else in the village for the first time. 'Gave one food for thought.' Her eyes slid to Uncle Ben who stood rooted to the spot, the expression on his face the expression of a man who sees the guillotine ahead and realizes he's next in the line.

'Above rubies,' Nain said, busy with some wry thought of her own. 'Now that's the part that caught my interest.'

Guto and I walked on rapidly, stifling our laughter until we'd crossed the road and entered our own garden where we leaned against the wall, clutching ourselves and groaning with mirth. 'Food for thought and poor old Ben's the meal she's licking her lips over!'

'Red lips!' I bent double.

'Like rubies!' Guto chortled.

The others were returning, all save Uncle Ben. It being a Sabbath everybody used the front door, the women removing their hats as they entered. Nain wore her black chapel coat and the hat with a little white bow at the side. It was a most respectable outfit but, with her wiry dark hair and the rings in her ears, she still looked like a gypsy pretending to be ordinary. By the time Taid arrived Guto had recovered from his hysterics but I was still moaning softly. Taid saw me but considered it beneath his dignity to notice, or perhaps he was too elated at the turn events had taken.

When I finally went into the dining-room they were all discussing the wedding.

'No need for a long engagement since they are neither of them children,' Nain was saying.

'No point in waiting for Ben. Seeing that he's walking her home she's bound to ask him in for a bit of dinner.' Aunt Ellen had forgotten how cross she had been about the sermon.

'I'll put some in the oven just in case,' Nain said, dishing up.

'May would be nice,' Aunt Catti said.

'That's when Flora's expecting,' Aunt

Marget reminded her. 'Best to wait a month or two after.'

'I think we must leave things to take their course,' Taid said judiciously. 'No need to embarrass him by asking questions. We won't mention it when he comes in. Ben's a grown man. He'll do the thing in his own way. Not one word, mind.'

We said not one word, though it was mid-afternoon before Uncle Ben returned and then it was only to change out of his Sunday suit. I had just come back from Sunday school and was on my way upstairs when I heard Nain calling.

'Have you eaten, Ben?'

'I had a bite,' came his answer.

'There's plenty left!' Nain sounded anxious as if 'a bite' wasn't enough to sustain him.

'Eat it yourself, Mam! You're looking a bit peaked,' he called back.

He'd eaten at the widow's, I supposed. That could only mean the affair was progressing. I was dying to ask if I could be a bridesmaid, but when Taid said 'not one word', that meant complete and utter silence.

'Going out again?' That was Aunt Marget, very casual.

'Over to Mark's,' Uncle Ben said. 'I'll probably be late.'

'Gone to ask him to be best man,' Aunt

Ellen said, encountering me on the landing as the door closed again on my uncle. 'Ben doesn't waste time once he's made up his mind to something. He was just the same when I took him to the dentist.'

The dentist not being my favourite subject, since I was due for my annual examination during Lent, I murmured something vague and climbed up to my attic. On the Sabbath playing out was strictly forbidden. The see-saw and swings were chained up lest any godless child decided to take a ride; not a single shop was open (though it was rumoured Mrs Pitman would sell a packet of cigarettes through the back door) and everybody went to worship two or three times. In between, unless one was preparing, eating or clearing away a meal, there wasn't a lot to do. Sewing and knitting were frowned upon; anyone who hung out washing went straight to perdition the first chance the good Lord got and though tinkering around with the insides of cars was regarded as harmless, playing hopscotch, marbles, cricket, tennis, reading anything except the Bible, or skipping were forbidden. I never bothered with hopscotch and marbles, had never played tennis or cricket, and considered myself too sophisticated to bounce around on swings, but on this one day in the week I always had an urge to indulge in all those activities one after the other.

In the attic I opened my Bible at Kings and then, flat on my stomach, proceeded to cast a gigantic Hollywood epic. Barbara Stanwyck would make a lovely Bathsheba — or Claudette Colbert who was, I had read, in the habit of taking baths in milk. I had not yet cast King David. Most of the actors I'd seen on screen were either too old or too short. It was a pity Guto wasn't an actor. He was rather as I pictured King David to have been — tall and straight with sun dappled hair. I sighed, pushing away the thought of the girl on the tennis court, and bent my attention to the problem of casting Michal. Now that would be some scene! David dancing naked before the ark and the Princess Michal hanging out of the window, scorning him. Shot from a distance with lots of fog, I decided, for I was not only casting manager but cameraman, director, producer and the girl who sold ice-cream during the intermission.

When I went down to tea, which was held early since we had to put another hour in at chapel, Taid asked me, as he always asked me, if I'd learned anything interesting at school during the week. He didn't really want to know the interesting things so I didn't tell him that our Latin mistress had a bad crush on the French master or that one of the sixth-form boys had been suspended for smoking. I told him instead about the nature walk we'd taken and the spelling bee where I'd come top. I didn't mention the arithmetic test. I'd got sixteen out of thirty for that, but in our family if one couldn't get the highest marks one was expected to get the lowest.

'If you can't win then fail gloriously!' Taid had declared.

When I'd given my weekly report I fell upon the heaps of buttered scones, the bara-brith and the tinned salmon. It was possible to get fresh salmon but nobody in our family would touch it. We liked our salmon cut in chunky bright pink rounds and dripping with oil.

We were nearly half-way through the meal when we heard the door open and then Uncle Ben walked in. He had on his ordinary weekday clothes and there were smears of grease on his hand, but he looked different somehow. We all felt it as we looked at him though we couldn't have said where the difference lay.

Then Taid, forgetting his self-imposed rule of silence, cried,

'You've gone and done it then!'

'I've gone and done it,' Uncle Ben said heavily.

'When's it to be then?' Nain asked.

'Next few days.' Uncle Ben accepted a plate of salmon.

'Next few — ! What's the big hurry then? Have you disgraced the Sabbath and now she's insisting you make an honest woman of her?' Taid demanded.

'I'm not getting married,' Uncle Ben said.

'Not getting married? Of course you're getting married! It was all decided,' Taid said.

'Not by me,' Uncle Ben said calmly. 'I walked Rhiannon Evans home and had a bit of dinner with her — she's a good cook. Not as good as you, Mam. She doesn't get her roast potatoes as tasty as you do.'

'Nobody gets potatoes as I get them,' Nain said, stating the fact modestly.

'Never mind the bloody potatoes!' Taid roared. 'What happened then?'

'I came back to change and then I walked over to Mark's. That's a champion little engine in that Ford, Guto. We had it purring like a kitten before we were through.'

'Never mind the — what about Rhiannon Evans?' Taid said through his teeth.

'Oh, she's keen on me — keen on the idea of me, to be more accurate. Quick on the uptake she is too, understood everything that was said in your sermon and filled in the gaps herself. She was a bit forward for my liking.'

'What did she do?' Aunt Marget and Aunt Catti leaned forward as one.

'Asked me if I'd take a look at her loft, thought there might be dry rot there. And then she kept offering to hold the ladder steady while I climbed up. Anyway I got to thinking about it all while I was fiddling with the engine and I made up my mind on the instant, so I borrowed Mark's car and I went to Bangor and joined up.'

'Joined up where?' Taid said blankly.

'He means the army,' Nain said and her voice was suddenly very small and frightened.

'Don't be daft, woman!' Taid said. 'You can't join up in the army on Sundays!'

'The Recruiting Office opens for one hour, so I went in and joined up,' Uncle Ben said.

'You're over age,' Taid said.

'I didn't give them my real age,' Uncle Ben said with a touch of scorn. 'I knocked off five years. When I take my birth certificate in I'll change the three on the date into an eight. The Recruiting Sergeant was a Scotsman.'

'What right have the Scots got to entice our boys away?' Nain said, flags of scarlet flaring in her cheeks.

'He's doing his job, Mam — and he wasn't enticing anyone, just sitting behind his desk,'

Uncle Ben said patiently. 'I'm to go for the medical tomorrow.'

'He'll never pass it,' Nain said, gazing wildly round at us. 'Not a chance of passing! Delicate as a baby he was. Never thought we'd rear him.'

'And what happens to the farm and your work on the estate while you're tripping off with Scotsmen?' Taid broke in. 'Mark never learned one end of a cow from the other, and I'm not as young as I was. Where's your sense of responsibility?'

'You can still do a full day's work,' Uncle Ben said, 'and since Guto left school you've got another good pair of hands. And while we're on the subject you might as well all know that Mark's planning to join up as soon as Flora's had the baby.'

'Getting me to manage the garage while he's running round with a gun, I suppose?' Taid said with heavy sarcasm.

'He'll get a couple of the older men to keep the business going while he's away fighting,' Uncle Ben said.

'Personally I blame Rhiannon Evans,' Aunt Ellen said. 'If she hadn't started that silly nonsense about paying a fee to take our cattle to the river this would never have happened!'

'You should have stood your ground and refused to be bullied!' Aunt Marget said.

'He ran away from that sow,' Taid reminded us.

'He's still running from one if you ask me,' Guto put in.

'Nobody did, so don't be cheeky!' Nain said.

'The boy's got a right to express an opinion,' Taid said, thumping the tablecloth. 'Speak the truth and shame the devil! If you'd been a bit harder when they were younger, Ben wouldn't have run from that pig in the first place. You spoiled them rotten, all of them!'

'I knew it would end up as my fault,' Nain said. 'Wait five more minutes and it'll be my fault Poland was invaded!'

'I don't recall your speaking out very loudly about it at the time!' Taid snapped.

'Oh, there's nasty!' Her eyes flashed and the gold hoops glinted dangerously. 'When did I ever have time to go into politics? You're the only one who's allowed to say anything round here!'

'Is that why you've so much to say when you go trailing off to see those gypsy cousins of yours? Clack, clack over the teacups!'

'Gypsy yourself. There's Romany in the Petries too!'

'That there is not!' Taid was on his feet, his beard bristling. 'The Petries are descended from cattle thieves, not bloody gypsies!'

'Infantry I've joined. There'll be a chance to go to France perhaps,' Uncle Ben said. 'Mark fancies the navy.'

'Mark can't swim a stroke,' Aunt Catti said and burst into tears.

'What are you crying about?' Aunt Ellen said. 'The war'll be over before they've been issued with their uniforms.'

'Better look out for vacancies in the Foreign Legion, boy,' Guto said in a fair imitation of Taid's voice.

Taid reached out and cuffed him in an absent-minded fashion. Aunt Catti, still weeping, cut herself another piece of bread and spread it thickly with butter. Nain sat down and poured more tea, her hands shaking.

'At least one thing's clear,' she said. 'With Mark and Ben away fighting, that Hitler hasn't got a bloody chance! Not a bloody chance!'

'I'll have another cup of tea if there's any left in the pot,' Taid said. 'Better have a cup yourself, Ben. They'll put bromide in it once you get into the army, you know.'

'What for?' Aunt Marget asked.

'Ask your brother later.' Taid glanced in my direction. 'We have chapel in ten minutes.'

Amid the clatter of knives and forks I sat mute. All about me the world was changing. I hoped that it hadn't begun to change because of my bright idea, but I decided sensibly that it was silly to wear a hairshirt on everybody else's account.

'Finish up the salmon, Ben. You won't get meals like this in the army,' Aunt Ellen said.

'If he passes the medical,' Aunt Catti dabbed at her eyes.

'Of course he'll pass!' Nain cried. 'I'd like to see anyone try to keep him out! I'd just like to see anyone try!'

5

'It will have to come out,' Mr Williams said.

His voice sounded somewhat muffled as my ears were still ringing from the noise of the drill.

I stared at him, appalled. All I could think was that I wouldn't be twelve for another fortnight and already my teeth were crumbling away.

'Ellen!' Mr Williams opened the door and summoned my great aunt. 'I've filled one tooth but the back molar will have to come out.'

'Nonsense!' said Aunt Ellen.

'The tooth's rotten. It's too far back to show and it won't interfere with her chewing.'

'Are you trying to tell me the Lord put a useless tooth in Nell's mouth just so you could have the sadistic pleasure of tearing it out?' she enquired.

'I'm telling you that it has to come out. I can take it out right now.'

'Without gas?' She looked horrified. 'That's against the law surely.'

'It's quite legal. What do you think, Nell? Shall I take it out now?'

I hesitated. The only experience I'd had of tooth pulling had been when my milk teeth loosened and Guto had kindly tied long threads of cotton round them to the barn door and then banged the door.

'We'll have to think about it,' Aunt Ellen said. 'Perhaps we'll get a second opinion.'

'Get six opinions,' Mr Williams said, looking offended. 'Opinions don't alter facts.'

'We'll let you know,' Aunt Ellen said grandly, taking my hand and sweeping out.

'Got to have it out?' Nain looked horrified when we told her later. Her own teeth gleamed as white and even as did every other tooth in the family. 'Are you sure you heard him right, Ellen?'

'With my own ears,' Aunt Ellen said.

'Good God! Nobody in our house ever had to have a tooth pulled before. I had an uncle once who had to have a leg off, but he had all his teeth. Mind you, he managed very well with a wooden leg except when it was damp.'

'My legs are fine, Nain,' I said hastily. 'Honest!'

'It looks alright to me,' Aunt Marget said, peering into my mouth a few minutes afterwards.

'It's on the other side,' I closed my jaws long enough to say.

'Does it hurt?' Aunt Catti poked it experimentally.

'It didn't before,' I said.

'Hurting's got nothing to do with it,' Aunt Ellen said. 'When something is dead it doesn't hurt!'

'Perhaps it's only dying,' Nain said hopefully. 'I'll pound some cloves and make a paste for it.'

'Mr Williams seemed very certain,' Aunt Ellen said, 'though I didn't give him the satisfaction of agreeing. Once you start telling a dentist he's good he goes off to Colwyn Bay and puts his prices up!'

'And just before your birthday too,' Aunt Catti said sympathetically.

'It will be with gas, of course,' Taid said as we were sitting down to tea.

'He said it wasn't necessary,' I informed him.

'Of course it's necessary! Everything is done with gas now,' he said impatiently. 'What's the use of having inventions that aren't used? With gas it doesn't hurt at all.'

'How would you know?' Nain said to him. 'You never had a tooth pulled with or without gas.'

'Will you have it out before your birthday or afterwards?' Aunt Marget enquired.

'I don't want to have it out at all,' I told them.

'All the talk about it's putting her off,' Guto said.

'Unless it's a premonition.' Nain looked serious. 'Do you have a premonition, Cariad?'

It would have solved everything to say that I had because premonitions were taken seriously in our family, but it was terrible to lie about having one so I shook my head.

'Has anyone else had a premonition?' She shot enquiring glances all round the table. 'Or dreamed of a horse with fleas?'

Nobody had, though I was hoping.

'Better get it over with and have it out in the morning,' Guto said cheerfully.

'Have it out yourself!' I scowled at him.

'Saturday would be better, then she wouldn't have to miss school,' Taid said.

Typical! I thought bitterly. Saturdays were the best days of the week and my grandfather was heartlessly condemning me to a painful one.

'Saturday's too far off,' Aunt Marget said. 'Anyway one of us will have to take her in. A week day is better for that.'

Saturday was the best day in the week for everybody else too.

'There's no need for anybody to take me,' I said loudly, 'because I'm not going to have the tooth out.'

'You can't walk round with a dead tooth in

your mouth,' Aunt Ellen protested.

'It'll turn black and poison the root and then the poison will spread right through your system,' Aunt Marget warned.

'I'm not going,' I said obstinately.

'It's been decided,' Nain began.

'It was decided that Uncle Ben was going to marry Rhiannon Evans,' I argued.

My uncle had not left the village yet, though he'd passed the medical. He was waiting to be told which unit to join and meanwhile spent all his time over at the garage when he wasn't working on the estate or the farm.

'You're not frightened of having the tooth out, are you?' Nain asked.

'Of course she's not frightened!' Taid said loudly.

'Yes, I am. I am frightened,' I interrupted.

'Well, I am surprised at you!' His tone was dark brown with disappointment. 'Fancy a Petrie being afraid of a little old thing like having a tooth out. I'd be ashamed to feel a twinge of fear.'

'You've never had a tooth out,' Nain repeated, 'so how can you talk?'

'If I was going to have a tooth out,' he said impressively, 'I would walk in with my head held high and never a tremor.'

'Why don't you then?' Nain mocked.

'Why don't I what?'

'Go and have one of your teeth out when Nell has hers done, if you're so sodding brave!'

'There's nothing wrong with my teeth!' he growled.

'It would set a good example, Dad.' Aunt Marget titled her head and gazed at the ceiling.

'Like a sacrifice,' Aunt Catti echoed. 'You wouldn't mind going if Taid was going too, would you?'

'Not a bit,' I said meanly.

'Right then, it's decided!' Nain slapped her hand flat on the tablecloth. 'Tomorrow morning the pair of you can go and get it over with.'

We set off the next morning in the trap since Taid scorned buses. I had six large handkerchiefs folded up in my pocket ready for the blood and Taid had the expression on his face of an early Christian riding to the latest Roman circus. We neither of us talked on the way. Taid wasn't one for casual conversation at the best of times and this wasn't the best of times.

When we reached our destination he drew up and sat frowningly in his seat.

'Would you like to go for a bit of a drive round first, Nell?' he asked.

'I think we ought to go straight in and get it over with.' I echoed Nain demurely.

'Yes. Yes, you're quite right.' He pulled his hat further over his brow and climbed down. 'Mind, coming like this without an appointment — it's possible the waiting room is packed out and he won't be able to fit us in.'

The waiting room was empty. Taid, looking round at the unpainted wooden chairs, the table with its pile of old magazines, its notices warning people to clean their teeth three times a day, said, 'Well, you think he'd try to attract patients, not discourage them!'

'We ring the bell on the table and then he comes out,' I said.

'No need to be in such a hurry!' Taid snapped. 'Mr Williams is probably having a cup of tea. We ought to give him time to drink it. We'll go for a bit of a walk first and come back later on.'

'Taid Petrie, good morning to you!'

The inner door had opened and Mr Williams appeared on the threshold, pulling on his white coat.

'We've come to have our teeth out, but seeing you're busy we won't bother you,' Taid said.

'Nell was in yesterday and I told her then that back tooth would have to come out,' Mr

Williams said. 'Have you come to have it done?'

'We've both come to have a tooth out,' Taid said.

'You're suffering from toothache? I don't believe I've had the pleasure of attending you before.' Mr Williams rubbed the palms of his hands together. They made a little rasping sound like the drill.

'I wouldn't like to say I've got toothache,' Taid said scrupulously, 'but I want you to take out one of my back teeth.'

'If you'll sit in the chair I'll just take a look,' Mr Williams began.

'I'll tell you which one to pull,' Taid said moving to the chair and surveying it with suspicion. 'Where's the gas?'

'Gas has to be ordered.'

'Ordered?' Taid's look of suspicion changed to one of outright disbelief. 'You don't have gas here already?'

'It has to be ordered,' Mr Williams said again.

'Well, in that case, we'll come back another time.' Taid took a step away from the chair.

'Mr Williams can do it without gas,' I said.

'Oh.' Taid frowned at me.

'If you'll sit down,' Mr Williams said patiently, 'we can find out which tooth is troubling you.'

'I didn't say any of them were troubling me,' Taid said, sitting down reluctantly. 'I'm having one out to encourage Nell.'

'You want me to extract a perfectly sound tooth?' Mr Williams gaped. 'I can't do that!'

'They're my teeth, aren't they?' Taid said. 'I'll decide whether I want them in my mouth or not. Now do your job and we can get out of here. There's a war on, you know!'

'Go and sit in the waiting room, Nell,' Mr Williams looked up to say.

I went reluctantly, leaving the door open a crack. There were smothered sounds from within and then a yell that iced the marrow of my bones. A moment later Taid marched out, holding a tooth aloft. Behind him, at the basin, Mr Williams was holding a bleeding hand under the tap.

'I'm afraid he's not in a very good mood,' Taid said. 'Reflex action on my part. I bit him a little bit.'

'Did it hurt?' I asked.

'Well, though I say it myself I've got pretty strong jaws for my age,' Taid said complacently.

'Did having the tooth out hurt?'

'It wasn't pleasant. Not pleasant at all, Nell. I think we'll get your Nain to make a clove paste to loosen your teeth a bit more. No point in bothering Mr Williams if we can get it to fall out by itself.'

He took a shilling from his pocket, laid it on top of the magazines with a lordly air and taking my hand led me out into the street again.

A few days later Uncle Ben got his orders and all arguments about teeth were smothered by the advice heaped on him from all sides.

'Don't volunteer for anything. No sense in being a dead hero.' That from Uncle Mark, gripping his brother's hand tightly.

We had all come to the station at Bangor to see him off, though he'd asked us not to bother. We were not the only ones seeing people off to the war. The platform was crowded with relatives and friends, wearing their best clothes, cracking jokes, laughing a lot. Here and there among the bustling groups, like small quiet islands, people stood alone or in couples, silent with all the words spoken and nothing left to do but wait for the train.

'They'll give you a uniform and a gun when you get there, I suppose,' Guto said.

'And teach you how to use it,' Aunt Marget said and laughed. My uncles were two of the best shots in the district.

'Mind you use it on the right people,' Taid said, with a menacing look. 'It's the Germans you'll be fighting, not the first man who calls you Taffy.'

'I wish you'd stop talking about it,' Aunt Catti said and burst into tears.

Aunt Catti cried easily. She cried at weddings and funerals, at birthday parties and christenings and she'd drenched me with tears when I passed the scholarship. Aunt Marget cried with her now, the tears sliding gently down her cheeks.

'No need to get into a state,' Uncle Ben said. 'I'm only going to Aldershot.'

'Three weeks' training and then across to France,' Uncle Mark said. 'I envy you, boy!'

'You'll be in it yourself soon,' Uncle Ben told him.

'You in the army and me in the navy,' Uncle Mark nodded.

They grinned at each other and Aunt Flora joined Aunt Marget and Aunt Catti in their weeping. From the shape of Aunt Flora it wouldn't be long before we were seeing Uncle Mark off too.

'They say it's very bad over in France now,' Aunt Ellen said. 'The Germans are pressing forward very fast.'

'I don't think they'll be sending Ben there,' Nain said. 'He doesn't speak one word of French.'

'Makes no difference,' Taid said. 'They

send them anyway.'

'All that French food — terrible for the stomach,' she mourned.

'All the Petrie's have strong stomachs, Mam,' Uncle Ben reminded her. 'It's kidneys and consumption that gets us.'

'That's true.' She brightened.

'Make sure you have 'Welsh' on your identity papers,' Taid instructed. 'If you're taken prisoner you can say the English forced you to fight.'

'And don't mention that you're gypsy,' Aunt Ellen cautioned.

'What's wrong with gypsies?' Nain said sharply.

'Hitler doesn't like them,' she said.

We all studied Uncle Ben anxiously. Strictly speaking he was not full blooded Romany but Poshrat and I, being one generation further on, was Didicoi, but the Germans probably wouldn't appreciate the subtle differences in tribal status. Neither of my two older uncles wore hoops in their ears though Guto had small ones and many Welshmen were thickset with black curly hair. All the men in our family were tattooed from wrist to elbow, but then again many Celts were.

'I don't plan on being taken prisoner,' Uncle Ben said. 'Why go looking on the black side?' He broke off abruptly, staring at us.

Rhiannon Evans in a blue spotted dress and a hat with an eye veil had just come onto the platform and was gazing round with a seeking look. Then she saw us and, holding herself very straight, walked down the platform.

'Good afternoon, Taid Petrie. Nain.' There were spots of colour on her cheeks and her voice was pitched rather high.

'Mrs Evans.' Taid answered for us all.

'Thought I'd come and give you a bit of a send-off,' she said casually and thrust a small parcel into Uncle Ben's hand. 'Gingerbread,' she said, 'in case you have a fancy for a bit of a chew.'

'Thank you. That's very good of you.' My uncle had flushed scarlet.

'It makes all the difference to have a good send-off,' she said brightly. 'Guto be seeing to the farm now, I suppose?'

'And taking the cattle to the river,' Taid said with meaning.

'You're welcome to drive them across my field,' she said, magnanimous in defeat. 'No sense in neighbours falling out at a time like this. We've all got to stick together.'

'I believe you have the right to ask for a fee.' Taid too could be magnanimous.

'Good gracious, I wouldn't hear of such a

thing!' she cried. 'No indeed! I'd be obliged if you'd not mention it again.'

'Very good of you, Mrs Evans,' Nain said. 'And the gingerbread was a lovely thought. Perhaps you'd give me the recipe some time? I never had much luck with gingerbread.'

It was a barefaced lie, but we were interrupted by the shrilling of the train whistle as it snaked through the tunnel and drew up alongside. There was a surge back as doors opened and steam gushed, then a surge forwards. Men in uniform shouldering kitbags, men in suits with cases and holdalls, hurrying to claim a decent seat, returning to hang out of the windows, their hands clasping other hands.

All the women in our family were weeping now, including me. No nonsense about stiff upper lips interfered with our enjoyment of our emotions. The men gripped elbows and shoulders, dry-eyed.

'Don't get tangled up with any Frenchies! Take your bromide regular!'

'Don't go missing chapel now! There'll be chaplains out there, I daresay.'

'Mind you write to us! Mam will worry if we don't hear!'

All about us the noises of departures and the same words repeated. On the opposite platform the town band had begun to play loud and ragged and my cousin, Johnny, jumped up and down waving a small flag. The guard waved a bigger one and ran up along the train, slamming doors, shouting 'Heads in! Mind your heads,' before swinging himself aboard. The train began to huff slowly; clasped hands loosened; fragments of sentences rose into the smoke.

' — forget to write.'

' — get a weekend before embarkation.'

The train leaned into the tunnel and was gone, leaving us on an emptying platform. We groped for handkerchiefs and mopped our faces.

Nain said, 'If they ever find out he's over age they'll send him back.'

Uncle Mark and Guto clapped their arms about each other's shoulders and went off together.

'Up to mischief,' Aunt Ellen said. 'You remember the Lloyd George affair?'

Nain, her eyelids still damp, threw back her head and pealed out the laugh her daughters had inherited.

The statue of Lloyd George was in the main square in Caernarvon. The politician with waving hair and flowing cloak stood before a steep side-road that led between the ramparts of the ancient castle and a row of eighteenth century horses. On the left was a discreet Gents toilet, tucked away behind a grille. A couple of years before my three uncles, spurred by the occasional wildness that Taid swore came from Nain's side of the family, went into town with a pot of bright yellow paint. The next morning the citizens awoke to find a line of yellow footprints leading from Lloyd George to the Gents and back again.

'Well, we'd better get on back,' Taid said, jamming his hat more firmly on his head. 'Who is coming with me in the trap and who is going in the car?'

'Mark's not here,' Aunt Flora said.

'He'll remember he's got a wife and child in an hour or two, I daresay,' Taid said sarcastically. 'Ellen, you had better drive the trap and I'll take the car. Mark and Guto can walk or get a lift. So, who is coming with me?'

He looked round challengingly. Nobody spoke a word. Taid rode and drove horses better than any man I'd ever seen, but his car driving made strong hearts quiver.

'I'll come with you,' Aunt Flora said, 'and Johnny.'

She was a small, fluffy-haired woman with a meek face and voice, but we respected her courage on this occasion.

'The girls will have to go with you, Ellen,' Taid said.

'Nell and I will walk over to Menai Bridge and get a lift from there,' Nain said smoothly. 'You'd better offer Mrs Rhiannon Evans a ride. It's the least you can do when she's been so reasonable.'

'Right then!' Taid strode off to overtake Mrs Evans with Aunt Flora lumbering behind.

'There's room in the trap, Mam,' Aunt Catti said encouragingly, but Nain shook her head.

'I need to walk,' she said. 'You'd better get tea started, Marget. There's cold lamb and a bit of a trifle.'

What she meant was that, having just seen her son off to war, she could not endure to start cooking for the rest. She needed, for a brief while, to be among her own kind and it was a measure of her loving that she chose my company.

We came out of the station and plodded up the hill past the little bookshop, then veered away from College Road towards the suspension bridge. It was a sign of her unhappiness that she did not once mention the university. Instead she talked about herself which was rare.

'I remember when I first saw this bridge

after J.P. and I were married,' she said. 'I'd come from Ireland to Holyhead, of course. Duw, it was a bad crossing. To tell you the truth I was homesick before we landed. For two pins I'd have turned round and gone back. Mind you, it was a bit easier for me, knowing that I'd cousins here. The Petries all seemed a bit grand, keeping their sugar in bowls with little lace covers on and putting a farthing in the Missionary box whenever one of them used a bad word. Afraid to open my mouth I was, though they were very civil. Mr Petrie was a fine preacher and Mrs Ceridwen very open-handed even when times were hard. But they were strict in their ways, a little bit old-fashioned. They thought your Taid was a bit of a tearaway.'

I thought their outlook must have been very narrow indeed if they'd thought that.

'Anyway when I saw the bridge,' Nain said, puffing slightly for we were still walking uphill, 'I was really impressed! All glinted with sunlight and looking so delicate and yet motor cars drive across it today! I told myself then, if there are things as clever as that made in this country, then it's worth staying. And now it's my home, of course. I have the security my own parents never had. They never slept under a roof in their lives! My father — Tada, we called him — was the best

109

horsebreaker in Ireland. He liked horses better than people, I think, and yet he was very fond of my mother and she wasn't a bit like a horse. She was pure Romany with fair hair and eyes the colour of the sea. Not many people know the original gypsies were fair. The dark hair came after they started intermarrying with Spaniards and such. She used to dance at the fairs and markets up and down Ireland, like a pale flame with little bells in her ears and on her ankles.'

Her voice had taken on the singsong cadences of her youth. It always did as we neared the camp where those of her cousins who had not yet gone to war maintained their households.

We crossed the suspension bridge in silence. It was ill-luck to speak on a bridge. It was also ill-luck not to count ten backwards if you had to go back for something, to stumble going down a stair, to see the new moon through glass or to go in and out of a strange house by the same door. It was good fortune to stumble going up a stair, to see a black cat or a load of hay coming towards you, or to hear your name called when nobody had spoken. Life was full of omens and protective devices and it was courting trouble to ignore them.

We turned down the lane away from the

town to the stretch of land, part common and part beach, where the wagons and tents stood. The ponies were corralled at one end and lurcher dogs tumbled with children between the fires. There had been some trouble recently over the leaping bonfires in which rabbit and hedgehog were spitted and baked in clay and round which the families gathered to warm themselves. Now because of the blackout regulations, the meals had to be cooked early and the fires damped down before darkness fell.

We paused at the first caravan where Mama Sarah, pipe clenched between her teeth, sat on the steps surveying her domain. She was a nutmeg of a woman, probably near a hundred though neither she nor anyone else knew, and immensely wise though she had never learned how to sign her name or taken a ride in a bus or motor car. Sarah did, however, know what the weather was going to be like in a month's time, where the thickest shoals of fish could be found and when there were corpse candles flickering on the wind. She could rid a house of vermin by catching a mouse in the palm of her hand and speaking over it words that came from some language lost in time, then letting it go and within an hour the house would be free of its unwelcome visitors.

Nain greeted her with hands laid palm to

palm and sat down on the lowest step. I sat on a little stool placed near and for a full five minutes there was silence. Then Sarah took her pipe out of her mouth and said, 'Charlie and Joe went off this afternoon.'

'Ben too,' Nain nodded.

'And Mark's to follow when his wife's had her babe? She keeps well?'

'She's big.'

'Carrying before her or all round?'

'Mainly before,' Nain said.

'Ah! then it may be another child,' Sarah said. By that expression she meant a boy, but on Mona boys were referred to as girl-children until they were seven or eight years old. It was the worst possible luck to admit one had given birth to a boy.

'That's as God wills,' Nain said.

'So mote it be!' Sarah made the sign of horns with her dark hand. 'What other news?'

'All well. Marget is still waiting to name the wedding day. She's a fancy for a pure silk dress, but there's no virgin silk to be had.'

'Emyr won't fight?'

'He's forty and his occupation is a reserved one, a schoolmaster,' Nain said.

'That's a good match for her,' Sarah approved.

'When it happens! Emyr's a bit slow getting to the point.'

'He'll come to it before long,' Sarah said.

'Before I'm laid out, please God,' Nain said fervently.

'War hurries things up,' Sarah said. 'No sign of Catti getting a husband?'

'She could take her pick,' Nain said proudly.

'Not for much longer. Men are getting scarcer now the war's here and some won't come back.'

'You can see something?' There was a ripple of fear across my grandmother's smooth face.

'Nothing that others can't see when they hear the wireless or read the papers,' Sarah said and leaning down, took both my hands, turning them palms up, her sharp eyes clouding as she turned her gaze inward to that place within herself where past and future met and mingled.

I sat very still, hoping she was not going to see anything bad, but she said merely, 'She will have lovers one day, this one. Lovers but little contentment from them.'

'And Ben?' Nain said.

'Ben will be spared to take a wife, I think, but I cannot see so clearly these days.' She dropped my hands and her eyes were sharp again.

'So mote it be,' Nain said softly.

'So! We are moving south soon,' the old woman said.

She did not refer to herself but to those in the camp who planned to travel to the borders selling their horses, their plaited flowers, their carved love spoons and pegs.

'After the fair,' Nain said.

She referred to the one held annually at Menai Bridge and regarded as the most important event of the year.

'Of course after the fair,' Sarah said. 'The older men will have to stir themselves with the young 'uns going to fight.'

'It's a hard world,' Nain said.

'Always was,' Sarah said placidly. 'You'll feel it more being a house-dweller. I admire the way you've stuck to it all these years, but I don't envy you.'

Nain shrugged, not attempting to argue. There was to her no irony in the fact that her three-storey house and garden were scorned by an old woman who lived in a caravan.

'You'll eat and drink,' Sarah said.

It was a command, not an invitation. To refuse hospitality was an insult no gypsy would forgive.

We went to the fire and took tin cups full of thick stew and a hunk of bread each from Anne Boswell whose turn it was to cook. She was a fair Romany, third or fourth cousin to Nain, with a ripe-hipped figure and breasts like melons under her high necked bodice. Married women dressed modestly and covered their heads with triangular scarves, but younger, unwed girls were permitted to let their hair swing free and to wear frocks that dipped below their collarbones.

People were drifting in, some standing to eat, others relaxing with crossed ankles on the trampled earth. They ate quickly, being careful not to touch themselves below the waist until they were finished lest they render themselves taboo. I followed suit as I always did, replied to the occasional greeting, listened to the quick patter of Romany Welsh. Nain fitted in here more than I did, for in the camp she was the exile returned and I was the distant kinswoman. I was with them but not of them, tamed into a school blazer and a leather satchel. I knew they were proud of me, but I knew also they pitied me for the burden of civilization placed on me.

Nobody except Mama Sarah mentioned Uncle Ben or those who had gone away on the train to Aldershot. It was not good to talk about absent relatives too loud or too often, lest the forces of evil pay heed and seek them out.

'You'd better take one of the ponies,' old

Leni said, jerking his head towards the animals. 'Guto can bring him back.'

It was getting darker and the fires were being damped down, the black curtains being drawn closely across the windows, children being sorted out from the dogs. Several of the men were grouped round Mama Sarah, listening while she gave her orders to those who were bound on a poaching expedition. The last sparks rose up to illuminate their faces, dark above knotted red scarves and the gold in their ears.

Nain was heaved up to the back of a pony and I was whisked up behind her. She rode bareback, using only a bit and a bridle rein, and I clung to the belt of her coat as we trotted along the shore line and then through the maze of twisting lanes to the main road.

'Good to be on a horse again!' Nain said, clicking her tongue. 'I hope the old bugger got everybody home in one piece!'

And then she began to sing a very jolly song and I knew her heart had run grieving after the train all the way to Aldershot.

6

Every year there was an argument as to whether I ought to be allowed to attend the fair and every year I went anyway. The trouble was that the event was not entirely respectable. The girls who travelled round with the sideshows were not the sort of girls one prayed one's son would marry. As the day wore on and more strong drink was consumed behaviour became less controlled, tempers flaring, old grudges breaking out. The local police kept well away, though Constable Petrie was there in force, his cowboy hat pushed back, eyes narrowed as if from the glare of an Arizona sun.

We did not go *en masse* as a family to the event and Aunt Ellen never went at all. In her opinion, the entire affair was an open invitation to rape. Nain went in the morning with my aunts to buy a few things and to try her luck at the hoopla and my aunts usually returned in the afternoon, Aunt Marget with Emyr, Aunt Catti with her current admirer. My uncles were in and out of the place all day and they were always there in the evenings, two large, thickset men eyeing the sequinned ladies and giving the impression it was merely indolence that prevented them from slinging a couple over their shoulders and bearing them away.

In the past the argument had been resolved by Guto's taking me for 'a couple of hours' which we generally stretched into four or five, returning home after dark to be scolded. That problem wouldn't occur this year since, because of the blackout regulations, the fair had to close down at six o'clock, but it was possible that my youngest uncle had plans of his own for that day and didn't want me tagging along. Ever since I'd seen him with the girl on the tennis courts it had seemed to me that he was moving further away into the adult world.

However when the discussion reached fever pitch he broke in as usual, saying, 'I can take Nell for a couple of hours early on before it gets too rough.'

'Only a couple of hours now,' Nain cautioned. 'I don't want either of you getting a bad name.'

We promised faithfully we would not stay longer than the allotted 120 minutes and we would do our utmost not to get a bad name.

For days beforehand the talk was all of the weather. If it rained the fair would be a failure with money lost and a day's excitement curtailed. This year there was an added twist to the discussions. Everybody knew that Hitler was only waiting for a spell of fine weather so that he could launch an invasion, so to wish too loudly for sunshine smacked of the unpatriotic.

Uncle Ben was in France, though he had not come home for his embarkation leave. Having put the family through the trauma of one farewell I suppose he was unwilling to do so again. He was not, of course, allowed to tell us that he was in France, the censor being strict about such matters, but a code had been worked out before his leaving and in the one letter which had arrived he'd enquired tenderly after Cousin Fiona.

Uncle Mark was going because he had a couple of bicycles he was hoping to sell at a good profit, but he wouldn't bother this year with the entertainments. It wouldn't be the same without Ben's company and anyway Flora was due any day. Aunt Flora never went to the fair and Johnny, being marked for the pulpit, wasn't allowed to go either. I was glad about that and ashamed of myself for being so.

The day was fine, which might speak of the dreaded invasion, but would certainly ensure profit all round. Aunt Ellen had locked herself in her room and loaded her shotgun

119

for fear of lecherous strangers. I glimpsed her once or twice looking out of the window to see if any were approaching. Nain went off with my aunts to do her bit of bargain hunting. They were all hoping to find that elusive roll of pure silk for Aunt Marget's wedding dress.

'Though in my opinion it's a load of nonsense,' Taid said. 'If she'd wanted silk she could have had it any time these past eight years instead of waiting until everything was rationed! It's an excuse to put it off again if you ask me!'

He and I were in the meadow where he'd gone to see his cattle. They knew him and came crowding round, lowering their heads to rub against his side, their eyes moist and adoring. Our cows were milk and breeding animals. When they became old they were pensioned off. When any were sold it was Uncle Ben who took them to market. Taid would as soon have thought of eating one of his own children as of sending one of our beasts to the slaughterhouse, though he was not in the least sentimental about other people's livestock.

'Do you think there might be an invasion soon?' I asked.

'Not on Mona.' He frowned slightly, the idea displeasing him. 'Of course if it should happen we will be ready.'

As he was ready for the coming of the Lord, I reflected. On the morning of fair day he did not, however, blow the trumpet.

'The way I look at it,' he'd said, 'there's due to be a lot of sin hanging round the district today so it's not altogether prudent to attract the attention of the Almighty.'

'They say Mr Churchill is going to be Prime Minister,' I said.

'Next to Lloyd George there's no man I'd rather see,' he affirmed.

'Aunt Ellen says he used to be a bit of a warmonger,' I said.

'Pity more people weren't, then there wouldn't have been a war! Have you done your homework?'

'Last night.'

'Your Nain and your aunties will be back soon. You'd better run on up to the house and see if Guto's ready to take you.'

Taid who would not have been caught dead at the fair, though in his youth he'd been to many such, turned to address a spotted cow who was butting him gently with her horns.

'And unless you give a bit more milk, Delilah, you need not expect friendly treatment from me, so you can stop trying to coax me!'

I left him standing there and ran through

the springing grass, seeing Guto already hovering by the gate.

'Mam's back,' he said. 'I'm taking the trap, so if you're ready — '

'I'll just tell them!' I shot down the steps into the kitchen where my grandmother and aunts were laying their purchases on the table and lamenting, as they always lamented, the money they'd wasted.

'Why didn't you stop me buying these fancy jars? I've so many jars already they won't be filled till the day of judgement!'

'They looked prettier on the stall!'

There was no white silk among the articles on the table. That meant either another postponement or Aunt Marget would have to settle for something else.

'I'm just off, Nain,' I said and was through the door again before she could start warning me of the perils that abounded. These ranged from having my money stolen to eating unwashed fruit to having a needle stuck in my arm and being abducted by white slave-traders.

'You took your time,' Guto said, as I reached the trap. He was looking at his watch.

'I didn't know you were in a hurry.' I climbed up. 'Can I take the reins?'

'On the way back. It won't matter if you have us in the ditch then,' he said, unfairly because I drove very carefully when I was allowed.

'I haven't had dinner,' I said, hintingly.

On fair day nobody had dinner. We ate fish and chips out of newspapers.

'You want chips?' He glanced at me.

'I wouldn't say no,' I said, my stomach grumbling.

'I may run into a friend,' Guto said. He sounded slightly embarrassed, as well he might since he always took me to the fair and tradition was sacred in our family.

'Oh?' I tried to sound very casual.

'It's a girl,' Guto said.

'You should have told me before we started out,' I said crossly.

'Well, it wasn't a definite arrangement. She said that she might look in sometime.'

'She?'

'You wouldn't know her. Her name's Olive — Olive Rushton.'

I didn't know her but everybody had heard of the Rushtons. They lived in a large house over at Benllech and the three daughters had all gone to boarding school. Olive was the youngest of them and the prettiest it was said. Aunt Catti hadn't been entirely straightforward when she'd told me that Guto was going out with an Olive something or other. She must have known it was one of the

Rushtons. My world was crowded with small betrayals.

'She's a bit grand, isn't she?' I said nastily.

'She's not a bit grand,' he contradicted. 'Really grand people don't act like that at all.'

'Oh, you've mixed with a lot of them then?' I said.

'You did say you wanted chips?'

'I've got sixpence so I can buy my own if necessary,' I said loftily.

'That won't leave you much to spend at the fair.' He gave me his sudden, glinting smile and said, 'Don't act so snooty with your uncle! If we meet Olive you won't mind her coming round with us, will you?'

'No, of course not,' I said brightly, though I knew that I would mind. Always before it had been Guto and me at the fair, with no third person. It would have been better if he'd met her later, instead of using my presence as a way to avoid gossip. And there would be gossip, no doubt about that. The Rushtons were outside our sphere. David Rushton was a magistrate and played golf, which proved he belonged to the idle rich.

'Perhaps Olive would fancy some fish and chips,' Guto said as we clip-clopped along the road.

I thought that if the Rushtons ever ate fish and chips it wouldn't be out of vinegar and oil soaked newspaper but from plates, with knives and forks, where it didn't taste half as good, but I had the sense not to say it out loud.

'There's Olive!' Guto exclaimed.

I couldn't help muttering, 'What a coincidence!'

Guto didn't apparently hear. He drew rein with as much flourish as if the amiable pony had been a spirited war horse and said, 'Hello, Olive! How are you then?'

'I'm fine, thank you.' She had a very clear voice, with scarcely any accent at all.

'Is that Nell?'

'My niece,' Guto said.

'She's very pretty, just like you told me,' said Olive Rushton.

'You're pretty yourself,' I said, going red.

She was not pretty. She was exquisite. Close to, her figure was slight and her features delicate and she had skin as white as milk. It was the kind of skin that redheads often have but her hair was pale gold, drawn back smoothly from a centre parting and falling in ringlets against her long neck. In contrast her eyes were honey brown, upward titled, with long dark lashes that cast feathery shadows over her cheekbones.

'We're all pretty,' said Guto, laughing with relief and embarrassment mixed up together.

'Nell and I were thinking of getting some fish and chips. Do you fancy some? My treat!'

He was doing Ben's work now as well as his own and Taid had given him a rise in pay — but not until Nain had threatened to report him to the town council for keeping slave labour.

'I'd love some,' Olive said promptly.

'We eat them out of newspaper,' I told her.

'It's the only way to eat them. They don't taste half as good from a plate,' she said.

Guto tied up the pony and we went into the tiled fish and chip shop. There was a high, chrome-topped counter with glass in front of it through which we could see the long marble top with the bags of transparent white paper and piles of newspaper, the bottles of vinegar, the cruets of salt and pepper, the dish full of hot, squashy peas. On left and right were the fish, gutted and beheaded and ready to be dipped in the vat of batter and then, dripping through a long-handled wire basket, lowered into the boiling fat in the deep, square pans at the back.

Maggie and Gladwen, who looked like sisters but were mother and daughter, stood behind the counter. Dressed alike in white overalls with red hair tied up under jewel bright turbans, they took orders and executed them with a rhythm and economy of movement that was a delight to watch. Maggie was twenty-three and looked thirty and Gladwen was forty-one and looked thirty too. It had been a toss-up which one Uncle Ben would fancy, but he'd gone out with Maggie since Gladwen had buried two husbands already.

'Three fours, three plaice and extra peas, Maggie, if you please,' Guto said, not consulting Olive and me.

Translated that meant a shillings worth of chips, three pieces of the best fish and cone of peas. It also meant that Guto and Olive Rushton had eaten fish and chips together before since he already knew her preference.

'Right away, bach!' Maggie floured the fish, immersed them in batter, flipped them into the wire basket, lowered them into the sizzling oil. At her side Gladwen was scooping once-fried chips up, swivelling on her heel to lower them into the spitting oil. Both she and her daughter had sweat beading their faces and darkening under their armpits. The heat rose, quivering on the air.

'How's Ben then?' Maggie fashioned cones.

'Fine, as far as we know,' Guto said.

'He's in F — ' I stopped, my mouth snapping shut as my eyes met the stern warning on the poster on the wall. CARE-LESS TALK COSTS LIVES.

'On the Maginot Line, isn't he?' said Maggie, who obviously didn't read posters. 'Some of our boys are being shipped to Singapore. Terrible long way but they do say the Japanese are turning a bit nasty. Vinegar, salt and pepper?'

We nodded, our eyes on the bouquets of vinegar soaked chips, the cone of bright mushy peas, the half-wrapped fish hidden under the brown batter coating with its flaky surface.

'That'll be two and threepence. Remember me to Ben when you get the chance.'

'Thanks, Maggie.' Guto shepherded us out and across the side yard to the low wall where we clambered up and sat in a row, eating our dinner, Guto then Olive Rushton, then me.

Glancing sideways I was fascinated by the dainty manner in which she ate, pulling out each chip between the tips of thumb and forefinger, taking neat, quick bites at the fish. She was wearing a pleated grey skirt and a cream blouse with short sleeves and she didn't get a crumb or speck of oil on her.

'That was good!' She let out her breath in a long sigh of satisfaction and rolled up the newspaper into a tight ball. 'Where shall I put this?'

'I'll put them in the waste bin,' Guto took

my discarded wrappings as well and bounded to the corner.

'I'm not butting in or anything, am I?' Olive asked in a low voice. 'I'd not want to do that, but I've not been to the fair before and Guto said —'

'It wouldn't be so much fun without you here,' I said nobly, but the moment I said it the sentiment became truth.

She had charm, I suppose, and it reached out and touched all on whom she chose to exercise it and her spell worked because the charm was real and not assumed. It was the charm that a kitten has or a small child. The kitten and the child have nothing to do but be themselves and she was like that too.

'What are we waiting for?' Guto demanded, swinging back to us. 'Let's go to the fair!'

So we went to the fair, arms linked, striding down the road to the common where the tents and booths, the roundabout, the swings, the shooting arcade and the hoopla stand had been erected.

We were not the only ones. There were more people here than in previous years despite the numbers who had gone to war, as if for one day people had resolved to ignore the fact that the Germans were getting ready to invade us as had the Romans and the

Vikings, that place names had been obliterated and trees hidden at the side of the road to slow down enemy tanks, that a grey barrage balloon hung like an inflated elephant in the clear sky and that we had all been issued with identity cards and there were gas mask drills once a week at school. On this one day nobody wanted to talk about serious matters. They wanted to aim rifles at wooden ducks, throw hoops over coloured poles to win a kewpie doll and ride on the boat swings that stood on end fourteen feet above the ground.

There were local people here and visitors from Bangor, Holyhead and Caernarvon, pale-faced evacuee children who thought food grew in tins and ran screaming from grass snakes, tinkers in black brimmed hats and the Lovells, Boswells and Bohannas. There was the clown on stilts who leaned from a great height to shake hands; pens filled with snorting piglets and fluttering hens, booths where you could buy genuine imitation diamonds and gold bracelets that went green after a couple of weeks; brooches made from seashells; paperweights; white rock with WALES FOREVER going right through the middle; and clouds of pink candy floss that shrank to a wad of sugar in the mouth.

We were jostled and hustled, importuned by a girl in a sequinned bathing suit who begged us to come and see a genuine Egyptian mummy and a giant with bulging biceps who wanted to pit his strength against all comers. We were hailed by a couple of Bohanna men who swaggered past full of whisky with feathers stuck in the bands of their hats. Once, briefly, we were separated and I stood on trampled grass, surrounded by laughing, eating, shouting faces and bodies pressing me into a smaller space. Then I ducked down and scrambled through and Guto caught me and spun me round while Olive clapped her hands and cried, 'Gosh! You gave us a fright, vanishing like that! We're going to buy gingerbeer. My treat!'

The gingerbeer was amber and fizzy and tasted like nothing at all until it reached the roof of one's mouth where it exploded into a million tingling bubbles. Olive wiped the neck of her bottle carefully before she drank and I did exactly the same thing. Had she decided to stand on her head I would probably have followed suit, for by this time I was as much in love with her as Guto was. To me she had become, in the space of one afternoon, the epitome of everything that was sweet and beautiful and worthy of admiration.

It no longer mattered that there was an

extra person with Guto and me. Olive completed us, not coming between, but binding together. She was sixteen and that age immediately became the perfect age to be. She thought Clark Gable was the handsomest actor on the screen and I knew at once that she was absolutely right. She had taken typing lessons and I resolved to take them too as soon as I possibly could.

Guto shot all the ducks twice and won us both ridiculous teddy bears, one pink and one blue, and would have paid a third time had the man not begged him to stop before he won all the prizes. We failed on the hoopla because by then we were all three giggling too much to aim straight. We went on the swing boats, strapping ourselves in, swinging gently, then faster and faster until sky and grass changed places and everything whirled round together. I heard someone screaming, and recognized my own voice, and gripped hands with my companions as we flew like birds, higher and higher.

When the momentum slowed and stopped and Guto helped us down we staggered as if we were drunk, dizzy because the ground was still rocking beneath our feet and then we weaved to the side where the ground sloped up into a bank and sat down heavily, gasping for breath.

'Does anyone want another go?' Guto looked at us both and we shook our heads.

'That was the best ride I ever had in my life,' I said.

'Do you go on them every year?' Olive asked.

'For the past two or three years. I was too little before.' I did not add too cowardly.

'Guto said you were eleven.'

'Twelve,' I said, hurt. 'Twelve and two weeks, as a matter of fact.'

'You look much older,' she said generously.

'Our Nell was elderly at two,' Guto teased.

'I have my birthday in July,' Olive said. 'I will be seventeen then.'

'You look older too,' I flattered back.

'Guto and I have our birthdays in the same week,' Olive said. 'Isn't that amazing?' We agreed that it was amazing.

'Some things are meant,' she said mysteriously. 'I'm a great believer in destiny.'

'Oh, so am I,' I said fervently. 'And ghosts.'

'Did you ever see one?' she asked.

I shook my head, wishing that I could offer a story that would make her shiver.

'Neither did I.' She looked crestfallen.

'I read a book once,' Guto said, 'that said ghosts are not dead people but like moving photographs, impressions we leave on the atmosphere. That's why they repeat the same actions over and over again in the same places.'

'But people talk to ghosts,' Olive objected, 'and sometimes the ghosts talk back, so it must be more than that.'

'If any ghost talked to me,' Guto said, 'I wouldn't stay around to hear the rest of the conversation!'

We all giggled again.

'How about some ice-cream?' Guto suggested.

'I'll pay for it,' I said, my conscience pricking. 'I haven't spent anything yet.'

'Put it in the Band of Hope,' he said kindly. 'Do you want wafers or cornets?'

We choose cornets and he sauntered away to get them.

'Isn't he splendid?' Olive sat, hugging her knees, gazing after him. 'He's the first boyfriend I've ever had.'

'You must have had loads of chances,' I said enviously.

'Not really. I was always away at school until last year and then I took a shorthand and typing course and there was Christmas and then I met Guto. I'd seen him before, of course, but we bumped into each other one day and he helped me pick up my shopping. We got talking and there you are!'

'Destiny!' I said wisely.

'Wouldn't it be funny though if that book was true?' she said. 'We could turn round and catch a glimpse of ourselves doing something else.'

I didn't think it would be funny at all but I didn't like to say.

'Tell me about your family,' she urged. 'I love hearing about families. Is it true you've got gypsy blood? That's terribly romantic.'

'It is? Why?' I asked puzzled.

'Oh, I don't know.' She looked vague for a minute. 'In books gypsy lovers are always playing guitars and serenading their sweethearts.'

'Joseph Bohanna plays the accordion now and then,' I said, 'but I never heard of one of us playing the guitar.'

'And your Nain can work spells?'

'Yes, of course.' I was more puzzled than ever. 'Can't yours?'

'Mine sits on committees and my mother does voluntary work for St John's Ambulance.' She made a little grimace that paradoxically caused her to look more enchanting. 'My father plays golf and goes to the Rotary Club. They're dreadfully dull.'

'They sound lovely,' I said wistfully.

Oh, for a grandfather who didn't blow trumpets to remind the Almighty of what was promised in the Bible! I would have been delighted to caddy for him on a golf course instead.

'I am fond of them,' Olive admitted.

The manner in which she spoke sounded very upper-class English, but we had been speaking English all the afternoon. Most people slipped easily from one tongue into the other.

'You do speak Welsh, don't you?' I asked, suddenly suspicious. Some people who left the district for a long time came back claiming they couldn't remember a word of Welsh, as if loss of one's mother's tongue conferred some kind of social distinction.

'Of course I speak Welsh!' she said in surprise, reverting to it. 'I can speak some French too, but not much.'

'Can you speak Latin?'

'A bit.' As Guto returned with the ice-creams she looked up at him and said, 'Te amo, Guto.'

I suppose that he understood her even though he'd dropped Latin early, but even someone who had never learned one word would have understood what she was saying. There was, at that moment, a circle of radiance containing only the two of them and I was outside it, knowing loneliness.

Then Olive, without moving, drew me within the circle.

'Guto and I are planning to get married, Nell,' she said. 'You're the first person we've told.'

'Married?' I looked from one to the other.

'I'm eighteen in July and due to be called up then,' Guto said, squatting on his heels and handing round the ice-cream cornets. 'I'm going to volunteer for the RAF. When you volunteer you can choose which branch of the services you want to join. Ben's in the army and Mark's going into the navy, so I'm going in the RAF.'

'And we want to be married before he goes,' Olive said, softly breathless.

'They'll never let you,' I said.

'If I'm old enough to fight for my country I'm old enough to have a wife.' He answered me as he would have answered Taid. 'We plan to get engaged on Olive's birthday and married one week later on mine. We've got it all worked out. Olive's going to live at her house and do voluntary work, or get a job. It'll be over by Christmas and then we'll get a place of our own.'

I suppose I could have pointed out that they might as well wait until after Christmas in that case, but even I knew it would have been an absurd question. There was a trembling eagerness in them both which I could sense but not express.

'We don't want a big affair,' Olive said.

'Just a family wedding, in the chapel with Guto's family and mine. My parents won't mind if we're married in the chapel though they're Wesleyan, not Calvinist.'

'You've not told them?'

'Oh, my mother will have a little weep and my father will want to know if Guto will be able to support me properly after he comes out of the RAF,' Olive said serenely, 'but they won't object.'

'We'll have to have a family discussion,' I warned Guto. 'I'll say I think you ought to get married, that it's essential.'

'For heaven's sake don't put it like that,' Guto begged, 'or I'll find myself in the penance seat.'

'Don't say one word yet,' Olive warned. 'We want to go about it in the right way.'

'Aunt Marget's been engaged for eight years,' I reminded Guto.

'And I'm not Emyr Jones!' he retorted. 'I'm going to get round Mam first and then she'll make J.P. do what she wants.'

It was true though an outsider would not have guessed it.

'Plotting revolution then?' Constable Petrie, appearing suddenly out of the milling crowd, stood with legs apart, glowering genially at us.

'We wouldn't dare with you around,' Guto said.

'The presence of the law is a great deterrent to crime,' Constable Petrie agreed. 'It's been very quiet today. Only two arrests.' He sounded slightly disappointed.

'Someone is bound to strike a match after it gets dark,' I comforted.

'Well, as long as you're not getting into mischief.' He tapped the holster of his pistol meaningly. 'We don't often see you in these parts, Miss Rushton. How's your mam and dad then?'

'Very well, thank you, Constable Petrie.'

'Make sure she catches the night bus home. This is no time for young girls to be roaming about by themselves.' He lowered his voice and mouthed. 'Fifth columnists!'

'On Mona?' Guto said.

'Everywhere. It's a problem keeping track. Give my best to Nain and J.P.'

He pushed his hat further back on his head and strode off, an impressive rather than a comic figure.

'Olive and I thought we'd go to First House Pictures in Holyhead,' Guto said. 'Shall we drop you off at home on the way, Nell?'

'Unless you'd like to come with us?' Olive said with her quick and kindly grace.

'I'm not really in the mood for pictures,' I lied airily, 'but I'll take a lift home.'

They wanted to be alone and I was outside

the circle again. It was as it should be, but it made me feel raw inside.

'Want one more go on the swing boats?' Guto asked, rising and tugging Olive to her feet. She was licking drops of melted ice-cream from the tips of her fingers and laughing up at him and I wasn't surprised when he didn't wait for an answer from me but started back with Olive across the field towards the trap.

I swept my gaze round the panorama of tents, booths, swings and merrymakers. People were still streaming in and two of the Boswell boys had started a fight, but for me, the fair was over. There was a cloud over the day and outside that circle of radiance it was chilly.

'Promise not to tell,' Guto said when he dropped me off.

'You don't need a promise,' Olive said, giving me a women together look. 'I would trust Nell absolutely!'

So saying, she gave me back a little piece of the warmth we had shared and Guto lifted me down into the road and drove off again with Olive sliding her hand into the crook of his arm and bending her curly head towards his shoulder.

I watched them go, then holding the little piece of warmth tightly inside me, I turned and entered the house.

7

'It's my opinion that Flora's hanging onto that baby just to prevent Mark from joining up,' Aunt Ellen said.

'Well, small blame to her if she is,' Aunt Marget defended. 'No wife wants to see her husband go to war.'

'Oh, I don't know about that,' Nain objected. 'I'd have been glad to see the back of J.P. in 1914, but he was over the age then. Mind you, he knew exactly how the war should be conducted. It was a constant wonder to him that nobody thought to put him in the War Office. He'd have sorted them all out in five minutes flat.'

'Mark's like a cat on hot bricks,' said Aunt Catti. 'He wants to be where the action is.'

'There'll be action enough round his own place once Flora gets going,' Nain said crossly, 'without him running off to find more. It's bad enough having Ben out there and no news, without the worry about Mark going.'

'And Guto,' Aunt Marget said incautiously.

'Guto won't be eighteen for another couple of months,' Nain said, 'and it'll all have been settled by then one way or the other. Anyway, he's walking out with Olive Rushton and her father's a magistrate. He can pull strings!'

Nain was a firm believer in pulling strings.

'Are you sure Guto is eighteen next?' Aunt Ellen asked. 'I know what you are when it comes to dates. It's possible there was a mistake made and he was born a year later than we all thought.'

Nain considered for a few minutes, then thrust the temptation behind her.

'1922. I was there, wasn't I?' she said.

'It'll all be over by then, Mam,' Aunt Catti repeated reassuringly the phrase everybody repeated several times a day.

'Sooner or later,' Nain said. 'Get the teacup, Marget.' The teacup with its border of pink and blue roses and forget-me-nots was Nain's channel to the future. She and Aunt Marget had the 'sight', passed down in the family generation after generation. The gift lit on one or two women in each generation to use or flee as they chose. It was never taken for granted but it was not much talked about either. Nobody knew yet if it had alighted on me, though now and then Aunt Marget would invite me to look in the emptied cup and I would see the sodden shapes of the leaves swirl and twist into tiny pictures. Nain always scolded when she caught us at it.

'Leave the child to be a child,' she'd say. 'Why put the burden on her too soon?'

'Pour the tea, Catti,' Nain said.

Aunt Catti lifted the brown teapot and poured it in a steady stream into the big cup. I added milk and sugar and we sat down round the big table. Aunt Ellen, who disapproved of the entire business, walked out into the passage, closing the door with a sharp ping.

We each took a swallow of the tea. Then Nain turned the cup upside-down, turning it round three times to let the dregs trickle out.

'You can see anything, Marget?' She nodded towards my aunt.

It was not possible to read for oneself. Only the futures of other people sometimes showed clear.

Aunt Marget picked up the cup and turned it first one way and then the other. Over her face there fell a listening look. It didn't always happen but today it happened. Sleepy eyed, she talked in a stream of unemphatic, gentle phrases with scarcely a pause between them.

'Boats, many boats are sailing, many little boats and the aeroplanes flying low. Rattle of machine gun fire. Ben in the water holding a rope. Lines of men holding ropes and moving into deeper water, and the beaches still crowded. Men and little boats and the long ropes stretching across the sea. Ben will be — alright, I think? I can't see him so clearly now. I don't think there's any need to grieve. Not for Ben. Not for Ben. For another there's mourning. I can — '

She shook her head, raised it, the sleepiness jerked out of her eyes.

'Was there anything to see?' she asked.

'Nothing that made any sense,' Aunt Catti said. 'Boats and sea and Ben in the water, but he's in the army so what would he be doing in the water?'

Nain had taken the cup and was peering into it, but after a moment or two she shook her head.

'I've not the sight today,' she said. 'Well, we'll find out what it means in due course. Perhaps it was Mark you saw, learning to swim when he goes into the navy?'

'I don't know what I saw,' Aunt Marget said. 'Do you want to have a look, Nell?'

I looked but the tea leaves remained tea leaves.

'Tea leaves might not be your strong point,' Aunt Catti said. 'There are some who use cards.'

'If the old sod discovered a pack of cards in this house he'd divorce me!' Nain said, laughing. 'The Devil's picture book he calls it. Now, who's this?'

A figure had crossed the window and the door opened.

'Flora's started!' Mark cried. 'The waters broke and she's cramping every ten minutes.'

'Have you rung the doctor?' Nain was on her feet.

'I ran to get you first, Mam.' He looked younger than thirty-four suddenly.

'Run back and telephone the doctor,' she said briskly.

'You think I should have booked her in at the hospital?' Mark said anxiously.

'Everything was going normally when she had her last check-up, wasn't it?' Nain said. 'No, just give the doctor a ring to let him know. Marget, you'd better step up the road and tell Nurse Robson to get her bike out and herself on it. Catti, you come with me. Where's Ellen?'

'She's on her way to Flora,' Mark said.

'Right! Nell, run to the barn and tell Taid and Guto the baby's on the way and then go with your Aunt Marget to get the earth and the water.'

'I can do that by myself. I know what to do,' I said.

'You're sure? Marget, you follow on to the garage then! And you come after, Nell. Why does everything have to happen on a Saturday in this house?'

But she sounded pleased and excited. A third grandchild was a great event. Indeed, to my grandmother, the birth of any child was a great event.

I left them bustling around and flew across the meadow to the big barn where Taid and Guto were mending the door frame. At least Guto was mending it, knocking nails into the stubborn wood while Taid supervised from his perch on a fallen log.

'Auntie Flora's started the baby!' I called.

'Right then!' Taid stood up. 'Guto, leave that and go and help your brother. He'll be feeling bad.'

'I'm to fetch the earth and the water,' I said importantly.

'Fetch them then, girl! Don't stand there telling us about it,' Taid ordered.

I exchanged raised eyebrows with my young uncle to convey the impossible demands made by the older generation and ran back to the house.

'Here are the jars.' Aunt Catti, coat and headscarf on, a crowded basket hooked over her arm, stopped to give instructions to me. 'A couple of teaspoons of earth, that's all and half-fill the water jar. There's no need to dash everywhere! It might be hours yet.'

I took the two squat jars and, trying not to dash, went out again and walked fast up to the graveyard. It was the first time I'd ever been here by myself and it being a Saturday, the place was deserted. There were just me and the dead as I walked up the gravel paths, trying to decide from which grave to take the earth. Nobody had said, so it was something of a responsibility.

Charlie Williams, to whom Aunt Ellen had donated the vase of flowers from another grave, might not object if I took some soil. He lay beneath cracked slate but there was loose soil in the crevices. I knelt and, using a bit of wood, scooped some into one of the jars.

'Birth and death are two sides of the same coin,' Aunt Marget had said to me once. 'You can't have one without knowing the other is there. When new life is put into a cradle we sprinkle a little earth because everything that is born must die and out of everything that dies something is born.'

I didn't take much, not wanting to irritate Charlie Williams, and I screwed the lid back on with care before I rose to my feet again and hurried back through the gates and across the road to the lane that twisted down to the beach.

On this afternoon everything glinted and shimmered under a sky that was clear and blue with golden sun flecks dancing in the air. The water had borrowed colour from the heavens and even close at hand the waves had a turquoise translucence. I went to the edge where the large rocks dwindled into smooth pebbles and shingle and half-filled the second bottle.

'Sea water must be rubbed on a baby's back,' Aunt Catti had said. 'We Celts come from the sea and are bound to the sea. We need the strength of the sea when we are first born.'

Perhaps we had all been fish once, I thought, or mermaids. I knew that mermaids did not really exist, but I hoped that they might.

Armed with the bottles I went back to the road and set off for the garage. Halfway there Nurse Robson sailed past me on her bicycle, the skirt of her navy blue coat flapping behind her, beret rammed down over her eyebrows.

'Nell! Nell, has your auntie started yet?' Concepta John, untying her apron as she came, hurried from the Black Boy.

I nodded, holding up the two bottles, and went on importantly. There were several neighbours following me now, birth being a communal event.

By the time I reached my Uncle Mark's house everything was well under way. A large closed notice hung on the nearer of the two petrol pumps and a small crowd was already gathered at the gate staring up at the bedroom window where there was absolutely nothing to be seen except an occasional vague figure moving behind the net curtains. Nurse Robson's bicycle was propped against the front step and, as I entered the hall, I heard the keening of the women in the parlour.

It was not a parlour like ours. Aunt Flora always called it the lounge and she and Uncle Mark frequently sat talking here, one at each side of the fireplace with the tapestry fire screen Aunt Flora had been working on when she was expecting Johnny. She was fond of tapestry work. There were embroidered covers on every chair, a round tapestry cloth on the table in the bay window and six framed pictures made out of wool on the walls. Nain and my three aunts were sitting there now, scarves drawn over their heads, swaying backwards and forwards like cornstalks in a breeze. From their lips issued a rhythmic moaning, older than the most faraway time I could imagine. From time to time one or the other would break off and move over to the trolley against the wall where tea and sandwiches had been set out.

'Did you bring the earth and water?' Nain asked, breaking off from her moaning.

'I took the earth from Charlie Williams,' I said.

'Oh, Charlie was a nice old boy,' Aunt Marget said. 'He'll be very pleased to have the soil taken from his resting place. Put the bottles down, there's a good girl, and go and find Johnny.'

'Must I?' My face fell considerably.

'Take him for ice-creams.' Aunt Marget dug in her pocket.

I hesitated.

'It'll be hours yet,' she said. 'You'll be needed later to help drive ill fortune away. We're saving our voices a bit until then. You go on now and find Johnny.'

I went reluctantly into the hall and stood for a moment looking up the stairs. In the front bedroom above, Aunt Flora was giving birth. I heard voices and then a door closed somewhere and Guto came along the landing and looked down at me.

'We just got Mark to bed,' he hissed. 'Can you find Johnny?'

'I'm just going.' I went, deciding that when I did find my cousin I'd send him off to buy ice-cream and hang around near the house. It was not until the birth was imminent that the expectant father retired to bed in the spare room to moan and groan in pretended labour, encouraged by his male relatives, to

150

ease the genuine pangs being endured by his wife. That too was an ancient custom dying out even then in some parts.

I found Johnny in the garage sitting on the running board of an old van. I didn't like my cousin. Indeed the adjective 'obnoxious', which we'd recently learned in school, described him neatly, but he did look a trifle disconsolate as he sat with hunched shoulders, drawing patterns on the concrete with the tip of his gym shoe.

'Hi Johnny! I said, going in.

'They won't let me see Mam,' he said.

'The baby's coming. Only Nurse Robson can see her now.'

I sat down next to him on the running board and held out the coppers.

'You're to run and get a couple of ice-creams,' I told him.

'The baby might come.'

'It'll be hours yet,' I said wisely. 'Your dad's only just gone to bed. You can join the men when we've eaten our ice-cream.'

'Does it hurt to have babies?' He didn't look like the smug, intending preacher.

'It think it hurts a bit,' I said, 'but not much.'

'*Your* mam died,' he muttered.

'This is a second baby. People don't die having second babies,' I said.

'You're sure?'

'I'm certain sure! Go and get the ice-creams.'

He took the money and went, holding himself a little bit straighter. It was odd, but I had never thought of my cousin's being worried about Aunt Flora. I'd imagined he'd be jealous about the new baby, but not anxious. It was possible he might grow up to be fairly decent. He might even change his mind and decide not to be a preacher but something more sensible.

The garage was chilly and smelled of petrol and oil and car polish. The renovated Ford car was at the far end, brightly gleaming. Uncle Mark was so pleased with it that he had decided to keep it for himself and sell his current car instead, though his current car needed some of the dents on its side straightening out. Taid, whenever he drove it, aimed at lamp posts.

'Nell? Where's your Uncle Mark?'

I looked up as a couple of the Bohanna men came into the garage. They were third cousins or something, one near fifty and too old to fight, the other limping on a leg caught in a gin some years before.

'He's having a baby.' I stood up, politely.

'Good God! Now's not the time to be having a baby!' They glanced at each other in consternation.

'Can't Flora hold onto it for another week?' Jim Bohanna demanded.

'In a matter of hours it'll be here,' I told him.

'Then she'll have to get a move on,' Sean said.

'Is something wrong?'

I followed them as they went towards the house.

Inside the keening had temporarily ceased as fresh tea was brewed. Jim Bohanna stationed himself at the foot of the stairs and yelled up.

'Mark! How much longer d'ye reckon you'll be?'

'Depends on Flora.' My uncle's voice came from upstairs. 'She's having a bit of a sleep.'

'Having a bit of a sleep!' Sean echoed in disgust. 'Doesn't she know she's supposed to be in labour? She's got to make an effort quick, boy!'

'Why all the shouting?' Nurse Robson poked her nose over the bannisters.

'We need Mark, Nurse Robson. Him and his boat,' Sean told her.

'Nobody takes that boat without me in it!' my uncle yelled from the back bedroom. 'You want to go fishing you take your own.'

'Yours is a motor boat. It goes faster,' Jim shouted back, 'and we're not going fishing. We're going to France!'

'*What!*' There was a creaking of bed-springs, a concerted rush onto the landing as Taid and Guto appeared with Uncle Mark, hastily fastening his dressing gown.

'It just came on the wireless. Every boat is needed to pick up our men from France. They're stranded on the beaches.'

'It'd take twenty-four hours if we set out right now. By then they'll all have been taken off,' Nurse Robson said.

'By the English!' Sean nodded. 'I wouldn't trust myself in an English boat! There'll be Welsh lads out there.'

'Ben's there!' Aunt Catti erupted from the lounge. 'Marget saw it in the teacup. Long lines of men in the water holding onto ropes and Ben there.'

'Ben can't swim,' Sean said blankly.

'By the time you can get there he'll have let go of the rope,' Nurse Robson said.

'Your brother's drowning and you're lying around having a baby!' Jim accused.

Aunt Catti burst into tears.

'Lend us your boat and we'll go,' Sean coaxed.

'That boat stays in harbour until I'm aboard,' Uncle Mark shouted, rumpling his hair. 'Anyway she needs petrol.'

'Moss is filling her up now to save time,' Jim said.

'We'll need blankets and a hot thermos,' Taid said.

'We?' Everybody stared up at him though it was Guto who posed the question.

'You don't imagine I'm staying here while everybody else sails off to France, do you?' There was a threatening rumble in his voice.

'It'll be dangerous,' Uncle Mark said.

It was the wrong thing to say, acting as a spur and not a check.

'You think I'm too old and feeble to face a bit of danger?' Taid demanded.

'But the Germans might shoot at you,' Aunt Catti wailed.

'They're not likely to be waiting with flowers, are they?' he snapped. 'If they shoot we can shoot back.'

'You can borrow my shotgun.' Aunt Ellen had joined us in the hall. 'You might be glad of an extra weapon.'

'But there'll be thousands of troops there,' Guto objected. 'How are we going to pick Ben out?'

'You're not going to pick anybody out,' my grandfather said. 'Mark and I are going with Jim and Sean. If every Tom, Dick and Harry gets aboard there won't be room to bring anybody back! And if we don't spot Ben we'll pull someone else in and pray he's in another boat! But first Flora's got to do her duty and have the baby. Shouldn't you be in there with her, Nurse Robson?'

'You can't hurry nature, J.P.' Aunt Ellen began.

'Can't hurry nature?' He fixed us all with a steely glare. 'In the Petrie family I decide when things get done! Flora!' Before anyone could stop him he had paced across the landing and wrenched open the bedroom door. 'Flora, Ben's drowning and Mark's going to France to rescue our lads and be shot at by the Germans, so stop holding up the war effort and have that bloody baby!'

'That's done it! You've done it now, Taid Petrie!' Nurse Robson fairly scuttled past him, calling over her shoulder. 'More hot water, Ellen!'

Within the lounge the keening had started again, rising and falling like the wailing of a banshee. The Bohannas were halfway up the stairs, urging Mark back into the spare bedroom. Through the open front door I glimpsed neighbours crowding closer. I opened my mouth to wail with everybody else and then I heard it. Just over my head was the sound of a slap and a sharp, protesting howl.

The keening ceased as abruptly as if someone had just pressed a switch, but the crying went on. The house held its breath.

Nurse Robson appeared, her sleeves rolled

to the elbow, her face scarlet.

'It's a child!' she said loudly.

'Duw! That was quick,' Sean said, emerging from the back bedroom.

'It was Taid's shouting did it,' Nurse Robson said and vanished into the bedroom again.

Aunt Ellen went past me with a pan of steaming water and there was a burst of cheering from the neighbours. I went into the lounge and sat down on one of the tapestried chairs. Nain was pouring more tea for Aunt Catti who had stopped weeping.

'Better take up the earth and water, Mam,' Aunt Marget said, bustling in. 'I'm brewing up a thermos flask and cutting more sandwiches, so the men can get off quickly.'

Nain took the two flasks and vanished. I could hear voices and tramping feet overhead and the thin, high crying of the baby. Aunt Catti wiped her eyes and went through to the back kitchen to help Aunt Marget.

'Find Johnny and tell him to come and see his baby brother!' Aunt Ellen called down to me.

Johnny walked in at the front door as I reached it.

'You've got a — ' I began.

'A baby brother,' he interrupted. 'Mrs Concepta told me. I'm going up to see him.'

'What about the ice-creams?' I detained him to ask.

'I ate them both,' he said calmly and continued on his obnoxious way up the stairs.

'Don't you want to see the baby, Cariad?' Aunt Ellen enquired from the top of the stairs.

'I'll go up later when there aren't so many people about,' I said.

'There's a considerate girl.' She vanished again.

I wasn't in the least considerate. I already knew the baby was to be called William after Aunt Flora's father and would probably be a chemist when he grew up, though Nain still hankered after doctor. For the rest the infant would look like all the others I'd ever seen. For a 12-year-old I was sadly lacking in maternal instinct.

Guto came down the stairs, looking angry, and pushed past me in a way quite unlike his usual manner. He was annoyed about not going to pick up Uncle Ben off the French beaches, I supposed, and I felt indignant on his behalf. He'd be more use than Taid, I felt, though I wouldn't have dared to say.

A car drew up outside and the doctor got out and hurried up the path, brushing off various clutching hands and the odd, 'If you've one moment to look at my veins,

Doctor? Didn't want to bother you in surgery.'

'A child, is it?' he greeted me.

'A fine child.' Nain came, beaming, to the head of the stairs. 'About six pounds, I'd guess. Going to be wiry.'

'Can you clear these people out of the house?' Doctor Morgan, who'd trained in Cardiff and had very peculiar ideas, glared at the Bohannas who were draped over the banisters. 'Flora will want a bit of peace and quiet without half the neighbourhood tramping through her bedroom! The trouble with you people is that you don't move with the times. Primitive isn't in it!'

'We're going to France as soon as Mark stops congratulating himself on becoming a father again,' Jim said.

'I heard it on the wireless. The Germans chasing our lads into the sea. Not good at all. Nurse Robson, let's take a look at the afterbirth then!' He moved into the bedroom.

I wandered into the kitchen and helped myself to a couple of sandwiches. There was a great toing and froing. It whirled and eddied about me, but I was not part of it. I took another sandwich and wished, gloomily, that I were going to France.

The men were tramping through the hall with blankets in their arms and their shotguns over their shoulders. My aunts hovered with the thermos flasks.

From the stairs Nain raised her voice to say, 'Determined to go, are you J.P.? Sailing down the coast and across the Channel like an old Viking? What happens if you get shot? Or the boat sinks?'

'The boat's insured, Mam,' Uncle Mark said.

'Well, when you're all floundering in the Channel, don't be surprised if I say 'I told you so'!' she said crossly. 'And if you're set on going make sure you bring someone back even if it isn't Ben. It's not a pleasure cruise.'

'I'm doing my bit towards the war effort,' Taid said with dignity and stalked out.

'Silly old bugger!' said Nain. There was a singing in her voice.

I followed them as far as the gate and leaned on it, watching them diminish into the distance down towards the tiny harbour where my uncle's boat was moored.

'If we had a wireless,' said Aunt Ellen, joining me, 'we might have some idea what's going on.'

'Uncle Mark has one but it doesn't work very well,' I remembered.

'It might disturb Flora and the baby. Have you done your homework?'

The fate of hundreds was in the balance and Aunt Ellen wanted to know about homework.

'I did it yesterday.' I crossed my fingers behind my back.

'Go and do some more. Geniuses,' said Aunt Ellen, giving the word its full weight, 'cannot get too much homework.' She had twisted her head and was giving my crossed fingers a hard look.

I went slowly through the gate and down the road. An uncanny quiet had fallen over the village, like the beginning of the start of the day of judgement. It would serve Taid right for being a silly old bugger if Judgement Day was really coming and he was in France and missed it.

That was a strange weekend. Everything moved twice as slowly as usual and meals, for once, were skimped and unpunctual affairs. Guto had gone over to Benllech, partly to nurse his injured dignity and partly because the Rushtons had a wireless that worked more efficiently than Uncle Mark's did. Aunt Ellen had gone over to sleep at the house and take care of Aunt Flora and the new baby and Johnny and Nain plodded there every morning. In chapel there were conspicuously empty seats and the minister's sermon was all about crossing the Red Sea, so that if one didn't pay close attention one was left with the impression of the entire British Army marching dryshod across the Channel while, behind them, the waters poured in again to engulf the pursuing Germans. Much more interesting than the sermon was the announcement that the schools would be closed for a couple of days until the situation had been clarified. It meant I could go and help Aunt Marget and Aunt Catti in their tiny greengrocery. I enjoyed the warm, damp smell of ripe tomatoes and the fragrance of tart russets that pervaded the place and the importance of wearing a white overall and giving the right change.

More people than usual came in, all of them lingering to enquire, 'Any news of the lads then? Ah, well! No news is good news!'

'And that's a daft saying if I ever heard one!' Aunt Marget exclaimed. 'No news is no news. Nothing good or bad about it! They'll be on their way back by now, I imagine.'

'Unless they took a wrong turn and ended up in Ireland,' Aunt Catti said.

Their laughter was as warm and ripe as the tomatoes.

'Rhiannon Evans was in earlier, asking if we'd heard. You were over at the grocer's,' Aunt Marget said. 'If you ask me she's still keen on our Ben.'

'Well, she might wear him down yet. Guto's walking out with Olive Rushton might encourage him,' Aunt Catti said.

Aunt Marget glanced in my direction and said, 'Don't go spreading it round, but Guto and Olive are planning to get married this summer. It's a bit rushed but he wants to have everything settled before he joins up.'

'I already — '

'Not one word, mind,' Aunt Catti interposed. 'We've got to be diplomatic on account of the old man — with Guto being the youngest and all. It's my opinion J.P. will give his consent to make up for Guto's not going to France with the rest of them, but you can never tell what mood the old sod'll be in. Anyway, you're bound to be bridesmaid.'

'And for me too,' Aunt Marget promised.

I thought I would probably be too old to act as a bridesmaid by the time she and Emyr Jones were finally joined in holy matrimony, but I was too fond of her to say it out loud.

'I need another box for these sprouts,' Aunt Catti frowned. 'Run across to Steadman and ask him if he has a spare one — and see if my magazine is in yet. Not that it's worth reading these days. It's getting thinner every week.'

I went obediently across the road.

'Tell Catti I'll bring her a couple of boxes

as soon as I've checked my stock.' Mr Steadman was as round and genial as a gobstopper. 'Her magazine's not in yet. Everything's delayed on account of the political situation. When's your Uncle Guto getting married then? Before he goes in the RAF, I suppose. That's a good catch he's making if you ask me! But it's top secret as yet, I understand?'

'I thought it was.' I accepted a bit of liquorice root and went out reflecting it wasn't much fun keeping a secret everybody knew.

A figure in khaki, kitbag over his shoulder, was coming over the brow of the hill. I stood in the middle of the road, too startled to move, as it drew near and resolved itself into my uncle. By the time I began to move my aunts were ahead of me, pounding out of the shop.

'Where's the old man?'

'Why aren't you drowning in France? What are you doing back here?'

'I hitched a lift all the way from Southampton.'

'What were you doing in Southampton?' Aunt Marget demanded.

'He's deserted!' said Aunt Catti, tears welling in her eyes.

'I was lifted off in the first batch. Where is everybody?'

'Gone to France to rescue you in Mark's boat. Flora had the baby — six pounds it weighed — a child and Mark went with the Bohannas and the old man. When are you going back?'

'In about a week when my regiment reforms. The old man went too?'

'He insisted,' said Aunt Marget.

'Silly old bugger,' my uncle said calmly, 'Hello, Nell, have you done your homework then?'

8

'Lord, but we were in a tight spot!' Taid said, for about the twenty-ninth time. 'Planes coming in low and strafing the beach. Not that anyone could see the beach, mind! Nothing but a swarming mass of men, like bees crawling. The bigger ships couldn't get in close so they had to drop anchor off shore but the little vessels could sail in quite near. There were long ropes strung out and the troops were holding onto them. Very orderly they were too, waiting patiently! I'd been hoping we might spot Ben, but of course by the time we arrived he'd been rescued with the first batch.'

'He might have waited,' Constable Petrie said.

'Well, he was under orders I suppose,' Taid allowed, 'and then he didn't know we were on the way.'

'He ought to have realized you wouldn't leave him in the lurch,' Constable Petrie said.

'Well, he probably wasn't thinking straight,' Taid said kindly. 'It was hard for any of us to think straight. The water was pretty choppy and men were scrambling into the boats trying to hold their rifles over their heads. Everybody was mixed up.'

'You could have done with someone there to take charge.' Constable Petrie sounded wistful.

I was bored with the conversation and wandered off into the yard. The cell was empty.

'No sense in filling it up with petty criminals when the entire country is crawling with fifth columnists,' the Constable had said. 'I'm keeping a very close watch on the Petrocellis, I can tell you.'

The Petrocellis were certainly suspicious characters. To start with they came from Milan in Italy, which proved they were probably on the run from the Mafia. Had they come from Sicily then they would actually have been in the Mafia. That was the way things worked in Italy. Since the war began they'd been required to report at the police station every week, which meant closing down their ice-cream shop and trailing over to Constable Petrie who looked them over very closely, then stamped their papers and let them go with an expression on his face of regret because he hadn't arrested them. He was certain they'd give themselves away sooner or later, but their being Catholics made it more difficult since they had probably been trained in spying techniques by the Vatican.

I pushed open the door of the cell and sat down on the cool, stone step. It was a hot, still July with skies of electric blue and corn ripening too fast. The school holidays, which seemed to stretch ahead endlessly at their beginning were slipping away faster as the summer wore on. When the September term began I'd be in a higher form.

There had been some heated discussion about my report, which I'd carried home in a sealed envelope, heroically resisting the temptation to peek. Nain had entertained no such qualms.

'We'll steam it open and take a look before the old bugger sees it,' she said.

This she immediately proceeded to do, watched by the aunts.

'Conduct — excellent. Well, there's a good start!' Her teeth gleamed in her brown face. 'Let's see now. English literature, eighty-three per cent. Why no comment at the side?'

'Sir was in a hurry, I think.'

'More likely he left it blank because he didn't want to give you a swelled head. Catti, pass me the pen and ink.'

This command obeyed, my grandmother carefully printed in, 'promises genius', and blotted it.

'Sixty-one per cent for English Language,' Aunt Marget said.

'We'll make the other one into a seven so that it matches closer to the literature,' said Nain, doing so.

'Welsh, sixty per cent. We can make that into sixty-nine with no trouble. French, sixty-two. Latin, forty-five. Well, that's forty-three more than you ever got, Catti. History, eighty-three. Geography, fifty-one — he probably meant fifty-nine so I'll alter it for him. Science, ten? Good heavens, that's a definite mistake! The teacher gave you full marks and was interrupted while he was writing it down. Scripture, sixty-five. Mathematics, thirty-six — well, they're not important for a girl. Put it back in the envelope, Marget, and get the glue. You can take it up now, Cariad.'

I took it up and laid it before Taid in the parlour, backing out and leaving him to peruse it at leisure. It was, I flattered myself, quite a decent report even before Nain had amended it, but one could never be certain how Taid would react to things.

At teatime when we all sat down I stole a look at his face and saw that it was hard and forbidding, but he didn't say anything until we were on our second cup of tea. Then he frowned round our assembly and announced,

169

'I'm not happy about Nell's reports.'

'Isn't it a good one then? I thought she'd done very well in the examinations,' Nain said.

'It's a very good report, but it's clear to me they don't appreciate her! Full marks she got for science and the only comment was 'must try harder'. How can you try harder than full-marks? It was a very unfair comment in my opinion!'

'They probably rush the reports through on the last day of term,' Aunt Catti said.

'They're careless about adding the figures up too,' Taid informed us. 'They put her average mark as fifty-three per cent when it should be sixty-six. I think I ought to have a word with the Headmaster.'

'Oh not with his boy in the Fire Service!' Nain exclaimed.

'Well, what's that got to do with anything?' Taid demanded.

'The war being on and all,' she said vaguely.

'I don't see why my granddaughter should be penalized because there's a war on,' he retorted, his face beginning to redden. 'Anyway, think how bad it will look for the country if the Nazis ever get here and find out the inefficiency in the schools. I've a good mind to take it up with the Minister of Education.'

'I'll have a word with Emyr when I see him,' Aunt Marget offered.

'He doesn't teach Nell's class,' Taid said.

Emyr Jones taught senior French and woodwork and I never saw him at school save in the distance.

'He can make enquiries and sort out the muddle,' she said.

'Pity he can't sort out his marriage.' Taid couldn't resist a gibe as he passed the report over.

'If I had a silk dress I'd not hesitate,' Aunt Marget said.

'It was a pity you couldn't pick one up while you were in France,' said Aunt Ellen.

'Good God, woman!' He glared at her. 'I was under fire, not shopping. And we didn't land anyway. Too busy pulling the lads out of the water. Oh, you talk nonsense sometimes, Ellen!'

His temper had finally worn thin, but at least he'd shelved the subject of my report. With any luck he wouldn't remember it again either because the talk now was all of Guto's wedding.

I shifted into a more comfortable position on the cell step and reflected on the unpredictable ways of adults.

Everything that occurred in our family was the subject for long and acrimonious

171

discussion. Yet when my youngest uncle had calmly made it known that he intended to get married on his eighteenth birthday and then volunteer for the RAF nobody had said one word save in agreement. It was as if Olive had put them all under a spell. After one visit, when Guto had brought her home for tea, even Taid had been trapped in the powerful beam of her enchantment, the more powerful because she herself was not fully aware of it.

'A lovely girl,' Aunt Ellen said. 'Guto's lucky to have caught her. A girl like that would make any man proud!'

'They are young,' said Nain, 'but with the war on everybody has the right to grow up a bit faster.'

Unspoken was the thought that many of the boys who volunteered for the RAF didn't grow much older. There were always aeroplanes in the sky above now. They flew low, so low we could see the bombs strapped to the undercarriages, and when they returned they flew higher, freed of their loads. Very often more flew out than came back, but we didn't talk of it.

We talked instead of the wedding that was to take place in defiance of tradition from our house.

'I don't want a big affair,' Olive said, prettily earnest, 'and I do want to be married

172

in the chapel here and have Taid preach the sermon. My parents are not strict chapelgoers and they're quite willing.'

It was clear that her parents would not have raised the smallest protest had she and Guto planned to marry in a Hindu temple, hung round with bells and lotus flowers. Mr Rushton was a large, slow-moving man whose slight deafness occasionally led to some confusion in the magistrates court where he found it difficult to follow the evidence. Mrs Rushton was small and had the same kind of prettiness as the china shepherdess in the dining-room cabinet. They had driven over for morning coffee which had put Nain into a bit of a flurry since we didn't have any particular time of the day for a break. The huge kettle sang on the hob all day and anyway we usually drank tea.

But the Rushtons had been nice people and Nain, in her dark print dress with its scattering of little white flowers, had displayed a quiet and charming dignity that made me proud of her. Even Aunt Ellen had refrained from talking about her unfortunate experience but had sat, hair neat for once, nodding pleasantly every time there was a pause in the conversation.

'Olive is hoping to take a course in first-aid,' her mother said, 'since she's too young to be accepted in any of the services. It will keep her busy while Guto is away and there's the possibility he'll do his training at Valley, so he'll be able to come home often.'

'The time to think about is when the war is over,' Nain said, brightly optimistic. 'At the moment he's helping out on the farm here, but eventually he'll want a place of his own.'

'They'll be doing a lot of building after the war,' Mrs Rushton agreed. 'It might be a good idea to start looking round for a nice plot of land.'

'Let's get the war over first,' Taid rumbled.

'By Christmas,' said Mr Rushton who heard male voices more distinctly than female ones. 'I have it on very good authority it will be all over by Christmas.'

Being a magistrate and a member of the yacht club we assumed he was in a good position to know. Perhaps there were fifth columnists on our side too.

'Let's talk about weddings, not wars,' Olive begged. 'I want Nell to be my bridesmaid. You will, won't you?'

I'd never been a bridesmaid and the honour of it made me feel a trifle dizzy.

'She'll make a lovely bridesmaid,' Mrs Rushton said kindly. 'I thought pink would be nice, with a flounce on the skirt and a wreath of white rosebuds — of spotted muslin. Olive will be wearing the family lace, so muslin would be very suitable.'

She genuinely saw me as the kind of child who would look beautiful in pink muslin and rosebuds. Perhaps she was right and as I followed Olive down the aisle I would blossom forth into loveliness like her. It was something to anticipate anyway.

'Time to go home, Nell! We mustn't keep Constable Petrie from his duties,' Taid said, breaking into the dreaming vision of myself.

I hoped that the cleaning would have been done by the time we got back. The engagement party was on the following day and for the past week Virgin and Child Cottage had been four walls with a mess in the middle.

'I can't understand why it's necessary to turn out every cupboard,' Guto protested. 'Olive's parents aren't likely to be inspecting the linen closets, are they?'

'But I will know if they're untidy, won't I?' Nain said unanswerably.

The aunts, who enjoyed cleaning, joined in with a heartiness that left me cold. I was only grateful that all my female relatives were too plump to mount the ladder to my loft room with ease. It was impossible to move without falling over tins of Brasso, cakes of lavender polish, brushes, brooms and the antique carpet sweeper. Looking at the latter I remembered that as a very small child I'd had an imaginary friend called Prudence. Prudence had gone everywhere with me and had a place set for her at the table and then, one day, Aunt Ellen had unthinkingly sucked her up in the carpet sweeper. It had been of no use for my aunt to protest that Prudence had been invisible anyway. After she went into the carpet sweeper I never saw her again.

I climbed up into the trap next to my grandfather and said a polite farewell to Constable Petrie. He had been invited to the wedding, of course, though he had warned that it might not be possible for him to stay right to the end of the reception lest crime run riot while he was absent from his post. Though the wedding was being held in our chapel the Rushtons were giving the buffet luncheon in their house, which accounted for the fuss and bother over the engagement party. Nain didn't intend to be outshone either in hospitality or cleanliness.

With the ceremony only a week away the house bore an expectant air.

'The last time anything exciting happened here was when you were born, Nell,' Aunt Ellen said greeting us as we reached the front door. 'Mind you, it cast a bit of a shadow with your mam dying and your dad taking off for Australia before we could turn round, but it didn't alter the pleasure we felt.'

'And next year there might be another birth, if Guto doesn't waste all his time flying aeroplanes.' Taid climbed down and went past her into the hall, to be greeted by an anguished shriek from Aunt Catti.

'Take your shoes off, J.P.! You're trekking mud into the carpet!'

'Mud? It's not rained in weeks!' he retorted. 'I was thinking of praying for a spot of rain!'

'Not for tomorrow!' Aunt Ellen dived into the house. 'Well, there's mean of you! Starting to pray for rain on the day before the engagement party! Real spoilsport!'

I went through the garden and down the steps to the back of the house. The yard had been swept and lacked its usual quota of tramps and layabouts and Nain was hovering anxiously over a fresh batch of scones in the kitchen.

There was food everywhere. Every surface was covered with trays of fancy cakes, plaited buns, pies, scones, barabrith and jellies. The sliced tongue and ham and tinned salmon were on the cold shelves in the pantry and bottles of Nain's home-made wines decorated the floor. Some of the bottles were cob-webbed which meant they would have a lethal kick. However they didn't count as real alcohol.

'Do you think there's going to be enough for everybody?' Nain said to me. 'There'll be Flora, Johnny, the baby — well, we can't really count the baby — and Mark and J.P., Ellen, Catti, Marget, the Rushtons, Constable Petrie, Rhiannon Evans — it's a pity Ben had to go back to the army. You think they'd have given him a bit of a holiday after Dunkirk! And Mark starts his training the day after the wedding. I think he said he was going to Scapa Flow. Where was I? Rhiannon, Dilys, Ceri, Maggie, the Bohanna lads, you and me. Have I left anyone out?'

'Olive and Guto,' I said.

'The most important pair! Duw, I must be getting old! They say kidney trouble can affect the brain! Olive and Guto. The names go nice together, don't you think?'

'They belong,' I said.

'And she's a lovely girl. Pretty as a picture. I wish they were getting married without this old war hanging over our heads.'

'If there hadn't been a war they'd have waited,' I reminded her.

'They say 'marry in haste, repent at leisure!'' she said thoughtfully. 'It's not true in my opinion. I knew J.P. for years before he got round to asking me and I've been repenting my answer ever since!'

She put back her head and pealed her pretty laugh.

'I don't think Olive and Guto will repent,' I said, sneaking a scone under cover of her amusement. 'I think they'll enjoy being married.'

'I hope so, Cariad. Now if only Emyr and Marget would set the date I'd be very contented. It's a pity we can't get hold of any silk — she's set her heart on a silk frock. Have another scone. I can make more.'

'It'll be wedding cake next week.' I took an official scone.

'Two tiers, Mrs Rushton told me. They can save the top layer for the christening. I've a feeling they'll go in for a family quite soon. People do when there's a war on.'

Olive and Guto begetting. For some reason I couldn't understand I felt myself blushing. There were odd corners of the grown up world that were still dark and mysterious to me. Uncle Mark and Aunt Flora, Uncle Ben coming home late on a Saturday night with his shoes in his hand, the big bed with Nain's side so neat and Taid's a mass of rumpled coats. I was not certain if I wanted to explore these corners yet or not, particularly where my youngest uncle and his sweetheart were concerned. I had been part of the two of them ever since the day of the fair, but after the wedding I knew they would draw away together and leave me solitary again. And when that happened I would know that I was solitary though I had not realized it until I was part of a threesome.

'You'll look lovely in your bridesmaid's dress,' Nain said, reaching for a scone for herself and slapping her own hand away before she touched it.

Pink taffeta had been decided on, the net yoke outlined with seed pearls and more pearls edging a little lace cap. 'A Juliet cap,' said Mrs Rushton. 'They always look right somehow.'

Olive's dress was white lace and her Juliet cap had tiny white rosebuds and a long veil. She was going to carry white carnations and I was going to carry a posy of sweet williams. There had been some talk about Johnny's being a pageboy, but thank the Lord it hadn't come to anything!

I wouldn't wear the bridesmaid's dress until the great day itself. It would hang under tissue paper in Aunt Marget's wardrobe for another week. I had already worn it out with looking.

For the engagement party I had a sprigged cotton dress. That too was new and, though it couldn't rival the pink, it was very crisp and fresh looking. I had been taking an interest in clothes for some time and longed passionately to wear a brassiére instead of the liberty bodice that was scratchy in summer and inadequate in winter.

'Trampling dirt in and praying for rain!' Aunt Ellen said, coming into the kitchen. 'He's got no consideration at all!'

'He never did have,' Nain said placidly, not asking whom Aunt Ellen was talking about. 'Tell me what you think of these scones. I was afraid they might go a bit heavy, but they seem alright.'

Aunt Ellen took two and sat on the draining board, the only uncluttered surface, to test them.

'They're up to your usual standard,' she pronounced. 'I don't think you'd get them lighter without them floating away.'

'I always had a good hand with scones,' Nain said, looking pleased. 'Now the sandwiches will have to be cut first thing and covered with greaseproof paper. The cake is iced — I'm rather proud of the cake! Mind you, it won't compare with the actual wedding cake, but they had a caterer make that.'

'Has Olive bought the shroud yet?' Aunt Ellen enquired.

A faint shadow marred the serenity of my grandmother's face. The ancient custom

181

whereby the bride presented the bridegroom with a shroud had never found much favour in her eyes and with Guto about to go into the RAF, it was tactless of Aunt Ellen to mention it.

'Olive will do her duty,' she said, somewhat shortly. 'Have the last scone, Nell. Seeing that batch turned out fine, I might as well make another straight off.'

Reveille was almost at the crack of dawn the next day. One would have imagined that we'd all been twiddling our thumbs for a month from the way Nain galvanised the family into action.

'It's a catch-as-you-can breakfast in the kitchen and stack your dishes in the sink. Then everything can get washed up together! Ellen is going to cut the bread, Marget can butter and Catti can do the fillings. I want to give the silver a last bit of a rub. Guto! Did you take your bath yesterday or do you want it today?'

'I'm the cleanest man in North Wales, Mam!' He winked at me.

'Well, see that you stay clean! What time are you fetching Olive?'

'Ten o'clock. We're going to Holyhead first to pick up the ring and then we're driving back here. Mark's lending me the Ford.'

'By that time everybody will be here and

you can make a grand entrance! I like the affairs to be done properly.'

'I wish I could go with them to Holyhead,' I said to Aunt Marget.

'No indeed, Cariad. Choosing the ring is just for two people. It's a very romantic occasion.' She glanced fondly at her own ring.

'I'm astonished you can remember from so far back,' Taid said.

'You don't have to be so nasty. If I had a silk dress I'd be getting married tomorrow!' she flashed.

'Now that you've waited eight years you can hang on for a bit longer,' he retorted. 'Paying for this little lot is liable to land me in the bankruptcy court! And after we finally get you wed I suppose Catti will be rushing into matrimony! On the whole it might be a lot cheaper if you both stayed spinsters!'

Aunt Catti's eyes had begun to fill. The sandwiches would be damp enough without greaseproof paper if she wasn't careful, I thought, and slipped out of the kitchen before anyone noticed I hadn't been given a job to do.

Every available chair, except the parlour chairs, had been ranged round the dining-room walls. The table had been opened to its fullest extent and, in its centre, was the engagement- cum-birthday cake in all its glory of white icing with two white doves perched on top and silver hearts stuck round the edge.

'Nell! Go and put your frock on and be sure your socks are clean,' Nain was calling after me. 'You can change in your aunts' room.'

The hallstand had been cleared ready for guests' coats. I hoped they'd go home before Taid went to bed, otherwise they'd have to sneak into the bedroom and get their garments back.

Guto and Olive had already chosen the ring, I thought. Three little diamonds on a gold band — not very big stones but real. The ring was being made a bit smaller to fit Olive's finger. It would have been fun to have gone with them and shared in the grand entrance when they came back. I would have liked to make a fuss about it, but knew I was too old. On the other hand if I just happened to be in the hall when he left he might take me along as he usually did.

By the time I got down into the hall again there was no sign of Guto, but Nain and my aunts were bustling in and out, carrying trays of food. From behind the closed door of the parlour I could hear Taid's voice raised in petition.

'Praying for rain,' said Aunt Ellen with a

malevolent look. 'Silly old sod!'

There would be no rain that day. The sky was cloudless and the air was drifted with bees.

'Have you got your present for Olive?' Aunt Catti asked me. 'We mustn't forget it's her birthday as well as their engagement.'

I had a very special gift which I intended to give Olive as soon as I could snatch a private moment. It was wrapped in pink paper and tied with a long piece of silver tinsel and I was dying to see her face when she opened it.

'Come and count these plates for me, Cariad,' Nain begged. 'I want to smarten myself up a bit before I greet everybody!'

She never would look smart. She was too round and comfortable for that and all her shoes had to be slit to accommodate her swollen toes, but she could outshine even my aunts when her hair was tamed into a Madonna smoothness and her ripe, clear laughter made melody.

The guests started to arrive, dressed up as if it were Sunday and shaking hands as formally as if they had just been introduced. Taid had given up on the Almighty and, emerging from the parlour, proceeded to marshal people to their chairs as if he were about to conduct a service.

'He's bound to make a speech,' Aunt Ellen said gloomily to nobody in particular. 'He never could resist the temptation.'

At the moment he was too busy separating people who were perfectly happy talking together and urging them to talk to other people. The Boswells and Lovells were already eyeing one another. There was never much love lost between those two branches of Nain's relatives, though nobody was sure how it had begun. Everybody was hovering round the Rushtons who'd driven up in their saloon car and gave the impression, quite accidentally, that they were on their way to somewhere grander. Aunt Flora was thin again and laughed a lot, tinkling out her sentences as if nothing in the world would ever induce her to admit that she was worried about Uncle Mark going into the navy. Emyr Jones was handing round glasses of elderflower wine and fending off jests about long engagements. Everybody told me I'd grown and wanted to know what I wanted to be when I grew up. I wanted to reply 'taller', but feared it would be construed as a cheeky remark.

'Nell, walk up the road a little way and see if you can spot them coming,' Nain said. 'I thought we'd fill the glasses again and sing 'Happy Birthday' just as they arrived. Give a shout to warn us.'

I went through the front door into the road. It seemed I had a role to play after all. I walked with conscious grace, the stiff skirt of my sprigged print dress rustling. An army lorry passed me, raising a flurry of white dust as it tore along the quiet street. On the wrong side of the street too. As I registered that fact I heard the scream of brakes, the crashing of metal, the sound of a horn being sounded on and on and on.

Running to the corner, stiff skirt forgotten. Other feet pounding and passing. Tangled wreckage with car and lorry locked in deadly embrace. A soldier with blood on his face was crunching over the glass in the road. The wheels of the car were still spinning and Guto, all the colour gone from his face, was climbing stiffly through the place where the door hung loose, turning to hand Olive out. Olive sat motionless, her head flung back. Her eyes were wide open but she wasn't moving.

I could hear silence as the horn stopped blaring. It was like no silence I ever heard before. I stood forgotten, at the side of the road in the midst of the silence. Then a piece of buckled metal clanged to the ground and more people came running, running and shouting. Emyr Jones and Uncle Mark were struggling to prevent Guto from going back into the car and Mrs Rushton was screaming on a thin, high note.

One of the Boswells — Leni, I think — put his hand through the shattered side window and lifted Olive's head slightly. She was still staring at us but there was nobody behind her eyes.

'Neck's broken,' Leni said and he took the spotted red scarf from his throat and laid it over her face and settled her head back with great gentleness.

There were sentences whirling through the air and one of the soldiers was crying. I wondered why he was crying, because he wasn't anyone we knew and he hadn't been invited to the party.

I walked back to the house and nobody noticed me go, or asked me to do anything. It was like the fast reel of a film and in a moment we'd all come blinking into the daylight again.

When I reached the house where the door stood wide I went in and climbed the stairs without looking back. I concentrated on putting one foot in front of the other and I counted each step out loud, because the steps were real and their number never changed.

I went on climbing, up the ladder into my room under the roof where my aunts and my grandmother were too plump to mount. The summer heat had stolen the coolness of my eyrie and the sky beyond the sloping dormer glass was bright enough to make the eyes ache. The book of love poems I'd bought for Olive's birthday was still in its wrappings but I didn't touch it.

I didn't touch anything. I sat down on the mattress and I made myself very small, very, very small. I was cold despite the heat. The cold shivered through to my bones and I think I pulled a blanket round me, but I can't remember doing that. I simply sat, curled into my aloneness, part of nothing beyond myself.

I sat there while into my silence came sounds from below, a voice raised sharply, a door slamming, feet tramping up and down. I sat there while the brilliant blue of the sky faded into grey-blue and then into grey alone, the grey dulled and darkened into black and no stars appeared. I sat there while I waited for someone to call me down, to tell me it had never happened at all, that it had been a film or a dream. I sat there and nobody came. Nobody called my name or missed me and a terrible fear grew in me that when I did descend I would find nothing as it had been before and myself so changed that nobody would know me.

9

In my own mind, there was a clear division between the time before Olive was killed and the time that came afterwards, but for the rest of the world the year resumed its normal progression after the tragedy. For a month there was weeping and discussions as to how it might have been prevented and neighbours calling to offer condolences, but this was one death among many that summer. All over the island one heard of men being killed, of being reported 'missing in action' or taken prisoner. That Olive had been a young girl, not in any of the services, made her death more poignant, but there were so many events taking place that this too became part of the general pattern, a dark thread among many dark threads.

There was an inquest which I didn't attend and a court martial which I didn't attend either. I went to the funeral, of course, in my school uniform and stood, biting my lips and staring at the ground, among the mourners. Olive wasn't buried in our cemetery and there was an added sadness in that because she had been going to be a member of our family and now she never would be.

Guto had been sent to England to do his training as a flier and there was a certain, slightly guilty relief felt all round when he'd gone. He'd taken it very well in public. Everybody said how amazing it was, that he should act like a man instead of a boy, and of course going into the RAF would give him a change of scene and a new interest in life — as if the death of a sweetheart could be overcome by shooting down enemy planes. I thought that was a very silly way of looking at things but as nobody asked for my opinion, I didn't give it.

In a peculiar way there seemed to be a rightness about what had happened. All the love affairs that captured the imagination ended unhappily — Romeo and Juliet, Cathy and Heathcliff, Heloise and Abelard, Olive and Guto. There had been a moment now and then when I had felt shut out from the two of them, but in dying Olive had admitted me into that charmed circle forever. By the time Guto came home on leave he would be ready to share memories with me. An uncle whose entire life had been blighted would welcome a devoted niece.

Uncle Mark had gone too, clad in a rather jolly sailor's uniform. He had hoped for something dashing to do, but stationed at

Scapa Flow he spent all his time on minesweepers.

'A terrible dangerous job,' said Nain, valiantly concealing her disappointment that he hadn't been given command of a destroyer. 'The seas are full of those mines, you know, and they have to be tracked down and swept up.'

She made minesweepers sound like a bevy of kitchen maids fussily doing the housework.

'The place,' said Taid solemnly to me as we walked through the meadow one afternoon, 'is absolutely cluttered with women since the war started.'

He was right but I had not realized it until he spoke. Not only were my uncles gone but in the village one no longer saw young men except now and then when someone came home on leave. Aunt Ellen, in wellington boots and floppy hat, did the work that Uncle Ben and Guto had done and both Aunt Marget and Aunt Catti lent a hand when they weren't busy in the greengrocery. Jimmy and Sean Bohanna had taken over the running of the garage.

'Which they will do with an eye to their own profits I don't doubt,' Taid said wryly, never having had a very high opinion of Nain's kinsfolk. 'Mind you, one can't expect Flora to do it, not with two children and no head for business. And the government interfering all the time, trying to run everybody's affairs as well as the war. Making us all plant potatoes as if we were bog Irish!'

'They say 'Dig for victory',' I reminded him.

''Shoot for victory' would make more sense,' he retorted dourly. 'I never heard of winning battles with a spade.'

'They told us in school that Napoleon — I think it was Napoleon — said that an army marches on its stomach.'

'Duw! they teach you some funny things in that school of yours,' he said, shaking his head at me. 'Not to mention getting your marks all wrong. I never did get to the bottom of — '

'Here's Emyr Jones, coming to greet us,' I said.

'Come calling for your Aunt Marget, I suppose. It's a pity she can't put a bit of gumption into him. If they weren't already engaged I'd have asked him his intentions a long time ago,' Taid said irritably, raising his walking stick in acknowledgement of the other.

'How are you, Taid Petrie?'

My Aunt Marget's intended was, for a wonder, on foot instead of his motor bike. He was a neat, slim, sandy-haired man with none of the Petries' bright darkness. Taid had said on more than one occasion that he looked like a man hoping to be henpecked, but there were moments when I suspected Taid was wrong. Emyr Jones had kept Aunt Marget faithful to him and it was my opinion that they'd get married when they were good and ready and not in obedience to family nagging. It was not a very romantic affair after all, with my aunt already past thirty, and I thought it very likely there wouldn't be much begetting.

'Fine, praise the Lord!' Taid said promptly. 'Your bicycle broke down, did it?'

'I left it in Mark's for a bit of an overhaul. I was hoping to catch you.'

'Well, you've caught me,' said my grandfather. 'What can I do for you?'

'It's about the wedding,' Emyr Jones said.

'Which wedding?' Taid looked blank.

'Marget's and my wedding,' Emyr Jones said faintly and with pardonable surprise.

'Oh, *that* wedding!' Taid said, for all the world as if we were cluttered up with ceremonies. 'What about it then?'

'We thought the middle of next month.'

'You mean you've set a *date*?'

'October the fourteenth.'

'Rushing it a bit, aren't you?' Taid said with delicate sarcasm.

The delicate sarcasm was ignored.

'We've been sure of our minds for some time now,' Emyr Jones said.

'Eight years and nine months,' Taid murmured, but this too was ignored.

'We would have made it this month, but after the accident — it wouldn't have seemed fitting. However, now that the job has come up — '

'What job?' Taid gave him a sharp look.

'In Swansea,' said Emyr Jones. 'I've been offered a headmastership.'

'In Swansea? Good God, Swansea is crawling with English! You're not seriously thinking of going there, are you?'

'It's a step up,' Emyr Jones said modestly.

'Step up to what I wonder.' Taid frowned, prepared for an argument, then abruptly changed his mind, perhaps fearing that argument would further delay the long awaited marriage. 'Well, you're a grown man but I must say I'm surprised if you got Marget to agree to this.'

'Marget and I are generally in agreement,' Emyr Jones said, with the air of a man who knows he is scoring a point but doesn't wish to boast about it.

'October the fourteenth,' Taid said and pulled out his watch, peering at it as if he expected it to contradict him.

'Marget will be wanting you to be

bridesmaid,' Emyr Jones told me.

'Yes. That will be nice,' I said, politely but not altogether sincerely.

It wasn't that I didn't want to be a bridesmaid. It was only that by now, had everything gone in the way it was supposed to go, I would have already been a bridesmaid, following Olive Rushton, she in the family lace, myself in muslin with rosebuds on my head. The dress still hung in my aunts' wardrobe and I feared that, with new clothes so scarce, it would be pressed into service. It wouldn't be the same at all even though I loved my Aunt Marget and was glad she was going to be married at last. But that was mean minded of me and in our family it wasn't done to be mean minded.

'I'd better go in and break the news,' Taid said heavily. 'This will be the first time for one of my daughters to go into foreign parts. It'll come as a sad shock.'

'I think that Marget has already dropped a hint,' Emyr Jones said.

'Oh.' The word had a downward curve. My grandfather lifted a thick eyebrow and sniffed. 'Oh,' he said again and put his watch away.

'I'll go in,' I said and went as swiftly as was tactful. When Taid was thwarted in one direction, he was apt to kick out in another.

There were no signs of sad shock when I entered the kitchen. Nain was chopping turnips and carrots so quickly and deftly that one feared for the tips of her fingers and Aunt Ellen was soaking her bunion in a bowl of warm water.

'October seems a funny month to be married in,' she was remarking as I entered. 'Mind you, it's better than February. February's such a wet, dismal month and never could decide how many days to have.'

'October will do very well,' Nain said, with fingers flying. 'There's often a bright spell and perhaps by then the boys will be able to get some leave.'

'Not altogether. They wouldn't be likely to let them all come home together,' Aunt Ellen said, wincing as she pulled her foot out of the water and reached for a towel.

'Aunt Marget will be going to Swansea, won't she?' I said.

'Emyr's been offered a headmastership there,' Nain said. She sounded as proud as if he was already a member of the family.

'So he says.' Aunt Ellen pulled up her stocking and snapped the elastic garter back into place.

'Well, he'd not be likely to tell a lie about it,' Nain said placidly.

'Oh, I'm sure he's been offered a

headmastership,' Aunt Ellen allowed. 'They'd do that to divert suspicion.'

'Divert suspicion from what for heaven's sake?' Nain demanded.

'From the real work.' Aunt Ellen tied her shoe lace firmly.

'What real work?' Nain had ceased chopping the vegetables and was staring at her sister-in-law.

'Spying,' said Aunt Ellen calmly.

'Spying! Ellen, don't be so foolish!' Nain sounded quite cross. 'Whatever put that idea into your head?'

'He speaks French fluently,' Aunt Ellen said, 'and he's too old to go into the forces. No reason for him to go all the way to Swansea to get a headmastership. If he waits a few more years he'll get one in Holyhead. No, it's secret government work he'll be doing, you'll see — or rather you won't see, because he won't be allowed to tell. He'll be decoding messages.'

'But why not do that in Holyhead?'

'Swansea's nearer the battle zone,' Aunt Ellen said.

'I don't think I like the idea of our Marget getting mixed up in spying,' Nain said.

Her plump, pretty face had creased into worry lines.

'Marget won't be mixed up in anything,'

Aunt Ellen reassured. 'He won't be allowed to tell her one single thing.'

'Well, don't you go saying anything to her then — nor you, Nell,' Nain warned. 'Why, something like that might put her right off altogether — and her already thirty-one!'

'That's May,' I said aloud.

'What's May? Marget's birthday was in June,' Nain said.

'It's an idea I had recently,' I explained. 'I was thinking about eternity.'

'Well, that's not a very cheerful subject! Calculated to make you feel tired,' Nain scolded.

'I got to thinking,' I elaborated, 'that in God's reckoning seven years might be one month, so Aunt Marget is just coming into May.'

'They do say seven is a magical number,' Aunt Ellen agreed.

'It would explain why Noah lived so long — if one turned that around,' Nain said thoughtfully, 'with seven years being one month. I mean they say all those early people lived hundreds of years, but if seven of those years was one month — '

'Then Noah would have been about nine years old when he died,' Aunt Ellen said.

'If years were longer — or shorter?' Nain gave up, shaking her head. 'But it's a very clever idea, Cariad.'

'What I'd like to know is what happens when a body reaches eighty-four,' Aunt Ellen said. 'By Nell's reckoning they'd be at the end of December with no year left.'

'Then they start another year, a kind of borrowed one,' I said brightly.

'I've trouble enough dealing with the year I'm living through,' Nain said, 'and some people don't get very far along.'

She smiled at the beginning of the sentence and sighed at the end and for an instant the same thought was in our minds. If we turned our eyes swiftly in the right direction we might catch a glimpse of a slender girl with pale curls dancing on her shoulders and Guto's ring proudly on her finger.

'I don't know if Catti will feel like managing the shop all by herself,' Nain said.

I got the impression she had hastily cast about in her mind for a safe subject that would not twist the heart.

'One of the Bohanna girls might be glad to help,' Aunt Ellen suggested.

'Most of them are volunteering for the services or going into the Land Army.'

'I could help after school and on Saturdays,' I offered.

'You've your homework to do,' Nain said doubtfully.

'I can do it afterwards.'

'It wouldn't be wise to let your schoolwork lag behind and you with such a marvellous future.'

'Shakespeare used to hold horses' reins outside the theatre,' I said cunningly.

'Well, if he wasn't above earning a few coppers,' Aunt Ellen said decidedly, 'I don't think there's any reason why Nell can't help in the shop.'

'Provided it doesn't interfere with school,' Nain said.

'I won't let it,' I promised solemnly.

'And school starts again in a week!' She clapped her hand to her head. 'We've name tapes to sew on.'

I had been excited the previous year when I'd first entered the grammar school in all the glory of uniform, satchel, gym bag and the rest. This year I'd grown to fit my uniform and the tags had to be altered to denote Form IIA. It had become a chore, though I was not sorry to be going back to school. The summer had been too long and too muddled, change following change, soaring anticipation plunging into bitter grief.

'We've not seen the last of August yet,' Aunt Ellen said and she and Nain exchanged glances over my head.

I knew very well to what those glances

referred. We were approaching that time of year when Taid received his annual bonus for the work he'd put in as the Squire's bailiff. Since Uncle Ben had gone into the army Taid had revoked his deed of abdication and was not even regarded as semi-retired any longer. He would certainly receive the usual bonus and that meant he'd bring shame and grief upon the family, just as he'd done at the end of every August I could remember.

'Perhaps with the war on and the boys away — ' Nain's voice trailed away. A dozen wars and every man in Mona vanished to do battle wouldn't have stopped him.

'It's the pagan coming out,' Aunt Ellen said darkly, 'Sometimes I think one of those old Vikings stayed here long enough to rape a Petrie.'

'Or marry her?' said Nain who was of a romantic turn of mind.

'It would have been rape. The Vikings,' said Aunt Ellen firmly, 'went in for that sort of thing.'

'Well, I don't see the connection. J.P. has his faults, but I don't see him raping anybody,' Nain argued. 'The Vikings must have done other things.'

'They had berserkers,' I put in. 'I read about it.'

'What are — what you said?' Nain put the

chopped vegetables on to boil.

'When they went into battle the berserkers took strong drink after which they threw off their garments and charged naked into the fray,' I quoted glibly.

My grandmother and great aunt stared at me and with one voice begged, 'For heaven's sake don't tell your Taid!'

I swore that I would not, accepted a large slice of cake, and went out into the garden where Nain had insisted on retaining her flower beds despite the government instructions to plant potatoes. It was only a small garden, much smaller than the meadow, and as it was concealed from the road by its wall no Ministry informer was likely to glimpse our unpatriotic roses and geraniums.

A couple of days later, when August was so near its end that I began to imagine disaster had been averted, Taid came home from the estate with an expression on his face we had all seen in previous years. It is hard now to find words to describe that expression. One cannot call it fanatical since he was at all times fanatical; neither was it proud since Taid was already the proudest man in our community and would have given Cock Petrie a run for his money had that ancestor ever risen out of his tomb. It was as if all the qualities and characteristics that made my grandfather what he was were gathered together within the stern outlines of his face, glowing at the back of his dark, deep-set eyes.

'I shall not be at home for supper tonight,' he announced, standing in the doorway of the dining room.

'Chapel business?' Nain said, but her voice lacked all hope.

'I am going into Holyhead.' He spoke with a grave and stately defiance. 'A worker in the vineyard of the Lord is entitled to one evening out in the year.'

Vineyard was an unfortunate turn of phrase given our knowledge of the situation but nobody dared to pick him up on it.

The truth was that, on this one occasion in the year when the bonus came my grandfather, lay preacher and deacon of the chapel, forsook the service of Jehovah for the worship of Bacchus. He drove to Holyhead and, with the same singleminded ferocity as he embraced temperance on every other day, he proceeded to drink dry every public house between the causeway and the harbour. The more he drank the more ferocious he became but being the man he was, he did not waste that ferocity on aimless fighting like lesser mortals. Instead, with the last of the money, he bought a ticket to Dublin and boarded the ferry with the intention of invading Ireland

and bringing all the heathen Papists back to the true Methodist faith as practised in ancient Israel and Cybi Bay.

Nobody took this yearly event lightly. Nain, who had not the faintest objection to her cousins staggering back to the encampment at closing time, regarded her husband's dereliction as the deepest shame, a threat to the respectability she had won by marrying a house-dweller. Had he fallen from grace in Cybi Bay itself by entering the Black Boy she would not have minded it so much, but to have him regularly arrested the moment he set foot in Dublin and held for twenty-four hours until the boat returned with himself being bundled aboard by the Irish police was more than she could bear.

'I will see you later,' Taid said. There was already some of the majesty of intoxication in his face though he was perfectly sober as he turned and went out.

'And with the boys away,' said Nain, gazing despairingly after him, 'who's going to fetch him home from Holyhead? You know what a terrible temper he's always in when the mood's passed.'

Not even to us did she use the phrase 'sobered up'.

'I'm sure Emyr would be glad to help out,' Aunt Marget said.

'Emyr's not a member of the family yet so we mustn't impose,' Nain said tactfully.

'And J.P. would probably throw him into the harbour,' Aunt Ellen said, less tactfully.

'And he'd be in a worse temper if we sent Sean or Jimmy. I don't know why he has to do it,' Nain said. 'Other men get bonuses paid to them without having to go and invade Ireland.'

'But he won't be able to go this year!' I said, suddenly remembering. 'The regular ferry isn't running, surely, since the war started.'

'Duw, I hadn't thought of that!' Nain brightened with relief, then sank immediately into gloom again. 'He'll invade somewhere else where the police don't know him.'

'There isn't anywhere near enough to invade,' Aunt Marget said. 'There's the Isle of Wight. He knows the way there since Dunkirk.'

'But there's probably no ferry there either except from Southampton,' Aunt Ellen said.

'He might take Mark's boat and try getting to Ireland by himself,' Nain said.

'I'll go and dismantle the engine!' Aunt Ellen, gallant despite her bunion, was on her feet.

'There's no petrol in the tank anyway and she's a hole in her. Sean said he was going to get round to fixing it up before Mark comes on leave,' Aunt Marget said.

'Where's Catti? She might have some idea,' Aunt Ellen suggested.

'Gone to the pictures in Bangor. She'd only cry.'

'I could cry myself if I thought it would do any good,' Nain said. 'As if we hadn't troubles enough! The whole village will have seen him drive out and be laying bets on how soon the police bring him back. Every year it's the same and he never learns. He never even apologises, just buys some useless present I dint want in the first place and preaches a sermon on the evils of drink with not one word in it about sampling them at first hand!'

'Remember the parrot, Mam?' Aunt Marget said.

'Will I ever forget it!' Unexpectedly Nain began to laugh. 'It was before you were born, Nell! The old sod brought a parrot in a cage back with him. Very handsome bird it was too, better than his usual peace offering. Green and scarlet feathers! We spent a whole day trying to get it to say something before we found out it was stuffed!'

'And then Nain used more curse words than any parrot ever learned, alive or dead!' Aunt Marget said and went into one of her fits of silvery laughter.

'Well, since there's nothing to be done we'd better have supper,' Nain said at last, wiping her eyes.

Supper, with only the four of us and the empty chairs standing round, was no longer the meal it had been. I wondered if Aunt Flora missed Uncle Mark as much as we missed Uncle Ben and Guto. Tonight not even Taid was here. We were a house of women and though Nain and Aunt Marget went on joking about the parrot for a while there were spaces between their laughter and I knew that we were thinking of Uncle Ben somewhere in Italy — in the only letter we'd received he'd sent his love to Aunt Ida — of Uncle Mark sweeping up mines in the North Sea and of Guto flying spitfires across the Channel. We were all also thinking of Taid, bent on disgracing us while his sons were being heroes.

'Catti will be in soon,' Nain said. 'I'll put the kettle on.'

The kettle was always on, but she needed some excuse for being busy, which was foolish because it would be a couple of days before Taid returned, grim faced and with a temper to match his hangover.

'I think I'll stay on for a bit,' Aunt Ellen said to nobody in particular. 'Pity to break up the evening so soon.'

Usually she made her way across the meadow to her room above the stables shortly after supper for it took her at least an hour to check all the bars and bolts and prime her shotgun for fear of marauders in the night, but tonight she lingered, pouring herself another cup of tea and humming a tune under her breath as if she were staying more for our benefit than out of her own loneliness.

Aunt Catti came on the last bus, declaring the picture had been very good and Hugh had bought her a box of chocolates that must have used up his ration for months ahead. She had saved us the bottom layer and we took turns in choosing while Nain brewed up more tea all round and Aunt Marget, in a rapid undertone, brought her sister up to date on recent events.

'That means a couple of days peace,' Aunt Catti said, licking her fingers. 'I don't know why you take on so Mam, really I don't. Let the silly bugger have his fling.' With which observation she bit into a nut whirl, declaring she was ruining her figure, her skin and her teeth.

'Though Hugh says he likes a female with a bit of flesh on her.'

'You've been quoting this Hugh quite a lot lately,' Aunt Ellen observed. 'When are you bringing him home?'

'When I'm sure that he likes me enough not to bolt when he sees the rest of you,' Aunt Catti retorted. 'He's strict Baptist, so we'll have to prepare J.P. for the shock of that.'

'Better prepare your boyfriend for the shock of — what's that?' Aunt Marget cocked her dark head.

'Sounds like the trap, but it can't be!' Nain was on her feet, moving as fast as her bulk would allow through the hall to the front door.

In the moonlit street the trap had just drawn up and a female figure was alighting. We all crowded after Nain, staring at the recumbent figure in the back seat.

'Good evening, Mrs Rhiannon Evans.' Aunt Ellen was the first to find her voice. 'Would that be J.P. you have there?'

'We ran into each other in Holyhead,' Rhiannon Evans said calmly. 'I'd been visiting my late husband's cousin and missed the last bus, so Taid Petrie very kindly agreed to postpone his trip to Ireland in order to see me home. He's not feeling quite himself so I took the reins.'

We gazed at her in speechless admiration.

'Do you want some help in getting him out?' She was continuing. 'The late Mr Evans was occasionally not quite himself and I found it usually more convenient to leave him where he was, but you might require the trap taking round to the stables.'

'I'll come with you,' Aunt Ellen said. 'Climb up again, Mrs Evans! I can lead the pony. You don't want J.P. in the house do you Hannah?'

'Let him sleep it off with the horses.' Nain took a step towards the trap, sniffed the air, and took a hastier step back. 'Duw, but we're grateful to you, Mrs . . . .'

'Doing my duty as a good neighbour,' Mrs Rhiannon Evans said deprecatingly. 'He'll be himself again in the morning. The late Mr Evans always was.'

She climbed back into the driving seat and Aunt Ellen strode to the pony's head.

'Better come inside. We're showing a light,' Aunt Marget warned as the equipage with its unconscious burden was guided towards the lane.

In the hall we looked at one another.

'I think Ben made a big mistake,' Nain said at last. 'I think he left a pearl by the wayside — a real pearl!'

Shaking her head she closed and bolted the door.

10

The matter was not referred to again, Taid
making his appearance the next morning as if
he had not spent the night in the hay among
the horses but had been absent on business.
Indeed towards midmorning he harnessed up
the pony again and drove off in the direction
of the suspension bridge without telling
anyone what he planned to do.

'Gone to buy some damfool present,' Nain
said staring after him. 'He always does after
the drink takes him. I'm thankful it's only
once a year else the place would be cluttered
up with stuffed parrots and the like!'

When he returned later in the day he was
empty handed, however, though there was
about him an air of complacency which Nain
tried, but failed, to puncture by saying, 'Hah!'
very meaningly every time she glanced in his
direction. Taid merely lifted a bushy eyebrow
and strode into the parlour where, from
behind the closed door, his powerful voice
could be heard trying out various phrases for
the sermon he had begun to compose.

'It ought to be on the Good Samaritan,'
said Aunt Marget. 'Rhiannon Evans has gone

up in my estimation.'

'I shall make a point of telling Ben about it,' Nain said firmly. 'The trouble is I will have to use guarded language on account of we don't wish the censor to know everything that's private in the family.'

My aunt and I were preparing for our annual day out in Holyhead which I looked forward to very much indeed, though I went to school in Holyhead every day. But this Saturday was, like the Saturday I spent in Bangor with Aunt Catti, an event that never varied save in inessentials such as the weather and whether we had two or three slices of cake for tea and the town looked subtly different when I wasn't on my way to school.

It was the kind of mellow dark honey and pale wheaten day that people mean when they talk about St Martin summers they never knew but wish they had. Day out was a slight exaggeration as we always caught the one o'clock bus and returned at six but we packed a lot into those five hours did Aunt Marget and I.

Right on time the bus chuntered down the road and we climbed aboard, Aunt Marget in her navy dress and thin coat with white reverse, myself in the red cloak which I would not have admitted for the world was slightly too hot.

We travelled on the upper deck which carried with it a vague sense of danger since if the driver had tried to go under a low bridge, our heads would have been sliced off. That there were no low bridges between the Cybi Bay and Holyhead didn't diminish the relief with which we gained our destination.

We got off the bus at the bottom of the steep hill that rose up to the convent school. The pupils at that school exerted upon me all the glamour of forbidden fruit. They worshipped idols and gave all their money to the Pope, Taid said, and I used to slant glances at them as they went past, two by two, with their attendant nuns bringing up the rear. They looked exactly like normal schoolgirls to me, giggling and poking one another in the ribs whenever a boy went whistling by on the other side of the road. We were not so apt to do that in our school where the sexes were technically mixed, though we had separate playgrounds and didn't sit together in class. Some of the fifth formers were already going out together, but most of my crowd were in love with the Head Girl who had plaits wound about her head and was rumoured to wear nail varnish.

I saw one or two members of my form as we went up the steep street, but as it was not a school day we ignored one another by unwritten consent. My aunt and I made very slow progress, since we stopped at every shop and solemnly chose what we would buy if we had a thousand pounds each. We never actually bought anything but, by the time we gained the brow of the hill, I was the possessor of a very fine grandfather clock, a flatiron, a jar of bonbons, a pair of high-heeled gold slippers, an amber necklace, a set of golf-clubs, a squirrel coat and a number of artificial flowers.

We were bound for the house where Emyr Jones lived with his mother. Aunt Marget was a frequent guest here but I visited only once a year. Mrs Jones was a widow but not in the least cast down by it. I had the vague impression that she'd come into the world especially to be a widow and had been mentally measuring her bridegroom for his coffin as he slipped the ring on her finger. Not that she was gloomy! There never was a woman whom widowhood suited more as she opened the door of the neat, slate-roofed house that looked across the wide curve of the bay towards the mists of Ireland. She had been almost middle-aged when she'd begat Emyr, which meant she was nearly eighty though she was as brisk as seventy.

'Well, there's lovely!' Her smile doubled the wrinkles in her face. 'I was just hoping you'd drop in — it being the first Saturday. And the place not fit to be seen!'

The place was so clean that we could have eaten off the floor without the benefit of plates. Everything from the lace at the windows to the fire logs, gleamed, winked and sparkled.

'Emyr will be here directly,' she assured us, leading the way across a narrow hallway into a parlour that was used when visitors came. Perhaps it was used at other times too. Certainly it had a warm, lived in atmosphere though 'lived in' was, perhaps, the wrong phrase since the entire apartment was given over to relics of the dear departed.

Over the mantelpiece was a photograph of the late Humphrey Jones, gazing out of the frame with a hand on a globe of the world to signify, I suppose, his boundless ambitions. Indeed he had in his youth, gone on a walking tour in the Lake District that had ruined his feet. I never learned exactly how they had been ruined, save that it must have been serious since in the dozen or so smaller photographs of him scattered about the room his feet never once appeared. All of these photographs were framed with black sticky tape and in front of most of them were little bunches of everlasting flowers. Apart from the photographs of the late Humphrey Jones there was a framed text of the sermon preached at his funeral, a model of his tombstone very tastefully done in slate and a glass case in which were his fountain pen, his watch and a purple hassock on which he'd been accustomed to rest his ruined feet in chapel. In the midst of all this Mrs Jones presided over a table groaning with cakes and sandwiches and bright red jellies. She wore, as she always wore, a black dress and a black silk apron, a brooch woven from the hair of sundry deceased relatives and a black hat on her still plentiful white hair.

'You're looking peaky, Cariad,' she said to me as she always said. 'They're not working you too hard at that school, are they?'

'We've not started the new term yet, Mrs Jones,' I reminded her.

'No, of course not! I was forgetting! With Emyr taking over the Swansea headmastership at the start of November — silly to be starting in the middle of a term, but its something to do with the retiring headmaster's having to reach the right age or something! It'll be the kidneys with you then, making you a bit peaky! All the Lovells have kidneys.'

I agreed and we sat down to eat, having prudently skipped dinner so that we could stuff ourselves with a good conscience.

'And how is everybody then?' Mrs Jones folded her hands in her black silk lap.

'J.P. has a bad headache,' Aunt Marget said.

'Ah, it was his night for invading Ireland,' Mrs Jones nodded. 'He's back soon!'

'He never went,' said Aunt Marget and briefly related what had happened.

'Terrible pity Ben didn't take his chance in that direction,' Mrs Jones said. 'Very nice woman is Rhiannon Evans. Laid her Geraint out beautiful she did. I never saw him looking healthier. And good to him while he was alive too! There's some you can't say that about.'

'One could certainly say it of yourself, Mrs Jones,' Aunt Marget said. 'A devoted wife is what's said of you. Devoted, Mrs Jones.'

'As you will be, my dear!' Mrs Jones doubled her wrinkles again. 'Mind you, I'll not say that marriage is easy, no indeed! Your own mam could tell you that, I daresay, but if you're firm from the beginning about taking shoes off at the front door and taking turns with the washing up, then it's not hard to break them in. Very restless Mr Jones was sometimes, very plagued with ambition. There was nothing that man could not have done given his head. Nothing in the world!'

'Emyr's done splendidly, I think,' Aunt Marget put in.

'He had every encouragement. Every encouragement,' Mrs Jones said. 'From his father and myself when he was a boy and, during these past years, the prospect of wedlock has spurred him on something wonderful! Take another piece of cake, Nell. And another cup of tea to flush it down. People with kidneys should flush regularly in my view.'

I ate heartily, flushing it down, while Mrs Jones ambled happily through a monologue into which Aunt Marget dropped the occasional sentence. In the middle of it all Emyr Jones came in, obviously already broken in to marriage since his shoes were under his arm. He greeted me with a little bow as if I were a visiting young lady and not a lowly pupil at the school where he had been teaching. Marget he kissed on the cheek as if they had spent the last nearly nine years married instead of engaged. There was no circle of enchantment there to envy or to mourn. They were merely comfortable together, planning the occasion with as much passion as if it were a Band of Hope outing.

'If any of the boys get leave that will be marvellous, but it's not something to bank on. Catti was hoping that she could bring her new boyfriend, Hugh Price.'

'Not Hugh Coch?' Mrs Jones interrupted.

'He has got red hair,' Aunt Marget admitted. 'But it's not bright red — more ginger.'

'Then he'll be easier to break in,' Mrs Jones said, with a small sigh of relief. 'And Catti is the girl to do it! Plenty of spirit Catti has.'

'Marget has quite a bit of spirit herself,' Emyr Jones said in shy compliment.

'Enough to break any man into marriage,' his mother promised him.

Eating cake and flushing it down dutifully with tea, I thought suddenly that, in view of what had happened to Olive, I must be heartless to sit here enjoying myself in a room given over to the glories of mourning, but the truth was that Death and Mrs Jones kept such cheerful company together that one would have been foolish to be morbid. Indeed I had the impression that if the late Humphrey Jones were to be suddenly resurrected he would sit down and happily join in reminiscences of his own funeral.

They were, however, talking about the forthcoming wedding which would, due to the war, be a modest affair.

'With the boys away and everything in short supply,' Aunt Marget said, 'it wouldn't be the thing to have a big do. Mind you, Mam will lay on a lovely reception.'

'And Nell here is to be bridesmaid?' Mrs

Jones gave me an anxious little smile, as if she were doubtful of my kidneys standing up to the occasion.

'Couldn't have a wedding without Nell,' Aunt Marget said, smiling at me.

I was flattered by the remark, though I thought again of the muslin dress hanging unworn in the wardrobe. It was very foolish of me, but I could not endure the idea of wearing it. I could see only too plainly Olive clapping her hands as I was fitted for it and crying, 'Oh, but it will look beautiful!'

'Well, we must get on.' Aunt Marget was rising, dusting the crumbs from the tips of her fingers. 'We've the afternoon ahead!'

In fact about half of it was left, but Mrs Jones was rising too, kissing Marget with real affection as she exclaimed, 'We'll see you again before we see you in chapel, I hope! Duw, but it will seem peculiar when you're in Swansea! Nell will be big enough to come by herself next year.'

'Yes, well — ' Aunt Marget had paused, frowning slightly. Then she said, a trifle too loudly, 'As you say! Nell's growing up fast.'

'After Catti she'll be the next to start walking out with someone,' Mrs Jones cried.

I suspected she was already making a list of boys to be broken in to the rigours of marital bliss.

'I'll walk with you to the end of the road.' Emyr Jones picked up his shoes and opened the door. He was as polite in his own home as if he were visiting and I guessed my aunt wouldn't have much breaking in to accomplish. It occurred to me as we took our departure that it was just as well he was going to work in Swansea, otherwise I'd be in the awkward position of having to call the senior French master 'uncle'.

'Your mam keeps wonderful for her age,' Aunt Marget took his arm when we were in the street. 'She'll miss you dreadfully when we've gone.'

'She'll put black tape round our wedding photograph and be as cheerful as ever,' he returned and I was startled to see a decided twinkle in his eye.

At the end of the street we parted company from him, Aunt Marget waving in a very unloverlike fashion until the door closed upon him again. There was precious little romance, as I understood the term, in that relationship and I thought of Olive and Guto again and the muslin limp in the wardrobe.

'You won't want to wear the dress you were going to wear at Olive and Guto's wedding,' Aunt Marget said.

I knew she sometimes read thoughts, so I

ought not to have been startled, but I did jump slightly.

'Catti was bridesmaid when Mark and Flora were married,' she went on. 'We can alter her dress to fit you if you like.'

'You wouldn't mind?' In her place I would have hated my bridesmaid to wear a made-over dress.

'It's not as if I'm going to be wearing silk,' she said. 'You know, if I'd known there was going to be a war I'd have made my gown years ago, but I was always a bit superstitious about it. And it's the man that matters.'

She finished with a cascade of twinkling laughter but there was something wistful at the back of her eyes that made me wonder if she regretted being too old for romance.

Our next port of call was to the hairdresser, not to have our hair done but to spend an hour trying on wigs. We always tried on wigs when we came to Holyhead though I cannot remember why since neither of us had the slightest intention of ever wearing one. I didn't even know anybody who wore a wig though, as Aunt Marget said, they'd not be likely to advertise the fact.

The owner of the hairdressing salon was a young old gentleman — young in his flitting steps as he dashed up and down his salon, old in that he had been there for forty years to everybody's knowledge. He was called Mr Percival, though it was doubtful if his mother had called him that. He had no family anyone had ever known about and Aunt Marget was of the opinion he'd been washed up on the beach one morning clutching a hair dryer and a bag of curlers.

I never saw anyone having her hair done though Mr Percival was always terribly rushed, darting and swooping like a humming bird from one end of the salon to the other. He greeted us with much twittering delight, almost clapping his hands.

'My dear Miss Petrie — soon to be Jones — and Miss Nell. Little Nell, no longer, I see! You lovely ladies will be here to try on the wigs? They are here and waiting.'

They always were there and waiting, red, blonde, grey, white, black and brown, set on a row of wooden heads without noses. Some of them were long and curled, others short and fringed and there was one that looked like something Marie Antoinette might have worn, puffed high with three fat ringlets dangling over one shoulder. We tried them all on, as solemnly as if we intended to buy and Mr Percival acted as if he believed us, leaping about with mirrors and uttering little cries of approbation or censure.

'The blonde positively will not do! The

auburn now has a certain delicious sauciness. The auburn would suit you very well, dear Miss Petrie! And for Miss Nell, the brown? Yes, definitely the brown! With the fringe combed aside — there!'

I looked older with the wig on and my plaits tucked away out of sight. Looking at my reflection, arching unplucked brows, I felt strange and quite unlike myself as if the girl in the glass were someone I hadn't yet met but might become acquainted with very soon. I was not sure I wanted to know her and I pulled the wig off and said abruptly that we ought to be running for the bus, though if we'd strolled we'd have been in plenty of time.

'Not this year, dear ladies?' There was relief in Mr Percival's floating voice. 'Next year, perhaps?'

'Certainly! Why not?' Again Aunt Marget's voice was too loud. It was almost as if she didn't expect me to be around the following year! I was so overcome by the thought that she might know something I didn't know that I scarcely remembered to say goodbye to Mr Percival.

'It's my belief that he tries those wigs on himself when the shop's closed,' Aunt Marget said as we made for the bus stop. 'He'd have a terrible shock if he sold one! Not that he can make any kind of a living out of hairdressing. I think that he makes illicit whisky for a real living.'

She glanced expectantly at me. It was my turn to choose some outrageous occupation for Mr Percival, but my heart wasn't in it. I kept on remembering the echo of her voice pitched too loud, when she'd answered Mrs Jones and Mr Percival. It was as if —

'Did anyone in the Petrie family ever die young?' I abandoned the game to ask.

'Dozens, I shouldn't wonder,' she said.

'With kidneys?'

'And consumption. Mainly consumption before the drains were set right. The Lovells ran mainly to kidneys.'

As far as I knew our drains were fine on account of Aunt Ellen's always throwing boiling water down them. It was probably kidneys then, though I'd not yet begun to swell up. Perhaps it would be safer if I did. When a disease didn't manifest itself openly like a measles rash it burrowed inward and did all kinds of sneaky things.

'Is it really good to flush out the kidneys?'

'Six to eight glasses of water a day,' Aunt Marget said, waving down the approaching bus. 'Do you want to go upstairs, Cariad?'

If we veered off course and had our heads sliced off by a low bridge I'd avoid dying from kidney disease.

'Upstairs,' I said firmly and mounted the twisting stairs.

Perhaps dying young might not be so bad. If I died young I'd have fewer sins to explain away and I'd look remote and beautiful laid out with a rose — a white rose — between my hands and a bevy of weeping relatives. Then again I might be a bit swollen about the wrists and ankles.

'Seems funny to think this is the last outing we'll have,' said Aunt Marget.

I stared at her, bracing myself.

'On account of my getting married and going to Swansea,' Aunt Marget said.

She sounded calm and placid, so perhaps I had been imagining things after all. Nevertheless I determined to drink six to eight glasses of water a day just to stave off trouble.

When we reached home we saw a large van outside and two men in aprons struggling through the front door, with my grandfather directing them rather as if he was directing traffic.

'What on earth?' Aunt Marget rang the bell yards before our stop and pattered down the stairs in defiance of the notice 'Do not descend while bus is in motion'.

She was in the road the instant the bus stopped moving, with me at her heels, both of us gaping as the aproned men reappeared, got into their van and drove off with a lordly air.

'Now what has J.P. been up to?' Aunt Marget said under her breath and, clamping one hand on her hat and another on my wrist, dashed us both across the road and through the front door.

Nain was standing in the dining room, flanked by Aunt Ellen and Aunt Catti. They were all gazing in the same direction and, as we reached them, Aunt Marget and I gazed too.

'It's a piano,' Aunt Marget said blankly.

'An upright piano,' Aunt Ellen supplemented.

'Rosewood,' said Aunt Catti.

'With a keyboard,' said Nain, stepping forward and lifting the lid as if it might suddenly snap at her.

'A little present,' said Taid. He never beamed, but the muscles of his face relaxed. 'I had a very generous bonus from the Squire this year.'

'A piano,' said Nain. 'Well, I never thought I'd live to own a real piano! I'm speechless, J.P. I declare to you that I am speechless.'

'I went into Bangor this morning and bought it,' Taid said. 'I thought it was time we had a bit of music round here.'

'It looks very elegant,' Aunt Ellen said. 'I

must admit that it looks very elegant.'

'It was not inexpensive,' Taid said. 'I paid extra to have it tuned.'

'We can have a singsong round it,' Aunt Catti said. 'I could fancy a bit of a singsong now and then.'

'And hymns,' said Taid. 'The Good Lord likes to be praised in song.'

'Be lovely to have a bit of music with the boys away,' Nain said softly.

'Well, let us hear it then!' Taid rubbed his hands together. 'Who is going to play it?'

There was a brief silence while we all looked at one another and then everybody looked at me.

'Go on then, Nell,' Taid encouraged.

'I can't play the piano,' I said.

'Can't play?' He glowered at me. 'Of course you can play! Nothing to it!'

'I never had lessons,' I said.

'But you go to the grammar, Cariad,' Nain reminded me. 'They have music lessons there.'

'General appreciation,' I tried to explain.

'What's that?' Taid asked suspiciously.

'We listen to gramophone records,' I said.

'Listen to gramophone records!' Taid echoed. 'That's not learning music. I've a good mind to write to the school board!'

'Couldn't you give us a bit of a tune?' Aunt Catti said.

'I don't know one note from another,' I said.

'And who is to blame the child when she's not had the benefit of decent teaching?' Taid asked rhetorically. 'Let nobody blame Nell!'

'No indeed!' Aunt Ellen said, so heartily that I was bowed down with guilt.

'Can't Flora play a tune? I seem to recall Flora can play a tune,' Aunt Ellen said.

' 'Chopsticks' and 'the Dead March from Saul',' Aunt Marget said.

'I've heard there are natural geniuses who just sit down at a piano and begin to play,' Taid said hopefully.

'I don't think Nell's genius will lie in the field of music,' Nain said. 'I see literature for Nell.'

She made the *I* so bright we could all see it clearly.

'What's to be done with the piano?' Aunt Ellen asked.

'It'll do lovely for balancing spare cups on at the wedding reception,' Nain said firmly. 'And we can put photographs on it later on! That was a clever idea of yours to buy it, J.P. A very elegant idea in my opinion. Very elegant indeed!'

11

School had started again and we all told lies about the wonderful holidays we'd had, though in fact nobody had been anywhere or done anything very much. A certain morbid glamour hung about me because I had been involved, albeit as a bystander, in the accident, but nobody liked to refer to it directly and, in any case, nearly two months had passed and life had moved on. The first anniversary of the war had been and gone and there were grave doubts as to whether it would be over by Christmas. There was a large map on the wall of our classroom, stuck with white flags (for the cowardly Nazis) and scarlet ones (for the gallant Allies). It was alarming to see such a rash of white with the red like drops of blood scattered here and there. The evacuees who hadn't gone home had settled in, cockney accents and all, and were only beaten up now and then to remind them they were foreigners.

Most exciting to me was the forthcoming school play. To be sure it was not going to be a whole play. The lower, middle and upper forms were each rehearsing a one-act play, all of which would be presented on the same evening at the end of term. There were auditions, which sounded terribly professional, and rehearsals were to begin almost immediately since most of them would have to be squeezed out of regular lesson time. The upper school was doing a Welsh play about the bad old days when anyone caught speaking Welsh had to wear a notice with 'Welsh Not' printed on it hung round their necks. Privately we thought it was a tactless choice since we were friendly with the English now, but our opinion was too lowly to be considered.

The middle school were doing the Agincourt scene from Shakespeare's *Henry V*, and the girls were knitting chain mail like mad.

We were doing the trial scene from Shaw's *St Joan*, and the competition for the role of Joan was so fierce that best friends weren't speaking. With a strength of purpose that surprised me I hadn't breathed one word at home. Anyway I was scared of saying anything in case I didn't get the role and Taid threatened to complain to the school board.

But after a couple of weeks of the autumn term had gone by, I alighted from the bus one Friday afternoon with an ecstatic, visionary expression on my face that ought to have told anybody that something momentous had happened.

When I went into the kitchen, however, nobody seemed to notice anything different about me, though I stood by the sink hearing voices until I began to feel dizzy.

'Take the potatoes upstairs for me, there's a good girl,' Nain said, dumping the bowl on me as if it were an ordinary day.

I clumped up into the dining-room, put the bowl on the table and turned to see Taid hovering. Taid had a soul above food when he was composing one of his sermons but when he wasn't composing a sermon he was apt to hover, especially when the scent of cooking drifted up from the kitchen.

'I'm going to be Saint Joan!' I blurted out.

Taid wrinkled his forehead at me in a puzzled manner.

'Only Catholics are saints,' he said, mildly enough, 'and your name isn't Joan.'

'In a play on the stage,' I corrected.

Taid gave me a look in which shock and horror fought for mastery, then raised his voice, thundering through the house.

'Hannah! Ellen! Marget! Catti!'

I couldn't remember when I'd heard him use my grandmother's Christian name. Nor could I recall ever having seen the other females in the family pelt up the stairs so fast,

Nain panting in the rear with a fish slice in her hand.

'Good God, J.P. what's wrong?' Aunt Ellen was demanding.

'This child — this godless child — has just informed me she is intending to act on a public stage,' Taid said, letting each word fall like a meteorite from the thunder of his voice.

'Oh, don't be so silly!' Nain gasped, between pants. 'You must have heard wrong.'

'Did you or did you not intimate to me that you are going to appear on a public stage?' Taid pinned me to the sideboard with the ferocity of his glare.

'I intimated,' I said weakly.

'This is your influence!' Taid swung round upon his daughters. 'Taking her to the picture house and addling her head with film stars!'

'I'm not going to be in a film,' I protested. 'I'm going to be in a play at school that's all! The trial scene from Shaw's Saint Joan. The lower school is doing it and I got the part.'

'Would that be George Bernard Shaw?' Aunt Ellen enquired. I nodded.

'An Irishman,' Taid said heavily.

'And where is this play going to be put on?' Aunt Marget wanted to know.

'In the school hall,' I told her.

'There! In the school hall it's going to be,' Nain said, so relieved that she poked Taid with the fish slice. 'Not on a public stage at all!'

'But the public will come to see it, I suppose,' Taid objected.

'For the war effort,' I said cunningly. 'Half the proceeds are going to the Red Cross.'

'It's patriotic, J.P.,' Aunt Ellen said.

'It's still on a stage. Why can't you hold a bazaar for the war effort?'

'Joan is the only female part,' I said, still cunning. 'We're doing the trial scene and she's the only girl in it. Everybody had to audition.'

'There'll be a lot of lines to learn, I suppose?' Aunt Ellen too, could be devious.

'So many I'm afraid of forgetting them,' I said.

'Of course you won't forget them.' Taid snapped. 'You always had a very good memory for getting things by heart.'

'Well, if I'm not going to be allowed — ' I let the rest of the sentence trail gently away.

'Don't put words in my mouth,' Taid said. 'We'll have a look at this play and then decide. Are we having anything to eat tonight or are we going to stand round looking at one another?'

'My haddock!' Nain dived kitchenwards again.

Haddock always put Taid into a good

humour, though he preferred to eat his fish on any day of the week except Friday lest he be suspected of Papist leanings. Fortunately, Nain had also done some little sausages which looked brown and glistening and reassuringly Methodist, heaped on a blue and white dish with rings of fried onion.

'This play now,' Taid said, when we were halfway through the meal. 'Would you have a copy of it?'

'In my satchel, Taid.'

'I'll cast my eye over it later,' he said. 'Am I right in thinking this person was burned at the stake?'

'Oh, not for real, J.P.,' Nain said quickly. 'Not on the stage.'

'She was burned by the Catholic Church,' I said.

'They burnt one of their own? Duw, that just shows you the depths to which they sink,' he said.

'Why did they burn her?' Nain asked. 'Was she getting Methodist ideas?'

'She went and drove the English out of France,' I said.

'We could have done with her in Wales,' said Aunt Ellen.

'And she wore boy's clothes and cut her hair — ' I broke off because Taid's eyes were beginning to bulge again.

'They won't want you to do that, will they?' Aunt Catti demanded in alarm.

'It will be faked,' said Aunt Marget. 'They can fake anything these days.'

I didn't see how they could fake tights, but I wisely held my peace.

'I will read it later,' Taid repeated, 'and then ask counsel of the Lord.'

Whenever he asked counsel of the Lord only one thing was certain. The Almighty never went against Taid's opinion. Aunt Catti threw me a reassuring wink and Aunt Marget brought in the apple pie.

Taid took my slender copy of the play where I'd already marked all the maid's lines in red and went with measured tread into the parlour. I thought it would probably take him quite a long time to struggle through the English and wandered out into the meadow. I was not given to wandering in meadows as a rule but Joan had done it all the time. It occurred to me that she had been about my age when she'd started having visions. I wasn't sure if I wanted to have an actual vision, but I couldn't help thinking it would be interesting.

The nights were drawing in fast despite the beautiful weather and a purple pall was spreading over the shoulder-high corn. The cows were already in, milked and patted by my grandfather, but the sheep were dotted about in the grass, their coats thickening for the coming winter. There was no light to be seen except the glint of the dying sun splashing crimson over the far horizon. Faintly in the distance I could hear the sound of an aeroplane and, nearer at hand, the rustling of the cornstalks as they bent before the breeze.

I decided that if I were not allowed to appear in the play I would die out of frustration. Petries and Lovells might go in consumption and kidneys if they chose, but I would go in frustration.

'The disappointment was too much for her,' they would say, filing past to look at me as I lay there. The play itself might even be cancelled out of respect, unless they gave the part to Olwen Pritchard. She'd read for it nearly as well as I had and her hair was bobbed already. If they did that I would haunt Olwen Pritchard to her dying day.

The aeroplane was coming closer, its sound diminishing the wind. I looked up into the darkening sky and saw it like a bright bird with wings outstretched. But the brightness of it was not borrowed from the setting sun. It flew so low I could see the flames licking along the undercarriage and the crooked cross on its side outlined in white fire. And then out of it blossomed two white flowers that dipped and swayed, then began to float, like umbrellas of thistledown.

I think my heart stopped beating altogether as the aeroplane curved ahead of me, the sound of its engines muted by the crackling of flame, hesitating for a moment before it plunged into the river and sent a plume of black smoke skywards.

'Nell! Nell, go for Constable Petrie!' Taid was bellowing at me as he ran, shotgun in hand.

Duw! But I couldn't have run anywhere! I was rooted to the spot as one of the cornstalks.

The white flowers had resolved themselves into two men, their parachutes streaming along the ground as they struggled out of the harnesses.

'Nazis!' Taid was roaring as he swerved towards them. 'Nell! Go and get Constable Petrie!'

I found the use of my legs and started up the main road. If we were being invaded then Constable Petrie was the one to be informed, but it really wasn't fair that I was the one who had to run all the errands in the family and miss the best bits.

I pounded up the road, passing various other figures, all going the other way. There was a great deal of shouting and Concepta was carrying a pitchfork. She had the goodness to call to me,

'I've rung up Constable Petrie, Nell! He's on his way!'

'Nell! Cariad, are you alright?' Nain emerged from the house, flapping her apron wildly as if she were driving chickens before her.

'Taid's got two Nazis down in the meadow and Constable Petrie's on his way. Mrs Concepta rang him on her telephone!' I changed direction and ran with her, down the road again, and through Mrs Rhiannon Evans's gate without a by your leave.

The meadow was dotted now with more than sheep. Three quarters of the inhabitants of Cybi Bay were there holding flaming torches making a wide circle about the two airmen. One was seated on the ground, holding his knee, and the other was standing with his hands in the air and his helmet at his feet while Taid fixed him with an unwavering shotgun and an even more unwavering stare and Mrs Concepta jabbed the air with her pitchfork.

'Is it an invasion, J.P.?' Nain enquired.

'Don't be ridiculous, woman!' He boomed the reply without taking his eyes from his captives. 'Our side shot them down and they went off course and landed here! And I'm demanding compensation for the shock to my system.'

'Not to mention Mrs Rhiannon's sheep,' said Aunt Marget.

'If Mrs Rhiannon grazed her sheep in her own meadow, they wouldn't have been anywhere near,' he began.

'Well, there's ungrateful!' Nain cried. 'Considering what we owe to Mrs Rhiannon, I'm humiliated to hear you say such a thing!'

'There's no sense in having an argument now,' he said, somewhat hastily. 'The point is we have captured two Huns and it's clear to me they have to be handed over to the right authority before they try something desperate!'

'They don't look very desperate,' Aunt Catti said.

She was right. The one standing up had fair hair and a round face. The one nursing his leg had removed his helmet and was older — about twenty-one to the other's nineteen — his hair dark and his face thinner.

'The Huns are sly,' said Taid. 'They sneak over borders when people aren't looking.'

He pointedly did not look at the sheep.

'Well, these two don't look as if they're sneaking anywhere,' Nain said. 'Did you take their pistols away?'

241

'Of course I took their pistols away! With the help of Mr Steadman Corner Shop,' said Taid, giving credit where credit was due.

'They must be officers,' Aunt Catti said. She had a bit of a weakness for officers.

'Probably high up in the Nazi hierarchy,' Taid said.

'Then there'll be a reward?' That was Elias Lloyd who had flat feet and a sharp nose for profit.

'Shame on you, Elias!' Mrs Concepta cried, jerking the pitchfork in his direction. 'To be thinking of profit when you're doing your patriotic duty!'

'Well said!' Taid approved, though he looked as if he was the one who ought to have voiced the sentiment instead of an Irish-woman and a publican's wife to boot.

'That one's hurt his leg,' someone pointed out unnecessarily.

'He ought to have medical attention. Shall I fetch Nurse Robson?' Aunt Marget enquired.

'Don't be foolish, girl. He's not going to have a baby, is he?' Taid said.

'I think Nurse Robson knows about other things except babies,' Aunt Catti said.

'They don't deserve medical attention!' Elias Lloyd said shrilly.

'According to the Geneva Convention they

are entitled to it,' Nain said.

'Good God! When did you read the Geneva Convention?' Taid exclaimed.

'I read about it,' Nain said doggedly. 'Anyway, it's only Christian charity.'

'Don't you try to tell me about Christian charity!' Taid jutted out his beard. 'They deserve to be shot out of hand. You hear that?' He addressed the German. 'You deserve to be shot out of hand!'

The airman smiled and gave a polite little bow.

'The man's an idiot,' Taid said. 'He can't understand what I'm saying.'

'Try English, J.P.' Aunt Ellen had come from somewhere beyond the ring of torch-light. I wondered what had kept her. There was more straw than usual caught in her bun.

'You ought to be shot!' Taid said loudly and slowly in English. The airman smiled again and gave another little bow.

'Idiots!' said Taid with satisfaction.

'Here's Constable Petrie!' Aunt Ellen cried. 'He'll know what's to be done.'

Constable Petrie it was, galloping across the meadow, his pistol in his hand, his ten-gallon hat at the back of his head. He slid from the saddle and erupted into our midst like a firecracker.

'Everybody keep calm now! Nobody move!

I have them covered! They won't get away! Put out those lights!'

Becoming aware of the torches, his voice rose to a shriek.

Hastily torches were dowsed, those who held them running to the river to quench them there. Suddenly we were all plunged into darkness with no moon and the sun vanished into blackness.

'Nobody panic!' Constable Petrie's voice rose above the ensuing babble. 'Spread out now like a fan and beat about you until you hear a yell! We will have them again directly! Spread out now!'

It was too dark to see anything at all but shapes. Within a moment there was a loud yell and everybody, including me, rushed to the spot, but it was only Elias Lloyd holding his behind and Mrs Concepta holding her pitchfork and looking, by the flare of a match someone struck, as if she wanted to laugh.

'Keep your pitchfork down, Mrs Concepta,' Constable Petrie advised. 'It's escaped prisoners we're after!'

The match was dropped with an oath as the blue flame seared someone's finger and then we all scattered again, dark figures against a darker landscape with now and then the bleating of a sheep.

'Better send the young ones home in case

they take hostages!' someone shouted.

'No need to put ideas in their heads!' Constable Petrie rebuked.

'They can't speak Welsh or English,' Aunt Marget shrilled.

'That's only their low cunning!' he retorted. 'Beat about you now and don't be alarmed when you hear me fire off my pistol. It will be into the air by way of encouragement!'

A moment later a couple of shots cracked through the dark and, as if on cue, the moon poked its tip from behind a bank of cloud.

'Everybody stand still! Everybody stand still!' Constable Petrie roared. 'Still as statues! Anyone who makes a bolt for it is our quarry!'

We all froze as the moon ventured into full view and summoned forth the stars, bathing us all in silver. On the grass, where we had last seen them, two uniformed figures waited, patient and bewildered.

'Good God!' Taid said blankly. 'They didn't even have the sense to try to escape.'

'Where would they be running and one with a hurt leg?' Nain asked.

'We'd better take them to the Black Boy and ring the military,' someone said.

'They came down in my meadow so it's to my house they will be going,' Taid said firmly.

'Isn't it bad enough they're Germans without leading them to the demon drink.

The prisoners were being pulled to their feet and by the light of the moon we all streamed back across the meadow and into our yard.

'We'll never get everybody into the kitchen,' Nain said. 'Pull some benches into the yard now. Marget, get the kettle going and bring up some of my elderflower wine. Mrs Concepta, you mustn't take what J.P. said personal! Will you step across to your own place to telephone the military and then you are very welcome here. Where's Nurse Robson?'

She was produced from the crowd and a path cleared up which she marched with her black bag.

'Someone bring in the parachutes,' Constable Petrie ordered.

'There's only one here,' said Steadman Corner Shop.

'Escob fawr! There has to be two! They didn't come down on one parachute now,' Constable Petrie cried.

'You think the Lord has given up working miracles?' Taid asked. 'Take the parachute you have and be thankful for it.'

'It's my duty to take everything into custody, see.' The Constable sounded unhappy.

I edged into the kitchen where two bottles

were being opened and pressed into willing hands. The airman with dark hair was seated with his leg on a stool while Nurse Robson slit up his trouser leg.

'Torn a ligament he has,' she announced, 'and some burns to his hand. Comfrey and cold tea is needed here.'

The fair-haired prisoner had been jammed into a corner with the table blocking any desperate move he might decide to make. Nain went over and set a large piece of apple pie before him and a tall mug of her elderflower wine.

'Feed anyone you would!' Taid said, noticing.

Her eyes flashed as brightly as the hoops in her ears and her voice poured ice all over him.

'It is our Guto I am feeding,' she said.

The other one was being fed too and both were eating heartily enough for two. Now and then they glanced at each other, not speaking, but in that look was gladness to be alive and regret to be out of the war.

'That will have to serve until we can get the military doctor to take a look at it.' Nurse Robson finished making a bandage and pinned the flap of the trouser leg over it neatly.

'Danke,' the airman said. His voice, gruff

and reluctant, sent a fresh shiver of excitement through everybody.

'He spoke!' Aunt Ellen said. 'The German spoke. He said 'Thank you'.'

'Since when did you learn to speak German, Ellen Petrie?' Taid asked, deeply suspicious.

'I know what thank you means in any language,' she answered loftily.

'What I would be more interested in knowing is what happened to the other parachute,' Constable Petrie said.

'Oh, do give over about that old parachute!' Taid said. 'Such a fuss about nothing. You shouldn't go enquiring into miracles too closely. It is like opening the cupboard in the Lord's kitchen to find out how he made the manna that fed the Israelites in the wilderness. Have another glass of wine now. I'd not offer strong drink, especially with you on official duty, but this is teetotal, from Nature's own bounty.'

'It's a good brew J.P. I am against the strong drink myself, but elderflower cannot be called so — as you say, Nature's bounty. Here's to victory!'

He drained the glass and held it out again.

'The Military Police are on their way,' Mrs Concepta said, putting her head in the door. 'Have you still got them safe, or did they get away?'

'Of course they are safe here! Constable Petrie is guarding them,' Nain said. 'It will not be Constable Petrie for much longer after this night's work either. There will be a promotion — a letter from the King perhaps, or from Mr Winston Churchill.'

'And God bless him too!' Steadman Corner Shop raised his tumbler and everybody drank deeply.

'They can't be so bad,' Aunt Marget said, hands on hips as she stared at the airmen. 'They drank to Mr Churchill as prettily as if they were Welsh!'

'To Lloyd George!' said Nain. 'Let us not be leaving out Lloyd George, God love him!'

'Aye! To Lloyd George,' Constable Petrie agreed and glasses were filled up all round again.

'The King!' Aunt Ellen's voice rose above the rest. 'To King George, God defend him!'

Glasses were filled and raised again and Constable Petrie fired his pistol out into the yard in sheer excess of high spirits.

'Better get those blackout curtains down. Far too much light,' Taid said. 'We don't want any more Germans dropping in.'

Curtains were hastily drawn and Dai put out his cigarette.

'More pie and the rest of the cream over here, Nell,' Nain said. 'No sense in letting it go to waste, is it?'

I did as she bade me. More people were crowding into the yard, craning their necks to see the Nazis. The one who had hurt his leg was smiling at Aunt Catti in a way that would have had Hugh Coch worried if he'd been there. The fair-haired one was wolfing apple pie as if he'd never eaten any before, but to be fair he never had sampled Nain's.

'Another toast while we are gathered together!' Taid said. 'My granddaughter Nell, is to play the leading role in a play about Joan of Ark, who was burned by the Catholics, at a performance in aid of the Red Cross at the grammar in Holyhead. To Nell!'

He had communed with the Lord and, as usual, the Lord had agreed with every word my grandfather said.

12

Aunt Marget had said many times that she wanted only a small wedding. 'No sense in making a big fuss with the boys away and Emyr and myself engaged for so long.' Her voice had been quick and bright, but there had been a wistfulness at the back of her eyes as if somewhere inside her a small girl was pretending not to mind that it would be a lean Christmas.

'Since you are bent on leaving the island and going among the English we will give you a good send-off at least,' Nain said firmly. 'I'll not have anyone saying that I don't know the right way to see my eldest daughter married and the one with the power of the seeing moreover!'

So, everybody who was anybody at all would be crowding into our chapel and then coming across the road to our house for refreshments. It was to be a real wedding, with everything done in the ancient manner, and Aunt Marget was busy making the shroud for Emyr Jones up in Aunt Ellen's room above the stables. The dress that Aunt Catti had worn when Uncle Mark married

Aunt Flora had been altered to fit me. It had a yellow bodice and a long yellow skirt but Aunt Marget sewed white flounces round it and made a short white cape so that it looked like a different dress altogether. I was to have my plaits wound round my head, just like the Head Girl, and from the scraps of yellow left when the dress had been cut down she had made little flowers to be stuck into my hair on long hairpins. It was going to look lovely when it was done but I wondered if anyone except me remembered the wreath of rosebuds I had never worn.

We seldom saw the Rushtons save on rare occasions when we were shopping in Holyhead where they did their shopping and on those occasions there was constraint in the greetings on both sides as if Olive's death were a shame to divide us instead of a bond of sorrow. Out of kindness they had not been invited to the wedding and I was glad that Guto wouldn't be there either. I knew that if everybody in the world forgot, Guto and I never would.

But the grief was dying at the edges like leaves in autumn. There were the preparations for Aunt Marget's wedding and there were the rehearsals for the play which was to be given at the beginning of December. I was to have my hair flattened and pinned tightly to my head to make it look shorter and I was to wear black stockings and a black tunic. I spent a lot of time dreaming through the classroom window that term, hearing imagined applause.

The day of the wedding coincided with our half-term which, praise be! was free for once of homework, though those who were in any of the plays were reminded to study their lines. As I had learned all the parts already accurately enough to put on a one woman show I was not unduly burdened and could concentrate on enjoying myself.

I woke up very early on that day before it was fully light and, for once in my life, didn't snuggle down into my nest of blankets but was up and climbing down the ladder. The house was still dim and I could hear Taid snoring under his mound of coats as I went across the landing and down the stairs.

Aunt Marget was up before me, brewing tea down in the kitchen and stirring the coals of the fire into redness. She was still in her dressing gown and her naturally curly hair was screwed up into metal curlers that must have been torture to sleep in.

'I was a bit restless,' she said, giving me an apologetic look and getting another cup. 'A bit nervous, to tell you the truth.'

'About going to live in Swansea?' I

accepted the cup of tea and sat down at the table, my shoulders hunched and the palms of my hands curved about the cup, woman fashion.

'That and getting married. Wedlock is a serious business,' she said.

'I'm sure that Emyr Jones is broken in to marriage,' I reassured her, hoping she wasn't having second thoughts. I was determined to be a bridesmaid if it meant pushing her to chapel with the end of Aunt Ellen's shotgun.

'Emyr will be master in the house as is right and proper,' she said. 'And after then Catti will take Hugh Coch and then — '

'I won't be getting married for years and years,' I assured her. 'So I will be here.'

'As to that — ' She stopped and drew a sharp little breath, changing her mind as she was about to plunge into a sentence and plunging into quite a different one. 'I know you will always be a good girl and keep us proud of you, Nell. I'll be sorry to miss you in the school play but your Auntie Catti will cry for both of us I've no doubt.'

'It's a pity none of the men are going to be here,' I said.

'It's the fault of that silly old war, Nell.' She shook her metal decorated head and drank more tea reflectively. 'So many of the boys from the village gone and some never to return and others prisoner — and it would not do to be saying this to Taid, mind, but I think the German wives and mothers weep too. Yes, I think that in the depths of me, girl, but I'd not say so loud yet until it's victory for us and the forgiving time.'

'Will it be victory for us, Aunt Marget?' I asked.

'It will be glorious victory after a long and bitter while,' she said. 'I see it plain in the tea leaves and you here to share in the rejoicing.'

'Why, where else would I be?' I demanded, but she was rising, bustling about as adults do when they don't want to answer a question.

'Duw, but look at the time,' she said, 'and me with loads of packing still to finish! You'd better get your face washed, Nell. J.P. will be blowing the old trumpet this morning, I'm sure.'

'I wish he wouldn't,' I said. 'It shames me to have to go with him and everybody knowing where we're bound.'

'Go with him without grumble,' Aunt Marget said. 'You and I know it's a daft habit but when Noah was building his ark there were those to mock and tell him it hadn't rained in a month of Sundays. Go on now! If I sit gossiping with you it will be another nine years before I'm wed.'

She didn't let me go at once but hugged

me to her and then pushed me gently away and turned to pick up the cups.

The morning wore on, slowly because mornings always went thus when something exciting was going to happen. Even the announcement of Taid's readiness for the Day of Judgement was less of an ordeal than usual because it filled up the space before I could get into my bridesmaid's dress. I was changing in the aunts' room but Aunt Marget had gone over to Aunt Ellen's room to get ready since it was bad luck for the bride to be running about in full view of everybody coming in and out of the house. There were thousands of them, it seemed, coming in with presents and with cakes and jellies and bara-brith and anxious enquiries as to whether the rain would hold off, though the sky was cloudless and a hot, bright October blue.

Oh, but my dress looked grand!

'Like a daffodil under snow you look!' said Aunt Catti, coming in to pin the yellow flowers so cunningly into my plaits that not a hairpin showed.

She looked lovely herself in a peach coloured dress and a little straw hat with a veil coming almost to the tip of her nose. Hugh Coch would have some trouble in taking his eyes off her.

In the room next door Taid was calling on the Almighty as he struggled into the wedding-cum-funeral suit. It was black and tight and for weddings had a flower pinned to the lapel. In the rooms below I could hear people coming and going with food and presents.

'What I would like to know,' said Aunt Catti, 'is why Mrs Rhiannon Evans has refused to come.'

'Has she? I didn't know that.' I stared at her.

'Said she couldn't make it as she had a previous engagement and last night she drove herself to the station and took the train to Llandudno. I believe Geraint had cousins there. Oh! I nearly forgot! Emyr left this for you as the bridesmaid present.'

She handed me a small box and inside, lying on cotton wool, was a silver bracelet with my name engraved on one of the links.

'Better than an identity card,' she said, fastening it on my wrist. 'Now you are really bejewelled.'

I already had small hoops in my ears and a topaz brooch that had been my mother's to fasten the short white cape.

Someone called up from below that the trap was ready and waiting. The Bohanna boys had been cleaning and polishing it for days and festooning it with white ribbons. Taid would drive it round by the road to the stables to pick up Aunt Marget and then drive back to the chapel.

I went to the window and lifted a corner of the curtain to watch the people stream through the open doors of the chapel. More women than men, though here and there was a uniformed figure on leave. I thought it was a sad thing that none of my uncles would be there to see their sister married. Then Aunt Flora, in her best blue, alighted from a car driven by Leni and they went, with Johnny trailing behind and William sleeping in her arms, across the threshold.

'There's a taxi coming!' I was justified in sounding astonished since taxicabs were for rich tourists at the best of times and this was the worst since petrol was so expensive.

'It'll be the bridegroom and the best man — and Mrs Jones Widow! Escob, that man must have money to burn.' Aunt Catti joined me at the window as Emyr and the sports master from the grammar helped out Mrs Jones who had so far forsaken her mourning as to stick a plume of lilac feathers into her hat.

'I told you he was going to do secret work,' said Aunt Ellen, coming in. 'Very highly paid it is. Constable Petrie is controlling the crowds beautiful!'

He wore a black cloak lined with scarlet to make his uniform more festive and stood, a long white stick in his hands, directing people to left and right.

'You look nice, Auntie,' Aunt Catti said.

Aunt Ellen had on her best grey coat and there were violets in her hat and a fur tippet about her long neck.

'I like to dress for a wedding,' she said, not without complacency. 'If it hadn't been for my unfortunate experience I might have been a bride myself. As it is I lend my presence and my good wishes. Someone will have to escort your mam into chapel.'

Normally it would have been one of the sons, but none of them was here and Taid had other duties.

'You and I?' suggested Aunt Catti doubtfully, but she knew as I did that it would not have looked right.

'She's sitting in the dining room like a queen,' said Aunt Ellen with pride and sadness.

'Now what is up with that child?' Aunt Catti demanded, staring through the window as Johnny emerged from the chapel and marched towards our front door.

'God love him, but he's going to escort her — and him not grown into a lad yet!' Aunt Ellen cried.

It was true. A moment later we saw Nain, in a flowered blue and white dress and a carnation pinned to the brim of her navy straw, being escorted with slow dignity across the empty road by my cousin, very erect in his grey shorts and blazer.

'There will be a man in our family soon again yet,' Aunt Catti said, tears standing in her eyes.

'Save the weeping for when the vows are spoken,' said Aunt Ellen. 'So! Time for us now. Take your posy, Nell. Wait just inside the chapel door until the bride arrives, then fall in behind her and Taid.'

My posy was of Michaelmas daisies, yellow-hearted and virgin-petalled. I held it at waist level and went down the stairs between my aunts.

In the chapel there was whispering and nudging and turning of heads; two vases of white flowers; the minister standing behind the communion table with the marriage service open before him; Emyr Jones looking round with apprehension on his face, in case Aunt Marget changed her mind at the last moment and sent word that she wasn't coming; the organist with his hands poised over the keyboard; Tommy Williams crouched over the bellows; the sun striking gold from the oak pews and benches.

'The bride cometh!' roared Constable Petrie and the organ wheezed and then crashed into sound.

The bride came, alighting from the beribboned trap, pausing for a moment to lay her hand on Taid's crooked arm and then sweeping into our midst, her face mysterious behind the folds of her long veil that depended from a circlet of waxy orange blossom on her dark head. Her bouquet was a sheaf of bronze and gold chrysanthemums, her gown high-necked, long sleeved, tight waisted, and as she passed by yards of parachute silk whispered after her in the train of her long skirt.

I fell in behind her, on hand to hold the sheaf of chrysanthemums and then the service began in the rich and rolling Welsh, the bridegroom answering slow and soft but Aunt Marget's voice strong and clear as victory bells. Nain was weeping softly in the front left-hand pew and Aunt Ellen and Aunt Catti were weeping behind her and the only one who wasn't admiring the bride was Hugh Coch. He was admiring Aunt Catti.

The ring had been produced and the words said and we trooped to the back of the chapel to sign the register, my name among all the rest to stand for eternity, and then Aunt Marget put back her veil emerging as rosy as dawn out of cloud and the organ competed with the choir to see who could render 'Calwn Lan' the louder.

Then we were outside the chapel, throwing our little packets of confetti and posing for photographs with everybody trying to get in front of someone else's head and Johnny being a nuisance everywhere. Constable Petrie was waving his white stick, his cloak swirling about him, and there was more kissing than at Christmas. My aunts were down to their last handkerchief and Mrs Concepta had flung her arms about Taid and he wasn't minding at all.

We went across the road where every door and window in Virgin and Child Cottage was open. My! But there was a lot of food. You would have been forgiven for imagining there was no rationing at all so thick was the butter on the sandwiches, so sugary the meringues, so plentiful the raised pork pies, the veal and duck salad, the mound of fat, cold sausages with the sprigs of parsley. The table in the dining-room held the three tier cake with the silver balls and white doves and blue bows of ribbon and the wedding presents were piled up in the parlour. Plenty of toast racks and letter openers they would have and a very handsome funeral urn from Mrs

Jones Widow, ready to contain flowers for whichever one of them went first.

There were tables set in the yard and a couple in the street and a constant rushing up and down the stairs between dining-room and kitchen. Nain had the place of honour next to the bridegroom and her expression was something to behold for it reflected her pride in the occasion and her constant anxiety that something unspeakable would happen in the kitchen unless she was there to supervise.

The best man read out a pile of telegrams, one from each of my uncles and one from the Headmaster and staff of the Grammar School and Emyr Jones who was now my Uncle Emyr Jones made a very neat little speech in which he said that he had plucked the fairest flower in the Petrie bouquet and everybody clapped except Hugh Coch who looked as if he wanted to argue the matter.

And then the bottom tier of the cake was cut with everybody cheering again as if they didn't know that one slice had already been separated from the rest ready for them.

Pieces of the cake were being passed, the unmarried girls wrapping up theirs in tissue paper to be placed under their pillows for dreams of future husbands. I ate mine because I guessed there'd be more cake to be saved soon from Aunt Catti's wedding. Anyway I was in no hurry to find out who my future husband was going to be.

'Mama Sarah is here!' someone called.

At first we couldn't believe it because Mama Sarah never left the camp, but there she was, borne like some ancient idol in a wickerwork chair slung between two ponies, those members of her tribe who were not already in our house crowding round her. She had put on all her bracelets and double rings hung from the lobes of her ears and glittered on every finger of her hands. There were coins, Victorian sovereigns, hanging across her forehead and her belt had links of gold.

There was a silence fell when her chair was set down. Taid and the minister glanced at her and then at each other with mutual disapproval, but they could not hold back the rite that was richer than church or chapel.

Two of the Bohannas held a broomstick and the rest of us held our breath. If a bride who was not a virgin leapt the broomstick she would give birth at once to twins as had the rainbow goddess, Angharad, in the lost times before the Romans and the Vikings and the English came.

'Daughter, came you to this marriage untouched by man?' Mama Sarah was demanding.

'Untouched am I,' said Aunt Marget loudly and the Bohannas stooped, holding the broomstick low and my aunt gathered up her trailing skirts of parachute silk and landed with a cry of triumph and not a twin in sight.

Then Mama Sarah took the coins from her brow and placed them about Aunt Marget's head, speaking the hissing tongue of the Old Ones as she gave her blessing and Nain came out with cake and wine for the honoured guest who wolfed them down, then signalled to her bearers to lift her chair between the shafts again and lead her back to her caravan.

The awe that had fallen upon us all lifted with the trotting away of the ponies and the minister came out of the house where he'd taken refuge from an older faith.

Dai Harpist began to play and we all begged Selwyn to sing. He was lame was Selwyn with a thick-soled boot on one foot to level his walking and a voice like the angels, but he was the shyest man on Mona and could not sing if eyes watched him, so he went behind the hedge and, after a moment, we heard the mellow, pure notes of 'David of the White Rock' rising into the blue October air.

'Nell! Come and help your auntie to change!' Aunt Ellen commanded and I went upstairs where Aunt Marget was taking off her veil and her silk gown, smoothing its folds with gentle fingers. Her going away suit was polka dotted in black and white with a red collar and her hat was covered with the red fabric and turned up at the side. And she was no longer mystical but still warm and lovely as she dabbed lavender water behind her ears and fussed because there was a mark on her handbag.

The luggage was being loaded up in the back of the trap and the unmarried girls had clustered at the foot of the stairs with hands outstretched. I flew down to join them but it was Aunt Catti who caught the bouquet and, whirling around, was out of the door and running hard to the graveyard with the guests after her in hot pursuit. She gained the family plot ahead of everybody and laid the great sheaf on the tomb below the rampant cock and called down a blessing from the ancestors upon herself and the man who would win her. We all knew who that would be and, after the comments passed, Hugh Coch's face was as red as his hair.

The road was crowded with people and the chattering was louder than starlings. Aunt Marget was being kissed by everybody who could come within touching distance and Taid was tapping his foot with his watch in his hand and reminding everyone that there was a train to catch.

That was the moment when the taxicab — the second we'd seen that day — nosed over the brow of the hill and coasted towards us. As it stopped my Uncle Ben got out, waved his hand, and bent to help Mrs Rhiannon Evans out. She had on a blue suit and a white hat with a veil and I guessed what had happened even before he said loudly, 'Come and give greeting to Mrs Ben Petrie then!'

'You're married?' Taid said blankly.

'First thing this morning in Chester and just got the train. It was a proper chapel wedding but by special licence, see. Costs more money.'

'Well, there's a sly one!' Aunt Ellen cried. 'Why not marry in your own chapel? Is there something wrong with it I'd like to know.'

'We didn't want an old fuss, it being Rhiannon's second and all,' Uncle Ben said, shifting from foot to foot under the assembled, accusing gaze.

'Have you been doing something that ought to set you in the Penance seat?' Taid demanded.

'Indeed I have not,' said Uncle Ben. 'I have two days embarkation leave, that's the reason.'

'Good God!' Jimmy Bohanna said. 'The

last time you embarked anywhere we had to come and fetch you. Where are you going this time?'

'They don't tell us,' Uncle Ben said, 'but I had a malaria jab.'

'The Middle East,' said the minister. 'They have malaria there shocking.'

'Well, come and give us a kiss, Rhiannon!' Nain was rising to the occasion magnificently. 'Well, this is a day to be sure. Two weddings and thank God plenty left to eat and drink!'

She didn't say any old nonsense about losing one daughter and gaining another, but she kissed Mrs Rhiannon and kissed Uncle Ben harder and then Aunt Marget, who'd scrambled down from the trap, had to be kissed too all over again and pushed back up to Uncle Emyr Jones and we began to sing and cheer and throw old shoes after the trap as Leni drove it away in a little cloud of dust.

'We've been writing back and forth for months,' Uncle Ben was saying, his arm about Mrs Rhiannon. 'We wanted a quiet affair and when this embarkation came up we took the opportunity.'

'Probably because Mrs Rhiannon didn't want twins,' Aunt Catti said naughtily in my ear. Widows taking a second husband had to swear no man had touched them since their first mate's dying.

'Into the house then!' Constable Petrie marshalled his flock. 'We will be drinking health to another bride and groom.'

It was like an encore with everybody tumbling back indoors and Dai Harpist sweeping his hand across the strings to underline the joy of the occasion. I had already eaten more cake than would be comfortable later on, but I took another piece anyway and squeezed myself into the kitchen where the returned prodigals were being toasted.

'We will spend the night at Rhiannon's place and tomorrow I will rejoin my regiment,' Uncle Ben said, 'so we'll not stay late.'

Mrs Rhiannon's place immediately became the pivot of everybody's erotic imaginings though Aunt Ellen was still muttering 'sly' under her breath.

'This old house is emptying fast,' Nain said. 'Soon it will be like a nest in winter.'

'I'll be here, Nain,' I began and saw the colour run up in her face and her eyes lower.

Perhaps it had been true after all then that I was doomed to die young. I felt perfectly healthy, if a bit crammed with cake, but I threaded my way to the sink and drank two glasses of water very rapidly.

They had begun to sing again, voices rising and falling, and Taid beating time with his hand. It might be hymns soon, I thought, slow and solemn, with the happiness of this day swallowed up in grief. I let the tears come into my eyes for the sadness of my own dying and drank a third glass of water to be on the safe side.

13

'It's one of those telegrams,' Nain said, turning it over and over between her fingers.

There was fear in her face and small blame when telegrams brought bad news as often as not.

'Better open it, Mam,' Aunt Catti said.

'It can't be Mark. Flora would have had a telegram about Mark and Rhiannon would have had one about Ben,' Nain said. 'Oh, not Guto!'

'Mam, open it!' my aunt urged.

'Perhaps I'll wait until after the Band of Hope meeting,' Nain said, preparing to put it behind the clock.

Aunt Catti took it from her and ripped it open. A moment later she raised a face radiant with relief.

'No need to worry,' she said. 'Guto is coming home on leave, that's all.'

'And sent a telegram to let us know! That boy must think money's to be picked off the beach,' Taid shouted from the top of the stairs.

'Listen to the old sod!' Nain jerked her head. 'You'd think he'd be grateful not to be hearing bad news, wouldn't you? It was considerate of Guto to let us know. Oh, you don't think it is one of those embarkations, do you, Duw. I couldn't stand another embarkation!'

'He doesn't say, just that he's coming with a friend.'

'I'll make up Ben's bed! Does he say when?'

'Tuesday,' said Aunt Catti.

'Today is Tuesday — or does he mean next Tuesday? And the sheets to be aired! Oh, he ought to have given more warning. Isn't it just like our Guto to be giving us no word except a nasty old telegram that makes no sense!'

She had begun happily bustling about before I left the kitchen. In the yard the buildings were grey with November and all the harvest was gathered in. The cows were still out in the meadow, for winters on Mona were much milder than up in the valleys. On the rare occasions there was snow it was only a light dusting blown away by the salt spray before night had passed.

I was happy that Guto was coming home on leave but there was a tugging of sadness inside me too. It would not be the same for him. It could never be the same for him without Olive there. His return would remind

272

us all of what might have been.

There had been more comings and goings these past months than I could remember in all my life. Uncle Mark, Uncle Ben, Guto — and their sudden arrivals muddled with the birth of Aunt Flora's child, not to mention Aunt Marget who had sent a long letter from Swansea, telling us all about her new home.

'In a place called the Mumbles,' Aunt Ellen said, having been first to open it. 'She says there are sandhills — well, I hope she doesn't go walking by herself on them. Terrible lonely sandhills are!'

So much changing, pulling apart the fabric of our world. And some things not told. There were secrets to which I was not privy but which concerned me. I had seen Nain's face on the wedding day and since then there had been sentences broken off abruptly when I entered the room and letters hastily folded and slipped into Nain's apron pocket. I was outside something of which I ought to have been at the centre. One day soon I would come right out and ask them what was going on and the only reason I hadn't done so yet was the fear of finding out.

'Nell! Nell, Guto is here!' Aunt Catti was waving me in from the back door.

I forgot about secrets and ran back, not

caring that my plaits were coming untied and there was a smudge of ink on my nose to prove that I had been doing equations.

He was already in the big, warm kitchen, the firelight glinting on his blonde sun flecked hair and the wings on his uniform. For a moment he was taller than I remembered him, part of the adult world, and then he caught me up and swung me round, set me on my feet again, crying, 'Bobbie! Come and meet my favourite niece!'

Bobbie was female. Bobbie had fair hair rolled up above the collar of her uniform and red lipstick on. That was the first thing I noticed, the roll of bright hair and the brighter lips. And then the brilliant blue eyes and the English voice.

'Guto has told me a lot about you, Nell.'

Guto had no right to go chattering about me to a stranger. I was a private person not a subject to be discussed. Everything inside me shrank and cooled as I put out a reluctant hand.

'How do you do, Miss?'

'You can call me Bobbie. Everybody does,' she said.

In that case she wasn't offering me any privilege. And Bobbie was a stupid name for a female. Short for Roberta, I supposed.

'Would you credit that I made up Ben's

bed for you?' Nain was exclaiming. 'Guto you said 'friend' in your telegram, so we took it you were bringing a man! I can make up Marget's bed in one minute so there's no harm done at all! Well, you're very welcome, I'm sure. Isn't she, Catti? More than welcome! And Guto bringing you down into the kitchen where nothing is fit to be seen!'

'I adore kitchens!' Bobbie cried, making a sweeping gesture as if to gather the walls into her embrace.

'Oh.' Nain sounded bewildered. In our family we didn't go around adoring people let alone kitchens!

'Let's go upstairs anyway,' said Aunt Catti. 'I've the bed to do.'

'I'm causing you a lot of trouble,' said Bobbie, not sounding in the least sorry.

'Nonsense! I shall enjoy having company,' Aunt Catti said, whisking out.

'You'll be wanting your supper!' Nain sounded relieved, the prospect of making a meal giving her an immediate aim in life. 'The rest of us ate early because J.P. is off to a deacons' meeting at eight, but there is plenty to spare.'

'We ate on the train,' Guto said.

'But I'd adore a cup of tea,' Bobbie said.

'I'll bring it upstairs then, yes?' Nain was in a flurry, her placidity ripped apart by a young woman with red lips. 'Go up and have a word with J.P. He'll want to hear something of what you've been doing before he has to go to the meeting.'

'He has been busy himself, capturing Germans, from what I hear,' Guto said, taking Bobbie's hand and urging her up the stairs.

'Nain! She has red polish on her nails!' My voice was low and shocked.

She made a shushing face and began delving in the cupboard for the best cups. By the time I got upstairs I had composed my own face, schooling it into what I hoped was a demure expression. Inside I was full of nervous anticipation for the moment when Taid saw those red nails and lips and ordered the hussy from the house. They were in the dining-room but far from ordering her out, Taid was sitting down at the table with them, talking in his slow, careful English.

'I paid a visit to London once but it was not much to my taste. No indeed!'

'Oh, Guto and I adore London,' Bobbie said.

I wondered when they'd been there together and felt cheated, remembering the hours we'd spent worrying about Guto flying on dangerous missions when now it seemed he'd been adoring London with red-lipped, red-nailed Bobbie.

'Well, times change,' said Taid.

I could scarcely believe my ears. The one thing that times never did, in Taid's opinion, was change.

'Come in, Nell. Don't swing on the doorknob,' he said a moment later.

Some things hadn't changed. I was almost grateful for the rebuke as I slowly entered. Aunt Catti came downstairs and joined us and Nain came in with the tea, Aunt Ellen arrived and there was a great deal of chatter and nobody seemed to think it strange that Guto had brought home a girl called Bobbie when his heart had been broken over Olive.

This girl was called Bobbie Fenton and her father was a retired naval commander living in Richmond. I thought it a pity that his daughter hadn't gone into the wrens as she chattered on about 'Daddy' and how cross he was to be retired instead of standing on the bridge of a destroyer in the middle of the Atlantic Ocean. She had a quick, high voice and she laughed a lot, displaying a gold filling in her teeth. She did most of the talking indeed and she rattled on so fast that I believe Nain and Taid were left behind once or twice. She frequently addressed a smiling glance towards Guto and Guto smiled right back.

'Escob! The deacons' meeting!' Taid was on

his feet. 'I will be back after an hour, I hope! Guto, you should walk over to see Flora. She'll be pleased to have your company and to meet Bobbie here. It's lonely for her with just the two children and that old garage.'

She was 'Bobbie' to him already and he'd not said one word even when she'd taken a cigarette out of the pack Guto brought out and leaned forward for him to light it.

'Come on, Bobbie! We'll walk over to Flora,' Guto said.

He didn't ask me to go with them but I wouldn't have gone anyway. There was no circle of enchantment to enfold me.

'Well!' said Aunt Ellen when they'd gone. 'Well indeed! What has possessed our Guto?'

I loved Aunt Ellen dearly at that moment.

'She seems very nice,' Aunt Catti said. 'Very smart and modern. An officer too and her not twenty-one yet.'

'She's older than Guto — more experienced from the look of her,' Aunt Ellen said darkly. 'I am surprised at J.P. for allowing it.'

'J.P. makes allowances on account of her being English,' Nain said.

'I never knew him make allowances for anyone before,' Aunt Ellen said scornfully. 'He must be going soft in his old age!'

'I've got homework to do,' I said, trying to change the subject.

'Go and do it then, Cariad,' Nain said vaguely, looking at lipstick stains on the cup. 'I must say that's a nice cheerful colour — not that I'd like to see any of my own wearing it! Don't be getting ideas, Catti!'

'I need someone to test me on my conjugations,' I said.

'And she was wearing a lovely perfume,' Aunt Catti said. 'Very expensive smelling.'

'French conjugations,' I said.

'And silk stockings! Did you notice her stockings? She must know someone who can pull strings.'

'Her father is a retired naval commander,' Aunt Ellen said.

'Probably knows people in the black market,' Nain nodded.

'Irregular French conjugations,' I said and slammed the door on my way out.

I did not, however, go and do my homework. I was too out-of-sorts, too ill at ease with myself and everything around me. Nothing was as it had been. I had expected that Guto would have had a sadness on him like frost in autumn, but he had been cheerful and obviously delighted with the friend he'd brought home.

I went up into the street and sat on the step, pulling the door close behind me so no light would escape. Across the road the deacons were meeting about something or other. I saw a faint glow from one of the windows in the chapel before someone pulled the blind and then the street was dark again.

'Well, there's a funny place to sit!' Nain said from behind me. 'Anyone who sits on a cold night is likely to get the rheumatics in their bottom.'

'I don't much care,' I muttered.

'No, I suppose when the heart is hurting the rheumatics in the bottom are not going to count for much,' she agreed and lowered herself gingerly to sit beside me.

'I don't know why he had to bring her,' I burst out. 'It's only four months since — '

'You think grief must go on forever?' She turned her head sharply to look at me. 'Grief has no date or time, girl. Once you have known grief it is with you always but you cannot wrap it round you like a cloak. You must screw it up into a tiny ball and hide it in the deepest part of yourself and hold your head high, smiling. When the spring flowers die we remember them until the blooms of summer come, yes?'

'I suppose,' I said. 'But everything is different from the way it used to be. I wish this old war had never started!'

'You and everybody else! But you are growing up, Nell. Everything inside you is changing and the world is changing with you.'

'I want everything to stand still,' I said and knew even as I spoke that it wasn't exactly true.

'That would be a dull old world!' Nain said, laughing. 'People go and — '

'In consumption and with kidneys,' I said. 'Is that what everybody is thinking about and nobody will tell me?'

'Duw, but what notion have you got in your head now?' she demanded and began to laugh with a weeping at the back of it. 'Nell! It is only you have been invited on a long visit after Christmas and we have been thinking about it.'

'A visit where?' I asked blankly.

'To the Lloyds — your mother's people. You have relatives on her side too who have not seen you since you were a little girl. Now there are letters coming to ask that you spend six months with them. Your grandfather Lloyd is dead, but your grandmother is still alive and — '

'Where?' I interrupted.

'There is the difficulty.' Her voice was troubled. 'She is living in Manchester and now the Germans are bombing the cities we are nervous to let you go, though she says there are shelters.'

'Why is my grandmother Lloyd living in

Manchester?' I demanded.

'She is English,' Nain said. 'From Manchester in the beginning, you see. She has visited here, of course, but you were too little to remember. It was decided that it would be better for you to stay with us until you were older, to give you a settled home and so that you would grow up Welsh.'

'I am Welsh,' I said.

'Your mam was half-English,' said Nain, patting my hand for comfort. 'The English have some very good points, you know. They make very good roads.'

'So did the Romans and we drove them out,' I reminded her.

'Well, they are fighting on our side, so we must give them the benefit of the doubt,' she said judiciously. 'And it showed a good heart in her to leave you with us for so long.'

'You said a visit,' I said quickly.

'A long visit. It is the fair thing.'

'In Manchester, where the Germans are bombing?'

'She wouldn't ask for you to go if there was any real danger,' Nain said.

'But I shall miss school!'

'They have schools in Manchester. You will go to one there for a couple of months.'

I was silent, wanting to protest but curious,

282

despite myself, about this English grand-mother who wanted me to go and spend a long visit with her.

'It would be a brave thing to hide your grief and go with a smile,' Nain said. 'Your Granny Lloyd could have had you backwards and forwards between us, but she was not selfish. Only now it's natural she is wishing you to spend time with her.'

'In Manchester,' I said.

'It's for you to say the last word,' she said. 'We are not sending you from here, Cariad. We would keep you with us for eternity and a day, but we have to consider others, yes?'

'I don't want to leave Cybi Bay and go to England,' I said.

'Nobody is saying you are wanting to go,' Nain said. 'It is whether you will go. We have put off the telling because of the trouble in our own minds. It will not be forever. Nothing could keep you from us forever.'

I was silent. If I had been told before Guto had brought Bobbie home I would have been much more upset, but changes were occur-ring everywhere and carrying me with them.

'Not to decide now,' said Nain, struggling to her feet. 'We'd not let you go until after Christmas anyway. It wouldn't seem like Christmas without our Nell! Duw, but I shall be getting a lot of post soon! Mark in Scapa

Flow, Marget in Swansea, Ben in the Middle East, Guto in the south of England — '

'And me in Manchester,' I said, knowing it had been decided already.

Oh, if I had wept and cried they would have been glad for me to stay at home, but there would have been disappointment in them too because I had not lived up to the unspoken standards expected of me.

'We won't think of it until — the meeting is over already!'

The chapel door had opened and sombrely clad elders were coming out, putting on their hats and risking quick gleams of torches as they went their separate ways.

'What in the world are you sitting here for?' Taid demanded, striding across the road towards us. 'You think midsummer has come?'

He went past into the hall without waiting for an answer, his step so jaunty that Nain and I looked at each other, then followed him.

'You had a good meeting, J.P.?' Nain asked.

'Very good, very good!' He rubbed the palms of his hands together, then said so airily that we knew it was deeply important, 'I am to make a speech on the wireless.'

'On the — ? What?'

'You're not hard of hearing are you? I am

to go to Bangor, to the wireless studios there to make a speech, a ten-minute sermon to be heard over the wireless. I have been invited by the deacons to represent this area.'

'And you not even a minister!' Nain exclaimed.

'Ah! They are wanting lay preachers and I think I can say without boasting that I have a certain name in that field.'

'True, J.P.' Nain nodded. 'I will give the devil his due and admit there is nobody I have heard who can preach with more hwyl than yourself!'

'What's that about a broadcast?' Aunt Ellen had appeared. 'Who will be hearing this broadcast?'

'Everybody who listens to the Welsh programme,' Taid said.

'In Cardiff too?'

'Anywhere in the world that the station can be picked up. It works through the electricity,' Taid told her.

'When is this to be?' Aunt Catti wanted to know.

'In two weeks' time,' he informed us. 'I have two weeks in which to compose a sermon.'

'Well, you've plenty of time. I've never known you short of a sermon or two at the drop of a hat,' Nain observed.

'This must be written beforehand and

approved. In wartime everything has to be approved.'

'And you will speak in Welsh?'

'Of course I will speak in Welsh! Can you see me giving the word of the Lord in English?'

'There are good things in the English tongue,' Nain said.

'I'm not saying there are not, woman! I am very fond of Mr Charles Dickens myself, but for preaching, Welsh is the finest language.'

'Saint Paul did his preaching in Greek,' Aunt Ellen said.

'That was before he went to Damascus,' Taid said and stalked into the parlour.

'Even speaking the Welsh they will be able to understand him all over Wales and in Patagonia,' Nain said.

'We will have to go to Flora's to listen to Mark's wireless,' Aunt Ellen said.

'And I must write a letter to Marget!' Nain clapped her hands to her head. 'Perhaps Emyr will have all his school listening! Oh, but that is a huge responsibility your Taid has had voted upon him. Mr Lloyd George made wireless broadcasts, you know. His voice was like a nightingale's.'

'He was born in Manchester,' I said.

'Was he really? Well, there! Manchester cannot be all bad then,' Nain said, descending kitchenwards.

'She's told you then?' Aunt Catti threw me a glance with tears in it.

'I have chosen to spend a few months with Granny Lloyd in Manchester,' I said loftily, 'but not until after Christmas and if there is any bombing I will be back very fast.'

'If there is any bombing we will be there to fetch you double fast!' Aunt Catti cried.

'And time enough to talk about it when it happens,' Aunt Ellen said.

But it was going to happen. I knew it in the heart of me.

'And after the wireless broadcast there is the play,' said Aunt Catti. 'We are all coming to see you in that! This family will be getting very famous indeed.'

'Better go and do your homework,' Aunt Ellen said.

'I'm hopeless at irregular verbs,' I said.

'If you work at them, are you likely to come top?' she enquired. I shook my head.

'Then don't work at all,' she advised, 'and come bottom. Better to be bottom than mediocre!'

It was a good philosophy. I threw all my intentions of studying out of the window and went down with them to drink tea in the kitchen.

Guto and his friend stayed for three days, but they spent a lot of time sightseeing like tourists. Bobbie adored everything she saw and was crazy about the castle. She was a pleasant girl underneath her silliness and so eager to please that it was impossible to dislike her, but I was glad we saw so little of her. She and Guto spoke a kind of shorthand together, full of odd phrases like 'wizard prang' and 'going for a blighty' and Guto had started to grow a moustache which made him look older. He was older anyway for all his high spirits, with a wary look about his eyes. Nobody mentioned Olive and I didn't know if he'd told Bobbie about her or not. I would have thought he'd forgotten her himself, except that he didn't take Bobbie to Holyhead and he didn't ask me to go with them anywhere.

When they left he was very gay and bouncy and Bobbie kissed us all and declared she had adored every last moment and they went off together in a taxi with all of us waving and telling Bobbie she would be welcome any time.

'But it will be a different one next time,' said Nain. 'Guto is sowing wild oats and I will hear no word against it from anybody!'

She looked fierce enough to hex and we none of us said anything, but we knew Guto — the Guto we had known — would never come again and we screwed up our grief and hid it deep inside ourselves.

14

Aunt Flora's sitting room was packed like a sardine tin. It was perfectly possible to listen to the wireless in the Black Boy, but most people wanted to sit with the Petries and get famous by association.

It was an odd thing but Aunt Flora had become more vivid since Uncle Mark had gone to war. I had always thought of her as being on the fringe of the family but I saw now that she was a dainty little woman with a quietness in her that no longer seemed dull. Johnny had grown a lot in the past few months but I still considered him to be pretty obnoxious. I was not tolerant about young children who seemed to me to lack all the charm of babies and not yet to have acquired the good sense of older people. On this occasion however he was under pain of death from the Lovell cousins to avoid opening his mouth until the broadcast was finished and Nain had put a small measure of her elderflower wine into William's bottle so that he was already happily asleep and snoring.

The rest of us crowded round the set which had a photograph of Taid by the side of it to remind us more forcibly of his presence. There were pies and sandwiches on the trolley and the big teapot was ready and waiting.

'If everybody was here there would not be a happier woman in Wales than myself,' Nain said, 'for say what you will J.P. is a wonderful preacher!'

'You must hand that to the old sod,' said Leni.

We all mentally handed it to the old sod.

I was glad that the two weeks were over, because it had been uncomfortable having to tiptoe everywhere and speak in whispers because Taid was working on his wireless sermon. Fortunately I'd had to stay late after school every day for extra rehearsals so had missed the worst of it. The school plays were to be held on the following afternoon and everybody was coming. Even Taid was lending his presence though he'd cleared it with the minister first. I had taken this afternoon off school and Nain had despatched urgent messages to her sons, ordering them to take an afternoon off from the war and tune into the studios at Bangor.

'Switch it on, Mam,' Aunt Catti said. Her eyes were big with expectation.

'It is for Flora to switch it on,' Nain said. 'I cannot fathom the electricity of the thing.'

Aunt Flora bowed her head in acknowledgement of the compliment and the click of the knob cracked the sudden silence. There were a couple of high-pitched whistles and a noise like the organ made sometimes when the bellows hadn't been worked fast enough and then, as clearly as if we were in the studios ourselves, the voice of the announcer telling us that Mr John Petric, noted Methodist lay preacher, would give the first of the talks in the new religious series.

'Of course first!' said Aunt Ellen and was hushed by everybody else.

Taid sounded grand. He had a trick when he was preaching of suddenly dropping his voice as if speaking in strict confidence to one particular member of his congregation. He did it now and it was as effective as ever. It was a good sermon too, shorter than usual because there was a limit on his time, but full of rich and sonorous phrases. He spoke briefly of war and then of the homecomings ahead and the joy that arose out of sacrifice and there was not a dry eye in Aunt Flora's parlour.

At the very end, just before the announcer told anyone who had just switched on too late what they'd missed, Taid said, 'Let us be sure that the Lord will bless Wales and her brave people as I send my good wishes and my prayers out to all of you and to my family and granddaughter Nell. God bless you all!'

Nobody heard the announcer in the babble of congratulations and hugging and weeping.

'As good as Lloyd George any day! Good God, but the Parliament in London could take lessons!'

'And Nell to be mentioned by name!'

'Because she is going to be the genius and go to the university, of course.'

'And her name before the public already!'

'If any old Nazis were listening it would put the wind up them proper! Duw, that talk has probably shortened the war!'

'I hope that you will live up to the expectations, Nell. It is a solemn responsibility to have your name mentioned over the wireless.'

'And Nell to be in the play tomorrow!'

'The entire sermon is to be published in the Caernarvon and Denbigh,' Nain said.

After that words failed everybody for at least two minutes and then there were the sandwiches and the cups of strong tea and mugs of elderflower to be passed round and phrases from the sermon pulled out of context and endlessly discussed.

'You must be very proud, girl, to hear your name spoken for people to hear even in Patagonia,' Aunt Flora said. It was nice of her not to mind that he hadn't mentioned Johnny or William. But I thought I knew why he had spoken my name. It was because when the New Year came I would be packing my cases and going on the train to Manchester. Nain had read bits of Granny Lloyd's letters to me and in all of them had been comments about how much they were all looking forward to seeing me and how they would take every care to ensure that my education wasn't interrupted.

'Your Granny Lloyd has a sister living two doors away and two other daughters and a son, so there will be plenty of family,' Nain had said.

I felt I would be meeting all these strange relatives soon enough without being forced to hear all about them before. So far none of them had any reality for me. They were two-dimensional figures like the paper dolls I'd cut out of the illustrations in Aunt Catti's magazine when she had finished reading it. When I met them there would be the time to know them.

'And the play tomorrow,' said Aunt Flora. 'I will be coming myself to see it. Ceri will look after the baby and Johnny has school in the afternoons. It will be a lovely outing for me, I tell you.'

'I shall look out for you,' I promised.

In fact I had already promised to look out for so many people that had I been faithful to my word, I'd not have had time to speak any of my lines.

First there was Taid to welcome home. He had strictly forbade any demonstration and would have been furious had anyone obeyed him. Instead, as he rode back in the expensive hired taxi deemed a suitable means of transport for a famous broadcaster, we stood in the road, marshalled into two lines by Constable Petrie who had ridden over from the next village to control our exuberance. The taxi came over the brow of the hill and we raised our voices in a resounding yell that rolled across the meadows down to the sea.

'Lot of silly fuss,' said Taid, stepping out and grandly paying off the driver. 'I tell you, it was quite easy, once I got the knack of talking to the microphone as if it was human. You didn't hear the papers rustling as I turned them?'

'Not one rustle, J.P.,' Aunt Ellen assured him. 'We didn't even hear breathing.'

'And every word clear as if we were in chapel,' Nain said, adding, 'But don't get a swelled head about it now. There's lots of people who talk over the wireless. Even Adolf Hitler talks over the wireless.'

'Not preaching the gospel of the Lord,'

Taid said dourly and went into the house to a chorus of 'Sospan Fach'.

Of course, it was not the last word on the subject that was spoken. Taid had to relate every detail of the occasion from the moment he was directed into a little, glass-walled studio with the microphone standing up in the middle of the table — 'like a phallic symbol' said Aunt Ellen — until the announcer gave him the thumbs up signal to tell him it had gone without a hitch.

When I slept that night I dreamed a crazy muddle in which Taid was speaking all my lines in the play and I was helping Constable Petrie to light a bonfire. I woke up laughing and then remembered that actresses were supposed to suffer from stage fright. No actress worth her salt bounced onto the stage dying to play her part. I couldn't wait to get there and I hoped fervently that it didn't mean my performance was going to be dreadful.

'Not nervous are you?' Taid asked, catching me on my way to the bus.

'I suppose I will be later,' I said.

'Nonsense, girl!' His brows rushed together. 'It is foolish to be nervous! No Petrie ever had nerves.'

'Only consumption — and kidneys on the Lovell side,' I muttered.

'We will all be there!' he called after me. 'Be sure to look out for me now.'

'I promise,' I said recklessly and ran to the corner, swinging myself aboard, thinking scorn of fear about a little school play.

We were busy all morning putting out the chairs and hoisting up painted flats and checking programmes and seating plans. The girls who were selling the programmes wore the stove-pipe black hats and striped skirts that tourists sometimes believed we wore all the time and the front rows were reserved for the Mayor and the Board of Governors.

I suppose it kept us out of mischief but I couldn't help wondering if Sybil Thorndyke had been obliged to lug chairs about before her opening performance. Certainly, there was no time to feel nervous with masters and mistresses rushing up and down and behaving worse than the first-formers.

The Welsh play was going on first, then the scene from 'Henry V' and finally, after the interval, the trial scene.

'The best is being saved for last,' we told one another. At all events the audience would have been mellowed by tea and biscuits during the interval and not in a bad mood to criticize.

I saw my family from the window of the form room where we had been exiled until our turn came. They had not come in a taxi, theatricals having less importance than religious broadcasts, but in our trap and Aunt Rhiannon Evans' trap and Jimmy's lorry. Taid having been persuaded into coming, was holding himself as erect as if he prepared to face a firing squad. His head was high and I was certain that at the first suspicion of orgy he would be up and preaching. Nain, in her chapel coat, walked behind with Aunt Flora and Aunt Catti and Aunt Ellen brought up the rear with Constable Petrie who had left crime to run rampant while he came to lend his august presence to the theatricals.

There were Lovells and Bohannas and even a couple of Boswells, but I missed Aunt Marget and the uncles. We were too many women now and even Taid could not entirely redress the balance. I missed Uncle Ben's shaggy familiarity and Uncle Mark's sharper look and Guto before he'd put on a uniform. My new aunt, Rhiannon Evans, was with them, but she didn't yet seem to be like a member of the family. One did not get to be a Petrie overnight.

There is nothing more frustrating than hearing applause and a mumble of words of which only one in ten is intelligible. We had watched the dress rehearsal and we knew that in the end the young quarryman won the hand of the quarry owner's daughter and the entire cast burst into song with the erstwhile quarry owner, who had been an English villain all through, miraculously becoming fluent in Welsh and singing louder than anybody else, but it was still irritating to be stuck away in a room smelling of chalk and sweaty palms instead of being in the blacked-out hall with the imagined scent of greasepaint.

The English and French Armies clanked out in their knitted chain-mail, with odds and sods from all the local farms to do duty as shields and swords. But there was no laughter as far as I could hear. The bare stage with the glow of a campfire reflected onto a dark backcloth, the boys sitting round, the young king moving among them evoked feelings too deep for amusement. Nearly every family had at least one member of it fighting in a more savage conflict.

There was a babble when the applause died down and a general scraping of chairs and shuffling of feet. I was already in the maid costume, black stockings, gymslip cut short, black sweater, hair wetted and plastered flat to my head with my plaits rolled under and pinned ferociously. Being the only girl in the cast I had a space of my own behind a couple of screens and mentally hung a gold star on them.

'Come on, Nell. The interval's over,' Miss Watkins English said.

Never was an actress more eager to tread the boards than I was. The school was reading the members of the Inquisition resplendent in the staff's gowns and mortar boards, the curtain trembling upwards.

The first lines were spoken and then someone gave me a push in the back and I was under lights that felt like searchlights with the enemy poised in darkness on rows and rows of chairs. Somebody was asking me if I was quite well. I felt like telling everybody that I wanted to throw up, but it was Joan of Ark who must answer that she had eaten fish sent by Cauchon which had disagreed with her. I heard a voice giving the correct line and recognized it as my own. Everything swung back into focus and I knew where I was and who I was. In that little space I was the maid, fighting for my dreams. I remembered my promise and shot a swift glance into the audience but all I recognized was Taid's beard jerking out as he leaned forward, silently mouthing the lines along with me. I hadn't realized that he must have studied the script as closely as I had.

Towards the end, as I sprang up defying them I heard a voice say quite loudly, 'Good!

You tell them, girl!'

It was Constable Petrie and, for an instant, I had a glorious vision of him running up to the stage and arresting the entire Inquisition, but he remained where he was and I was dragged off stage to the accompaniment of loud applause. My legs had turned to jelly and I couldn't remember one word of what I'd just said, but Miss Watkins rushed up the corridor and hugged me and on the stage the voices rose and fell bringing the trial scene to its close.

We were all on stage again bowing and I could distinguish all the family. Aunt Catti was crying, of course. So was Nain. Taid was clapping with his hands held up high and there was as much excitement as if victory had been declared.

'That was a play!' were Taid's first words to me. 'That was literature, Nell! That was great literature.'

'And nasty to burn her!' Nain cried, seizing me and examining my arms and legs as if she feared to find scorches.

'It was better than the pictures,' Aunt Catti sobbed. 'Duw! But I did enjoy it!'

'It was magic,' said Aunt Ellen. 'If I had had the sense to dress as a boy I might have avoided my unfortunate experience.'

'We are going to have tea at Flora's,' Taid

said. 'Rhiannon too!'

I climbed up into the trap, feeling as if I were in a triumphal chariot. As it was we made quite a procession going back along the coast road, singing as we went and sometimes the same song at the same time.

Aunt Flora had made a cake with the marzipan thick and the icing thin the way I liked it and there were tinned peaches she'd been saving for a special occasion and a sugared ham and Welsh cake bursting with raisins. It was a day of triumph and I was sick with disappointment to think there were to be no other performances. It was dark when we started for home, with Taid driving slow though the pony knew the road blindfold and our voices dying into the frosty starlight.

'Taid Petrie! Is that you, Taid Petrie?'

Tom Chapel Bellows who'd stayed to milk the cows since he had no interest in literature was stumbling along the road, holding up a lantern.

'No! it's Mr Winston Churchill,' Taid said with fierce wit. 'Of course it's me and why are you shining a light to guide every Nazi aeroplane for miles around?'

'Two of the cows won't get up,' Tom said.

'It's not going to change in the weather, is it?' Nain was asking.

'Which two?' Taid handed the reins to Nain

and clambered down.

'Ceinwen and Dilys,' Tom said. 'They look funny, Taid Petrie.'

'I will have them up in two ticks,' Taid said. 'Dilys has a streak of mischief in her wide as the Menai Straits. She will lead the others on unless you're firm.'

He pushed open the gate, taking the lantern from Tom, and tramped into the meadow calling his beasts.

'Are we going in, Nain?' I asked, for her hands were slack on the reins.

'There is a crying on the wind,' she answered me. 'I can feel it. Something has come that would best have stayed away.'

We sat there in the trap, with Mrs Rhiannon and the aunts in the trap behind and we listened to Taid's voice and felt the crying in the wind.

Then Taid came back and even in the darkness, before he lifted the lantern, I knew he had become old and the triumph of the day was flat and dead.

'Go into the house now,' he said.

'Is it bad, J.P.?' Nain asked.

'In the morning I will tell better, but it is very bad, I believe,' he answered. 'I will stay with my beasts tonight. Go in now.'

We went in silence. Aunt Ellen walked across to Aunt Rhiannon's place as soon as she had changed into her wellingtons so it was just Aunt Catti, Nain and me to sit in the kitchen. Outside, in the road, we could hear voices and the occasional gleam of a torch as someone came through our garden and down into the meadow.

'I will make up a thermos,' Nain said. 'It will be a long night, I think. That was Cwilym Vet's voice I heard then.'

I tucked myself into the corner, lest anyone notice me and get the idea I ought to be in bed, but nobody said anything to me as the long evening wore on. The apprehension in the house was as thick as tobacco smoke.

At some point Taid came in and stood, his eyes overbright, his voice harsh to speak the dreaded words.

'It's the foot and mouth. There's no doubt.'

'A little doubt, perhaps?' Aunt Catti said in a thread of a voice.

'Cwilym Vet is as sure as I am. We have both seen it often enough before. It's the law to inform the Ministry of Agriculture. Cwilym will telephone them in the morning. There is nothing to be done until then. We will go early to our beds and be up at dawn. Nell, you must stay from school.'

I nodded and Nain, glancing at me, said,

'Go to your bed, Cariad. No point in staying up.'

I went, leaving behind me the brief phrases of despair. The foot and mouth was the most dreaded of diseases, virulent in its effects, spreading like couch grass. I did not expect to sleep, but I slept and awoke several times, knowing something terrible had happened, but sleeping again before I remembered what it was.

In the morning, I did remember and when I came downstairs there were strange men already in the yard and the overpowering smell of disinfectant. Matting had been soaked in it and laid on the pavement before our front door, along the garden path and yard, at every entrance to our smallholding. Down by the river the Bohanna men were digging a wide, shallow pit.

Aunt Rhiannon was sitting in the kitchen. Her face was drained of all its natural colour and two patches of rouge stood out clownishly on her cheeks.

'My fault,' she was saying as I came in. 'I grazed my sheep in your meadow and they were infected.'

'It's not your sheep and our meadow,' Nain said. 'We are family together, Rhiannon, and you were not to know your sheep were infected. Blame yourself when there is something to be blamed, but not over this! Drink down your tea — now what is Dai Post doing here so early? If there's bad news you may bet your boots the vultures will gather!'

'It's a telegram for Rhiannon,' Dai Post said, coming through the back door. 'From the War Office.'

She reached up and snatched it from him, ripping it open, reading it aloud in a high, bleak voice. 'Regret to inform — missing, believed killed.'

The message splintered into groups of words, heard with disbelief.

'Not Ben,' Nain said. 'Not Ben. There is some mistake. He was over age to go. Not Ben.'

'It's not definite,' Aunt Catti said shakily. 'It says 'believed'. They're not sure, see!'

And then it seemed everybody on Mona was in our kitchen, weeping and storming and cursing Hitler, declaring it was a clear mistake and the War Office had no business giving people bad frights. Aunt Rhiannon went on sitting, staring into a cup of tea she hadn't even sipped.

'Oh, J.P.!' Nain's voice rose above the rest. 'This is a terrible day to be borne! Disaster comes in threes. I'm sick with fear for Mark and Guto.'

'They're driving the sheep into the pit for shooting,' Taid said.

'Oh, bugger the sheep!' she cried in fury. 'Ben is missing!'

'I will think about that when the day's business is done,' he answered harshly. 'There's not room in my mind for more sorrowing at this time.'

He broke off, lifting his head sharply as the firing began.

'Rhiannon, you must come with me to lie down,' Aunt Catti said and, for a wonder, she wasn't crying. 'It's not good for the child that is coming when you're upset.'

Two months wed — not quite two — and she was with child. I had fancied her too old.

'I'm not certain yet,' she said in a drained voice.

'It was in your teacup clear as day a month ago. Mam saw it plainly,' Aunt Catti urged. 'You will lie on my bed and rest. When Ben comes home he will be angry if you haven't been taking care of yourself.'

'Nell, come with me,' Taid said.

'No, J.P.!' Nain interposed sharply. 'It's no scene for a child.'

'You would let her go off to Manchester wrapped in cotton wool against the reality of life?' he retorted. 'She will come with me.'

Nain drew her apron over her head and rocked to and fro in silent keening.

I went with him through the yard into the frost-glinted meadow. Away to the river I could see leaping fires where the sheep were burning and the stink of their wool and flesh was carried on the wind. Taid had his pistol in his hand and there was granite in his face. At our heels the dogs followed, but he ordered them sharply to go back and they dropped to the grass, noses on forepaws, eyes bewildered.

'When good times are here we share them,' Taid said, 'and when the Lord afflicts us we bear the affliction together. That is the way of our living and it is the way you will take with you when you go to England.'

'But it isn't fair — ' I began.

'Who said everything had to be fair?' He was regarding me with scorn. 'You think life has to be fair like a game? Life has to be lived, that's all. I reared my beasts from when they were born and thought to have them die of old age. It is not for me to complain when my plans don't fit into the bigger plan the Lord made before he created us. Anyone who does that is a fool! I'll not have you grow up to be a fool!'

The cows were tethered loosely at the edge of a smaller pit. They had smelt death and were moving restlessly, but recognizing Taid they began to moo greetings and strain at the ropes.

'Dilys died last night,' Taid said. 'I'd not have wanted to kill that old girl.'

He gestured to me to stay where I was and

stepped forward. He spoke each cow's name before he fired and there was such loving in his voice as I never heard when he spoke to humankind. And then he turned and said, very clearly and firmly, 'Now I must think about Ben.'

He walked a little way and fell, as if the Lord himself had launched a stone from Heaven.

15

'It was his heart,' the doctor said. 'A massive heart attack at his age could not be fought off.'

'He was in his seventies, you know,' Nain said, dabbing her eyes.

'Eighty-one,' said Aunt Ellen.

'What!' Nain stared at her. 'What are you saying? Ten years older than me he was!'

'Fifteen,' said Aunt Ellen.

'You're telling me that I have been married to an old man for forty-two years?' Nain demanded.

'He said he felt five years younger,' said Aunt Ellen, 'and we promised not to tell. Mam and Dad and me.'

'I've been deceived all my life?' Nain shook her head in bewilderment. 'And him always condemning liars to the fiery pit! Duw, but he was a whited sepulchre indeed! Eighty-one! I cannot credit the perfidy of the man. Well, this is a shock and no mistake. You might have told me, Ellen.'

'He would have had my head,' Aunt Ellen said.

'Well, I shall take good care it's carved big

on the headstone,' Nain said. 'It will be carved deep too, for everyone to see it. Eighty-one! Well, the old sod!'

And she began to laugh and weep together, her confused emotions snarled like unravelled wool.

Our house was in mourning for more than Taid. The smell of burnt carcasses lingered still on the air, the meadow was empty and Aunt Rhiannon lay up in Aunt Catti's room fortified with constant cups of tea.

For three days, according to custom, I had sat in the parlour, in the big chair where the sermons had been composed, and related over and over again the last moments of Taid's existence. The telling of the death devolved upon the one who had been at the deathbed and in this case that was myself. It was a solemn responsibility for one so young and a tiring one too for nearly everybody on the island, as well as many from Bangor and Caernarvon and up in the valleys, filed in to listen to the telling to make the appropriate responses and to leave money on the table when the telling was done.

Hour after hour they filed through, hour after hour my voice rose and fell in reciting, hour after hour Aunt Catti and Aunt Ellen made tea and scones. We were technically in quarantine so those who came had to walk over the disinfected matting and wash their hands as they left.

Taid had been carried into the parlour and laid on the table until the time came, after the doctor had been, for him to be laid out by Nurse Robson and Aunt Ellen and coffined in the handsome oak on which he had been making regular payments since his retirement. I had gone with Aunt Ellen to look at him, but Taid was not in the laid out figure that stared upwards with closed eyes. There was nothing of him there, nothing of him anywhere. He was gone into nothingness, as if he had never been, and with him had gone all the life of the little farm.

The blinds were drawn down in every house and every shop had closed for an hour. The distance to the graveyard was so short that the minister had agreed to have the cortège wend its way to the far end of the village and then turn around.

'It will never be the same here again,' I said aloud. 'Nothing will ever be the same.'

'Nothing ever is,' said Aunt Ellen. 'Have you been in the world almost thirteen years and not known that?'

Women, save for the widow, did not attend funerals. Nain was dressed in her black silk with a black veil over her black hat. She looked like a picture I'd once seen of Queen

311

Victoria, though her face beneath the veil was prettier. Old Leni and Jimmy came to escort her into the black taxi that would follow the hearse. Wreaths had come in from all over — a handsome one from the Squire, a splendid one from the chapel elders, a cross of poppies from the local Red Cross. On the morning of the funeral Aunt Marget arrived and was allowed to get her hat and coat off before she was set to cutting bread for the ham sandwiches.

I went up to the landing and peered through the stained-glass panes to see the chapel in gold and turquoise and scarlet and then I went down to the dining-room to peep through a gap in the net and see the reality of black and white in the street where the long procession was forming up, men in dark overcoats with crêpe on their arms and hatbands, the coffin the only note of colour with its heaped wreaths and bouquets.

There was no music, only the steady tramp-tramp of hundreds of feet — the chapel deacons and elders first; members not only of our congregation but from Moriah, Bethel, Engedi and Sion; farmers with whom Taid had competed at sheepdog trials; those who still remained in the gypsy camp bringing up the rear with black feathers stuck in their caps. Tramp-tramp, carrying my childhood away.

'Nell! For shame to be sneaking peeps!' Aunt Catti said, moving me aside and taking my place. 'Go and make sure we've enough cups, for the world and his wife will be wanting tea.'

'In Ireland they have a party when someone dies with the corpse right there in the room,' I said.

'J.P. always said the Irish had nasty habits. Get on now, Nell!'

I went reluctantly to count cups and check that the jellies were setting properly. For all we knew this funeral might be for Ben as well as J.P. 'Missing' could mean years of waiting with hope growing fainter everyday and, at the end, not even a body.

'There will be the reading of the will,' Aunt Ellen said. 'He went over to Caernarvon special two or three years ago. Of course Ben and Marget weren't married then.'

'And Uncle Ben might — '

'Don't shape the words to make them true!' she broke in fiercely. 'Learn to endure, girl.'

I was tired of being told to endure. For the first time the prospect of leaving was all promise with nothing of threat. My shell had broken and I wanted to be free of it.

They were coming back from the burying,

Nain being handed out of the taxi as if she were made of bone china. The house burst into conversation.

'Duw! But that was a grand send-off! J.P. would have enjoyed himself!'

'And the Squire coming himself all the way from Chester!'

'The Rushtons sent flowers. That was good of them.'

'It wasn't J.P. driving the lorry that killed Olive.'

'Good of them all the same! And a good sermon — not to be compared with the broadcast, mind, but very sound.'

'There was nobody who could describe hell-fire better than J.P.,' Aunt Ellen said. 'Nell, where are your manners? Pass the sandwiches round. They'll start to curl at the edges and then we'll all be shamed!'

I hastened to do her bidding. Around me the talk eddied and flowed. On this day, we had buried a saint it seemed. And it had not been so, I thought bitterly. He had been full of small meannesses and vanities, flawed and never knowing it.

'The will is to be read,' went the word from mouth to mouth.

The solicitor from Caernarvon was among us, saying all the right things, acting as if he and my grandfather had been bosom friends when I doubted if they had met more than a couple of times. Nain, ankles swollen over the tops of her shoes, was escorted into the parlour, relatives following and the rest crowding the hall and stairs and spilling into the street.

'You would think he had a million to leave,' Aunt Marget whispered.

'I will leave out the legal terminology,' the solicitor said. He had seated himself in Taid's chair and it was too big for him. 'It is a straightforward document with no codicils. In my view it is a very fair and well-reasoned last testament.'

'Get on with it, man. Let's hear it!'

That from Constable Petrie who had covered his hat with black crêpe.

' "To my wife, Hannah Petrie, I leave the property known as Virgin and Child Cottage, to hold until her death after which it shall pass to my son, Benjamin, and thence through my younger male descendants.' That is to say there is an entail on the property. I understand that Mr Benjamin Petrie is — well, in that event the property would pass to Mr Mark Petrie unless — ' He glanced at Aunt Rhiannon who stopped looking tragic and achieved a coy blush.

'Go on,' Aunt Ellen said.

'The aforesaid property includes the land and the — the livestock,' the solicitor said.

'With the following exceptions. 'To my sister, Miss Ellen Petrie, I leave the stables and any horses that may be in my possession apart from the trap and pony which I leave to my wife, Hannah'.'

'Well, did he think I was going to make you walk into town?' Aunt Ellen cried.

'To my sons Benjamin, Mark and Guto I leave the sum of 500 pounds each and to my daughters Margaret and Catherine the sum of 500 pounds each provided they are married within one year after my death'.'

Looking at Aunt Catti I knew that Hugh Coch didn't stand a chance.

' 'To any male grandchildren living at the time of my death I leave the sum of 200 pounds each and to any female grandchildren the sum of 100 pounds each. The residue of my estate, after any death duties and funeral expenses, I leave to the Society for the Propagation of Christian Knowledge, on condition any sums due be spent on the distribution of Bibles in Ireland.' There will be about 300 pounds for that purpose.'

As he paused Nain's voice rose.

'The old sod! Grumbled for years about giving me housekeeping and dies rich! Oh, I knew he was sneaky — like all the Petries.'

'I'm not happy to be called sneaky,' Aunt Ellen said.

'You're not faultless in that respect,' Nain retorted. 'Eighty-one indeed!'

'I have not quite finished.' The solicitor coughed slightly.

'Duw! You mean he had more to leave?' Nain said.

' 'To my nephew Constable Petrie I leave my watch in the knowledge he will continue to spend his time in the furtherance of law and order'.'

'Diawl! I do my duty! One must not expect a reward,' Constable Petrie said. 'But fancy his remembering me! Well, that was handsome!'

' 'To my granddaughter Eleanor Petrie, I leave my trumpet and the responsibility thereof'.'

It was not to be borne! One hundred pounds and the trumpet that had shamed me for years. Responsibility for making a fool of myself for the village to hear, I supposed!

'Oh, but he must have loved you something fierce,' Nain said.

I stared at her, stared at her shining hazel eyes that were gentler than any cat's, at the tremulous sweetness of her smile. I knew then that she was wiser than any of us, the firm heart in the body of us and the understanding mind.

Aunt Marget had been gazing down into her cup and now, raising her head, she said in her sleepwalking voice, 'Ben is not dead at all.

He is in a hospital in Egypt with an arm broken. Lost touch with his unit for a while, but now is on the mend.'

Nain's bright hazel eyes held mine and she gave a little nod.

I rose and went to the wall and lifted down the trumpet and went from among them, over the disinfected matting, down the lane past the bus stop, to the bleak December shingle where the white sea-holly defied the wind and the little waves sucked at the seaweed.

I knew, with a seeing equal to Aunt Marget's, that my path would lead away from here and that the old ways had begun to die with the coming of the war and would fall into the earth of my memory and nurture new blooms to replace the flowers of springtime, but the roots of the summer flowers would be entrenched in everything that had once been and would never completely be forgotten.

I had no Bible but I called out as loud and strong as I could, 'Lord! If today is the day of Your coming, we Petries are ready.'

And then I blew the trumpet in a long and quavering note that set all the echoes dancing on the shining bridge of my childhood.

THE LUCK BRIDE

Maureen Peters

On the outskirts of a Romany camp, Abner, a gypsy, finds a new-born baby wrapped in a fine shawl. Named Kushti, meaning 'luck', she grows up to be a beautiful young woman. After Nahor, a half-Romany, saves Kushti from being raped, she falls in love with him. However, Abner reveals Nahor's threat to find and kill the man who had deserted his mother when she was pregnant. Because this is against Romany law, the young couple cannot marry. Then, when the tribe goes to London, Kushti's beauty attracts the attention of Edward IV and his court . . .

A CHILD CALLED FREEDOM

Maureen Peters

When Tansy Malone first looks into the eyes of Tom Wolf, she is swept by love. However, their ways seem fated to part, for Wolf is a half-breed Indian returning to his father's tribe, and Tansy has an elderly husband and a delicate sister, with whom she is setting out for the New World. A variety of experiences lie ahead as Tansy travels along the Sacramento Trail, towards California — and as she moves from the unthinking passions of a girl to full maturity, Tansy finds, at last, her true destiny.

TANSY

Maureen Peters

Fifteen-year-old Tansy's family find her hard to understand, though all of them — practical Bridie, gentle Kate and her brothers, Pat and Seamus — love her. Raleigh Devereux, the English youth to whom Tansy first offers her heart, treats her as a plaything. Michael O'Faolain, for whom she has affection, but no love, never comprehends her yearnings for the freedom to be herself alone. Not until the failure of the potato crop does Tansy come face to face with reality — and with the complexities of her own nature.